Summer Storm

Savage PRESS
Box 115, Superior, WI 54880 (715) 394-9513

First Edition

Cover design: Jillene Johnson

Cover photo: Kevin Ahlstrom

This is a work of fiction. Any resemblance to real persons is purely coincidental.

ISBN Number 1-886028-62-1

Library of Congress Catalog Card Number: 2003097166

Published by:

Savage Press
P.O. Box 115
Superior, WI 54880

Phone: 715-394-9513

E-mail: mail@savpress.com

Web Site: www.savpress.com

Printed in the USA

Summer Storm

by

Lori J. Glad

To

Mark

1

Fog drifted from over the water to cover the Lakewalk in a dismal curtain of mist. It was six-thirty at night and darkness already had fallen. Janine glanced down the wooden boardwalk and felt a pang of apprehension. Mist haloed the street lamps that lined the pedestrian path so their light did little to penetrate the darkness and fog. The gloom looked anything but welcoming as wisps of fog shifted strangely about.

She glanced at her watch with a sigh. The last minute stops she had made had put her behind schedule. If she didn't take the shortcut down the Lakewalk, she would never make the bus home. It was her only option of transportation since she didn't have enough money left for a cab.

There was nothing for her to do but make a run for it. The decision made, she rushed down the steps and moved swiftly along the first wooden boards. Running for the bus wasn't something she did often, especially in the shoes she wore for work. The heels made a tapping sound that echoed eerily through the stillness that always seemed to accompany a fog such as this. The old foghorn sounded by the pier with its blasting deep notes. Janine almost jumped a foot, startled by the familiar and much loved sound.

Janine slowed to squint at the hands on the lamppost clock near the Vietnam Memorial. Maybe this time her watch would be fast so she wouldn't have to hurry, but she couldn't see the hands. The fog obscured the face of the clock.

She spun around and began to run again. Her breathing was rapid, and her heart pounded in her ears. She heard the sound of footsteps somewhere behind her. She darted a glance over her shoulder but saw nothing. The walkway was deserted, which didn't surprise her considering the weather. Muffled sounds surrounded her, and the flesh on the back of her neck began to tingle. She hurried along, her sense of hearing heightened until she caught sight of the lights at the Fitger's Inn.

For the moment, she caught her breath knowing safety was within reach. A sensible girl, she didn't usually give in to images of boogie monsters in the dark. But she knew she had heard something, although it could have been the echo of her own footsteps. The fog disembodied everything.

Janine slowed to a brisk walk while in front of the hotel for propriety's sake but continued to glance behind her just to see if there was anyone lurking in the shadows. She realized how silly she was being and laughed at herself. She knew this place like the back of her hand, had traveled it continuously since it had been built by the city, and yet when that fog rolled in, she felt like the victim in a horror film. Giggling at the absurd image, she whirled back around ready to sprint for the bus again and almost barreled into a broad black shape shrouded in mist.

"Excuse me," the shape said, stepping quickly out of the way before their bodies collided. His words sounded different, with an accent. "Señ…Miss, are you alright? May I be of any assistance to you?"

Janine leaped sideways, truly startled out of her wits. Her throat closed like a vise. She lifted the edge of her purse and aimed it at his nose. If he made one single move toward her, she'd belt him.

"You almost gave me heart failure," she gasped out, her breathing even more erratic. "No, no I am fine…please let me pass," she exclaimed, flustered by her fear. Barely looking up at the man, she edged cautiously around him, as far from his intimidating form as she could get.

"Are you being pursued?" he questioned urgently, moving along with her. His footsteps matched hers as he searched her frantic face for answers.

Janine shook her head, feeling quite wild and disheveled. Mist dampened her clothes, her skin, and her hair. She was sorry to meet anyone in this condition, even a mugger. Incapable of speech, she turned and began to run.

2

The man frowned as he watched her figure fade into the darkness. He snapped his fingers, and two men stepped out of the shadows of the balcony above him. "Follow her," he demanded abruptly. The two, without hesitation, raced down the wrought iron stairway, jumping over the last few steps, and began to pursue the figure that had already disappeared into the fog.

The man listened to their footsteps and continued to frown as he reached into his breast pocket to finger a thin cheroot and place it between his lips. He lit the fragrant cigar and stepped into the shadows to watch the path where he'd first seen the girl running as if her life depended on it. Dressed in a skirt and heels, he didn't think any woman would do this unless she was being pursued by some kind of desperado. When nothing unusual appeared, he began to wonder if he'd been too hasty. American women had different customs. Maybe this was something they chose to do—like jogging.

He finished the cigar and tossed it into the railroad track next to the walkway. His men hadn't returned. Either they couldn't find her or she'd run where they could not pursue. Then he heard the brush of leather on stone and waited for them to come around the corner.

"What happened?" he asked as they walked to the balcony where he leaned against the damp railing.

"She boarded a bus," the taller of the two men informed him, as he brushed the water droplets from the lapel of his suit jacket and straightened the thin black tie around his thick neck.

"Nothing was wrong?" Alberto questioned. "Did she seem frightened?"

Galeno shook his head. "We didn't arrive in time to see her actually board," he explained.

"Then you cannot be positive that she did board the bus." Alberto frowned. "Tomorrow at this time, follow the same bus and see if she gets off."

With the order, the two men nodded, glancing at each other briefly. They were to be on board an airplane tomorrow at this time.

Alberto Casilda heard the laughter inside the banquet room directly behind them and sighed.

"I think I shall make my apologies to the hostess, and we shall return to the hotel," he said. He flexed his shoulders, the fine material of his shirt damp from the heavy mist. "I have lost my desire for socializing."

"Even before the meal is served?' Galeno questioned. "Is that considered proper?"

Alberto's frown deepened. "I will think of a suitable excuse," he replied, "even to suit your fastidious taste, Galeno."

"Then I will bring the car around, señor," Galeno said with a glimmer of a salute in his crisp movement.

"Gracias, Galeno, you read my mind," Alberto said.

Feminine voices could be heard through the French doors. A look of annoyance crossed his face, which he hastily masked.

"I shall need you, Ordando, to stay with me," Alberto directed the younger man, who wasn't as intimidating in appearance as his partner.

Ordando nodded and followed closely behind Alberto as they entered the brightly lit room through the verandah doors. After making an appearance, it took only moments for several giddy females of various ages to surround the two men and attempt to engage them in conversation. Alberto directed the questions asked of him to Ordando who answered readily. Quite naturally the attention turned to Ordando, whose charming white-toothed smile welcomed the feminine appeal of the women fascinated by the visiting Spaniards. Ordando's dark handsome features added immensely to his attraction as he engaged in light small talk about his home and what it was like in Spain.

Alberto carefully moved through the women to the edge of the small group until he found an opportunity to slip away and disappear onto the crowded dance floor. From the moving figures, he spotted his hostess and made his way to her side where he excused himself formally from the gathering.

The woman, Madeline Glenn, a social trendsetter in her late fifties, found herself unable to concentrate completely on the man's words. She couldn't get past his striking dark face, and then his teeth flashed in a momentary smile that was devastating to glimpse.

She found herself nodding mutely and agreeing to whatever he said without understanding a word of it.

"My husband will be sorry he missed you," she responded after several moments of awkward silence where she simply stared at his face when he finished speaking. "But maybe…ah…on your next visit you will be able to discuss business with him. He will be very interested to hear of any business venture you propose."

Alberto looked puzzled then bowed low and lifted her hand to press a kiss firmly against it. "Your kindness in including my party was very generous, and yes, if I ever return, I will call upon your husband, gracias señora."

Madeline's eyelashes fluttered like a pair of butterfly wings. She glanced around to see if anyone else had witnessed this old world form of gallantry. With a deep sigh, she watched the straight-backed figure with raven black hair as he strode swiftly from the plaza.

Alberto opened the mirrored glass doors and stepped into the cold night. It was spring, and he could see his breath in the air. He nodded a greeting to Galeno as he slipped into the limousine.

Galeno quickly took his place behind the wheel and pulled away from the curb.

"You will have to return later to pick up Ordando," Alberto told him, relaxing against the plush seat.

Galeno grunted but said nothing.

"If you were half as accommodating as he is then you would have all the señoritas flirting with you," Alberto teased with laughter in his voice.

"If I cared to I would," Galeno replied as he deftly turned the vehicle out of the parking ramp.

"You have more distinguished taste than our young friend, eh?"

Galeno shot a look over his shoulder that spoke fathoms.

Alberto chuckled low as he settled back to stare out the window. The street they traveled on was quite picturesque in a restored-to-yesteryears style. After a few moments, he didn't bother to look at his surroundings. In the past few months, the numerous places he'd traveled, the small cities he visited, all melded together. His visit to the north of America held some surprises for him. The stark countryside waited for the thaw of spring, yet life abounded in thick forests of pine and rolling hills bordered by deep-watered lakes.

He had been residing at the country estate of a friend until yesterday morning and found the area similar in appearance to his homeland. When his group moved to the downtown area of the city before they departed, Alberto felt restless, which is why he accepted the party invitation. Now, the feeling was gone, replaced by a feeling of nostalgia. It was time to go home. He was tired of traveling and hotels. The time had come to return to the hacienda.

Galeno stopped the car in the entry of the hotel, and Alberto stepped out. The hotel lobby was quiet with only the desk clerk standing at the counter when he walked through the double doors.

The young man with a tired smile handed over the messages Alberto requested. He nodded his thanks as he flipped through the papers and realized it was fortunate he'd decided to depart early, there were several requests for him to telephone home. Galeno joined him, and the two waited in silence for the elevator.

"I think father is ready for us to return," Alberto said, folding the messages and slipping them into his pocket. With a humorless laugh, he added, "I am certain I will hear the full extent of his urgency when I place a call to the hacienda."

Galeno nodded briefly in response.

"Is that the only sign of rejoicing I will see from you? Didn't you claim long before that the cold in this place was like staying in the mountains during the worst of a winter that never seemed to end?"

"It is caused by the lake effect wind," Galeno informed him knowledgably. A glimmer of amusement showed in the blackness of his eyes as they entered the empty elevator.

Alberto laughed out loud. "Really?" he said, turning to look at the man who stood several inches taller and carried almost one hundred pounds more than he of pure muscle. "Where did you learn this?"

"The weather channel," Galeno replied evenly.

"With over eighty stations available on the television set, you are watching the weather channel," Alberto remarked with a smile.

"It is not uncommon for this part of the Northland to experience snow at this time of year," the big man said as he folded his hands across his waist and gave him a look of satisfaction.

Alberto rubbed his forehead not sure whether he should be amused or irritated. There was something bothering him, and he couldn't place what it was.

"Fine, fine," he exclaimed. "Not that I'm surprised. I can feel snow in the air tonight."

The two suites on the highest level of the hotel were being used by the Casilda party, and a key was needed to access the floor from the elevator.

Galeno inserted the key, and the elevator surged past the level used by the hotel guests to the next floor. Alberto moved quickly down the hall intent on reaching the privacy of his room and the use of the telephone.

"I'm not particularly hungry, amigo, so you will not be called again," Alberto told him. He turned back with a grin. "But don't leave Ordando stranded at the party all night. We need him tomorrow."

Galeno nodded and gave a short bow. "Buenas noches, señor."

"Good night, Galeno."

Alberto shut the door and walked into the large room. He didn't immediately pick up the telephone. Instead he wandered out onto the balcony where he looked over the lake. He was astonished at how quickly the mist had disappeared. The air was crisp, almost biting at the higher altitude. But the view of the lake was magnificent. Black water stretched to the horizon. A few lights glimmered on its surface, yet otherwise it remained untouched by civilization.

Alberto was just beginning to realize how intriguing this huge freshwater lake could be when a horn bellowed from out on the water. It wasn't the foghorn again. He leaned forward to look past the buildings and watched as a large ship, lit up with small lights, floated into view from behind a building. He heard a higher pitched blast but couldn't see what it might be. The loud blast was returning the signal, and Alberto listened, trying to pick out where the sound was coming from. His eyes followed the ship, which was clearly visible. The ship was headed toward a trellis bridge silhouetted in white lights. He watched in amazement as the middle of the bridge began to descend after the boat passed under it.

Alberto decided right then he must investigate this fascinating downtown area for at least another few days before boarding a plane for home. With the lake and...the woman...she was the cause of this strong feeling of unfinished business. Not knowing for certain what happened to her was weighing on his mind. He needed to find out. Alberto returned to the warm interior of his room, his thoughts raced as he slammed the door on the cold air outside.

3

Janine breathed a sigh of relief as she walked into the bright sunshine and cheerfully left behind the chill of the public library building where she worked. She wasted no time undoing the buttons of her sweater, the warmth of the sun making the added protection unnecessary until she returned to work. In her hands, she carried a hardbound copy of *Ivanhoe* and a paper sack with her meager lunch in it. She hurried down the steps to the Lakewalk where, with any luck, she would find an empty bench to sit and soak up the sun. After the stormy weather that gripped the area for the last few weeks, the bright blue sky overhead and the warm southwest wind were welcomed by everyone. She hurried around the slow moving couples that walked with hands entwined or arms draped comfortably about each other.

Janine tried not to stare at them, but she was fascinated by these couples. They were in the midst of finding out whether they loved each other enough to spend the remainder of their lives together, or they were already in love and enjoying it. She had never been in love herself, and she didn't quite know how people knew when it happened. Was it something that struck them at first sight, or was it something they discovered after knowing a person for a long time? For now, it was a mystery...for her at least. Janine would never admit it, but she was an old-fashioned girl. She believed when she did fall in love it would be the real thing. A love that would last forever.

"Miss."

Janine continued on her way, barely registering the voice calling out in the crowd. Whoever it was couldn't be calling to her.

She spotted an empty bench on the beach and rushed toward it but was stopped by a strong grip on her arm. She glanced down in alarm to see long dark fingers wrapped around the light green cotton sweater on her upper arm. Without hesitation she shook it off.

"Excuse me," she demanded icily. Barely moving her head, she looked to see an incredibly handsome man who could not possibly be from Duluth. This she could tell from his sun-darkened skin and the refined bone structure of his aristocratic features. He had to be a visitor, and it was his hand on her arm. His was the husky, incredibly sexy voice that had called out. She recognized the resonance but couldn't for the moment recall why. She thought with a momentary excitement that he might be a movie star or a famous singer.

"Miss, pardon me for being so forward." His expression was meek, which looked so out of character with the strong features. She couldn't stop herself from being interested.

"No, that's alright. Do you need directions somewhere?" she inquired politely though she tugged on her arm to be freed.

He grinned and released her.

"Thank you," he said. He'd been right about the pretty señorita. He couldn't believe his luck when he saw her walk right past him. The shapeliness of her figure caught his attention before he actually recognized her, and he knew this meeting was more than coincidence. When Galeno and Ordando couldn't track her down for two days, he'd almost lost hope, but the nagging worry that something bad had happened the night their paths had crossed could now be laid to rest.

"It seems we are destined to offer each other assistance when it is not really needed," he said smoothly. The feeling they were already acquainted burned strong within him.

Janine stared blankly at him and knew that something wasn't quite right. "I am sorry, but I don't understand," she said hesitantly. "If you don't need any help, I only have a short time and there are things I must do." Janine nodded briefly and hurried away, obviously giving him the brush-off.

Alberto watched her, a slight smile on his lips. He saw her glance over her shoulder several times to be certain he wasn't following. She settled herself on the only empty bench in sight. She craned her neck searching the many people milling around the area and then, satisfied he wasn't in sight, she seemed to relax.

Alberto stepped backwards off the walkway to avoid the other groups of chattering people who hurried around him. They seemed to be in a great rush to get to the end of the walkway and then turn around and come back again. None of them bothered to take time to enjoy the immense expanse of blue-black water that stretched out to the horizon and beyond. From Alberto's observations of the last few days, they seemed to barely notice the lake's incredible beauty.

Alberto couldn't seem to stop himself from staring at the water, then at the woman with wind-tossed brown hair streaked with strong traces of gold when the sun was behind her. She nibbled at her sandwich but seemed more interested in devouring the book she was reading. Alberto strongly suspected it was a tale of romance. He reached into his pocket for a cigar but hesitated. He didn't want to offend her. Americans had such strange ideas about smoking, and he was determined to speak to her again.

Janine slipped her sweater from her shoulders without raising her head from the book. The sun was hot even though the lake gave off a coldness that lent a crisp smell to the air. She skimmed the familiar words of the book quickly. Her hair fell over her face as she shrugged the clinging material of the sweater away.

"Miss, if I could only have a moment of your time?" The voice interrupted her at the very moment an incredibly expensive pair of shoes appeared in front of her.

Janine sighed and dragged her eyes from the page then closed her book with a thump. She looked up and felt almost a chill of curiosity. What in the world could this gorgeous foreigner want with her in the first place? And why was he so persistent? She couldn't be imagining it, not this time. He deliberately was seeking her out.

"May I join you on the bench?" he asked with that now familiar smile.

It set her teeth on edge to speak with a complete stranger like this, but they were in a very public place and nothing could happen, could it? She set her book and the bag from her lunch next to her, making it clear there was a boundary between them.

"You don't remember me?" Alberto began. She sat in silence staring out at the water instead of looking at him.

Janine's face fused with color as she looked directly at him for the first time. Her own soft brown eyes, ringed with yellow-green, filled with astonishment at his question.

"Remember you? I've never met you before," she stated emphatically.

He shook his head, the thick black hair remained midnight

dark even in the sun. It confirmed to her he was not local.

"No, you just do not remember," Alberto corrected her.

"Sir," she protested quickly, her shapely eyebrow raised, "it is not likely I would forget meeting a man like..." Janine stopped. Floundering over the words she was about to utter to this man's face, she was mortified by her lack of discretion. She fell silent in confusion.

Alberto watched her struggle, his black eyes danced at the conflicting emotions he saw on her face.

"The other night on the boardwalk near the hotel," he prompted. "You have no idea how many anxious moments I have experienced since that time, wondering whether you arrived at your destination safely or not. It caused me much dread that I might have been of assistance to you and failed to do so."

Janine sat in stunned disbelief and openly stared at him. She did remember the man from the other night, but surely this couldn't be him. His body had seemed so much more massive and his face so sinister in the dark. It was the night she'd almost missed her bus. She didn't recall much about him, except he scared the living daylights out of her. And his voice. She also remembered being followed by two men after passing the hotel, but this man was definitely different.

"I have remained in the area since that night hoping to find you and know that you are safe."

"You have?" she asked, incredulous. His story sounded too unbelievable. She was definitely suspicious but couldn't think of any reason he would fabricate such an outlandish lie.

Alberto stood indignantly. "Of course! Why would you even think to question it? I am a caballero, and it is our sworn duty to protect anyone in need." Especially beautiful women, he added to himself as his eyes searched her face.

"I...I'm sorry, I didn't mean to offend you," Janine said breathlessly after she watched him transform before her eyes into just what he claimed to be. An aristocrat, who wore his pride of being a gentleman like he wore the tailored suit over his broad shoulders. Both fit him perfectly.

"As you can see, I am fine," she told him, shading her eyes with her hand as she looked up at him towering above her. She definitely didn't like the disadvantage.

"Yes, I can see that," he conceded.

Before Janine could dwell on exactly what he meant, she glanced at her watch and immediately bounced off the bench to her feet.

"Oh, no!" she cried frantically. Her lunch break was over, so she quickly tried to gather up her things. Alberto grabbed the sweater and tucked it around her arm, so it would stay in place. Feeling more than a little anxious, she looked up at him and walked away.

"I would like to introduce myself," he said as he easily kept pace with her.

Janine glanced up at him in horror. "But why?" she asked, not slowing her stride.

Alberto fell silent for a moment.

"I'm not quite sure," he replied, dubiously frowning.

"Then let it be," she quickly pleaded. "I thank you for your concern. It will be the highlight of my year that I was taken care of by a caballero." She smiled brightly at him. "I am honored, sir. Good-bye." She managed a quick wave even as she struggled with her belongings before disappearing into the throng of walkers.

Alberto stopped dead. He had realized immediately how attractive the señorita was but when she smiled, it was only too obvious. He grinned and debated whether he should continue to follow her and find out where she worked. He figured she must be on, as Americans call it, her lunch break.

"Only enough time to devour food and rush back to the job, a terrible custom," he thought, shaking his head. He didn't know why they allowed it.

Alberto decided he'd upset her enough for one day and following her wasn't necessary. The book she was reading. It was much too large to carry far, especially for someone who walked more than usual. She must work nearby, either in a library or maybe a used bookstore. If he wanted, he could send Galeno to find her.

"Yes," he thought, feeling pleased despite the abrupt end to their conversation. He did want to find her again.

He should be concentrating on the plans for his trip home, yet he returned to the bench the señorita had used and stared out at

Lake Superior. He agreed with whoever had named it. It was the most superior lake he had ever encountered. The lake intrigued him almost as much as the woman.

The woman. What was it about her? He could not for the life of him explain his interest in her. It was to the point that he couldn't even think of an adequate response to her simple question. Alberto reached into his pocket for a thin black cigar and lit it, inhaling the rich blend of tobacco with pleasure.

Alberto pictured Janine rushing headlong down the wooden walk in the fog. Then again today she rushed down the walkway. She looked like such a sweet, tender blossom. If kept in cool temperatures she would never fade. He smiled when he remembered how easily she disposed of him. Sweet-tempered blossoms had to have thorns to protect themselves. If accustomed to the cool weather, could one survive in the heat of the plains? Is that why these people lived in this inclement place?

Alberto shook his head at the direction his thoughts had drifted and flicked the cigar into the stones along the rocky waterfront. He stood and crushed it beneath his hand-tooled leather shoes and began to walk restlessly back to the hotel. His pace quickened as a plan formed.

4

Janine stood outside the library with a group of ten others waiting to board the city bus after a long day at work. The bus pulled up to the curb, but Janine stayed toward the back of the line as she dug in her bag for her pass.

"Where is that darn thing?" she muttered under her breath. She could not find her wallet anywhere, so she grabbed her coin purse and counted out the necessary quarters to put in the meter.

Her irritation at being unprepared made her movements clumsy. Without lifting her eyes, she closely followed the person in front of her and stepped onto the metal stair. Suddenly her shoe slipped. She stumbled, falling forward. Incredibly strong hands grasped her arms from behind and gently lifted her upright and pulled her safely back to the sidewalk.

Janine, relieved to be saved from a nasty fall, turned to thank the man behind her. She barely stopped herself from gasping out loud when confronted by another Latin man. But, he was immensely different from her caballero. Huge, he stood above Janine with a thick torso and muscular arms, dressed in a dark three-piece suit.

"Oh, thank you," she stammered.

He didn't respond verbally, but bowed. His skin was dark and his features blunt, unlike the caballero's aristocratic features.

Janine remained unmoving for longer than she realized.

"Get on or move aside, lady," demanded the bus driver.

She spun around, almost tripping again, but caught her balance with a nervous little laugh. The man followed her on board but made his way to the back of the bus, far from where Janine sat next to the front door.

Once the bus had moved past several more stops, she glanced back to see if the man was still there. He sat straight, his body swaying slightly with the abrupt movements of the bus. His shoulders blocked anyone sitting behind him. He stared straight ahead, unmindful of the people surrounding him or their curious stares.

Janine turned away to concentrate on anything but him. She tried to figure out how she could have run into two handsome Latin American men in one day. But she was positive this man on the bus was not connected to the caballero. It appeared he had money or at least dressed like it. He certainly wouldn't be with a man who rode the city bus.

Her imagination had run wild after what happened at noon today. She was having such fun imagining why the caballero had wanted to introduce himself. At times, she found herself wishing she'd accepted his introduction, just to see what would have happened, although he was probably just being polite and following the customs of his people. She hated to remember she had little or no experience with any kind of gentleman, so she would have no idea how a person was expected to act toward one. With a sigh of dissatisfaction, she sat back in her seat and stared out the window, ignoring the whirl of activity around her.

The bus slowly emptied of passengers until finally Janine pulled the cable and stood, wondering if she would be the first home tonight. She'd better think of something to make for supper. She forgot about the man who had saved her until she stood on the bus stop with several others and waited for the bus to pass so she could cross the street. Then it was too late for her to see if he was still a passenger. He might have gotten off at any time along the way through the back door.

The group at her corner dispersed quickly, each one going in a different direction. Janine headed straight down the hill toward the lake. The gray water spread out in front of her. It had remained a beautiful day with clear skies and warm temperatures, until now. This close to the lake she could feel the temperature dropping as the sun went down. She slipped her jacket over her sweater and thought about the caballero. Her steps quickened. She couldn't wait to tell her mother about him, just to hear what she thought of it all.

5

The evening meal at the Nielsen's was usually a rushed affair put together by the first person home from work. Janine didn't mind cooking because at least then there was variety. If Joan beat her home, then soup and crackers would be on the table. Tonight it was spaghetti. Canned sauce and noodles with makeshift garlic bread made out of leftovers in the bread box. It wasn't anything spectacular, but still better than soup. And tonight, food wasn't as important as the conversation.

"Answer the door," Joan Nielsen called loudly from upstairs.

Janine walked out of the kitchen wiping her soapy hands on a towel. "What'd you say?"

"There is someone at the door."

Janine frowned. "You expecting anyone?"

"No."

"Not a package or anything?"

"If you answer the door, you can see firsthand why they are there," Joan said impatiently.

Joan walked down the stairs rubbing lotion into her hands. She looked enough like her daughter for people to know they were related, but Janine was taller with a fuller figure than her mother. Right now, Joan was finding it hard to keep any weight on her body. She assumed it was all a part of aging.

Janine threw open the door. There was a faint light left outside and she could see the outline of a man on the other side.

"Good evening, miss," the man said with a heavy accent.

Janine smiled. She couldn't help it. How could she treat him like a stranger when he lifted her in the air as if she weighed nothing?

"Good evening to you," she said. "Did I lose something when I nearly knocked you over this afternoon?" A dimple appeared in her cheek when she smiled.

The man's expression didn't change, but she saw him relax.

"No, miss."

Janine smiled again. She had never been called "miss" so much in her life. It was nice, but incredibly formal.

"I would like to deliver an invitation to you."

"An invitation?" She stared at him in astonishment. The last thing she expected when she opened the door was to have this conversation with a mysterious foreigner in her sweat shirt and sweat pants.

"My employer wishes to invite you to the Mayor's Ball, which takes place tomorrow evening. He wished to invite you personally, but there wasn't time for introductions this afternoon."

Janine stared at him. Her mind raced.

"Your employer," she repeated. Why was she repeating everything he said? She sounded like an idiot.

The man didn't seem to notice, or if he did, his expression remained impassive.

"Yes, my employer is Mr. Alberto Casilda. He is the man who spoke to you this afternoon, and who spoke to you two nights ago in the fog on the Lakewalk."

"Alberto Casilda," she murmured. His name rolled off her tongue. At least she'd been astute enough to recognize him as a foreigner. Janine shook her head. Her thoughts muddled with confusion.

"Excuse me, miss," he said, pulling Janine out of her thoughts. His face was expressionless. "It is the same man. I can assure you of that."

Janine looked blank for a moment. "I know that," she giggled. "I wasn't disputing you, only trying to clear my head and figure out if I'm dreaming or not."

She couldn't tell for certain, but she thought she saw a glimmer of a smile cross the man's mouth. He held out an envelope. The thick calloused fingers showed this man was accustomed to more strenuous work than he was doing at present.

Hesitating briefly, she reached out and took the envelope. It felt like paper with a satin texture, not like any paper she'd ever handled. She held it in both hands then slowly turned it over. The back was sealed with a wax stamp that was the seal of the City of Duluth. The only reason she recognized it was because she worked at the public library, and the seal was displayed over the door.

"Do you want me to open it now?" she asked quietly, her heart pounded in her chest.

He nodded.

Janine slid the wax off carefully with one fingernail and took out the bulky invitation. It was the cleanest white color she'd ever seen with inlaid gold letters. Yes, it was an official invitation to the Mayor's Ball, an annual occasion she barely knew existed. It was something she never thought she would be invited to.

"I suppose you would need an answer right now?" She gave him a hopeful look, wishing it weren't true.

He nodded his head watching her closely. "If that is entirely convenient for you."

"No it isn't entirely convenient for me," Janine wanted to shout at him but swallowed the thought instead.

"It is awfully short notice," she said lamely after several minutes of reading each elegant line of the invitation. This was something that would definitely end up in her scrapbook she decided.

Joan silently walked up behind Janine to see what was taking her so long at the door at this hour of the night.

"Hello," she said, hiding her surprise at seeing the Latin giant.

At Joan's appearance, the giant bowed in the same manner he had to Janine.

Joan studied him briefly before asking, "What do you have there, Janine?"

"Mr. Casilda wishes to extend this invitation to everyone in the household," the man told them.

"But Mr. Casilda wishes us to give our answer now," Janine added, a note of desperation in her voice.

Joan read the invitation Janine handed to her.

"The Mayor's Ball? How lovely! I didn't remember it was tomorrow evening," she exclaimed. "Mr. Casilda has invited us?" she asked rather gaily.

Janine turned to look at her, wondering what she was up to.

Galeno nodded.

"Please tell him we accept," Joan said without hesitation.

Janine's mouth dropped open in surprise for a fraction of a second before she snapped it shut.

Directing the question to Joan, he asked, "How many shall I say will be attending?"

"Two," she said, then laughed softly. "Yes, he would want to know that. There are only two of us here."

"I will arrive with a car at whatever time is convenient for you," Galeno said.

"No!" Janine cried abruptly.

Both Galeno and Joan stared at her. She flushed crimson.

"We will find our own way," Janine explained. "Thank you very much."

He looked at Joan for confirmation. She shrugged her shoulders.

"As you wish." He bowed to them and left the two women in the doorway.

As soon as the door shut behind him, Janine turned on her mother.

"What are you thinking accepting this man's invitation?" she demanded shrilly. Her body was so filled with nervous tension she couldn't stand still. She spun away and paced quickly into the small living room. "I cannot go. I will not go," she muttered half out loud.

Joan, unperturbed by her daughter's explosion, followed her.

"You're just shy, Jani." Joan attempted to soothe her. "I was quite impressed with that man at the door. He had impeccable old world manners." She laughed. "Suddenly I realize how much I miss it. What was his name?"

Janine stopped dead.

"I don't know!" she exclaimed. "I can't believe it. I didn't introduce myself to him either. You have accepted a man's invitation to an exclusive ball, and he doesn't even know our names. This is absolutely ridiculous."

"Janine, it's time for you to get over this shyness," Joan quietly reprimanded her. "It's gotten much worse where men are concerned. You know it could cause you to end up an old maid."

Janine groaned loudly, casting her eyes up at the ceiling.

"Oh thank you very much, mother," she wailed. "That certainly takes the stress out of the situation. Are you so sick of having me around you're going to auction me off to the highest bidder? Which, in this case, I might remind you, would also be the first bidder."

Joan picked up the mail and began sorting through it.

"Don't talk so silly. You always act this way when a fearful new situation comes along. Remember to breathe deeply or you'll hyperventilate." She glanced over at her anxious daughter. "Or better yet, just calm down."

"Mother!" she shrieked, ignoring her sarcasm. "I will not go to this thing. I don't care what you say."

Joan opened a bill and read it, disregarding Janine completely. She settled herself on the couch.

"If I were you," Joan said, "I would begin thinking about where I'm going to find a suitable gown on such short notice." She glanced at her watch. "You still have three hours until the stores over the hill close."

"I don't need a gown," Janine declared stubbornly. She knew her mother was right, but she wasn't giving in…yet.

She took several deep breaths to steady her nerves. After several minutes of her mother ignoring her tantrum, Janine conceded.

"Isn't there something in the attic in one of those chests that might work?" she asked sheepishly.

Joan looked up and smiled at her daughter. Janine could look amazingly plain at times, but when she was happy and her eyes lit up, she possessed a real beauty that few people got to see. It had been so long since anything had riled Janine to this level of excitement that Joan had forgotten what she was like.

Their lives had become downright dull. Janine was too young to live this way. She'd had no rebellious teenage years. Her father had died when she was fifteen, and after that she had become more reserved than ever. She stopped socializing outside of school, and most of her high school friends left town while she stayed home and attended business school. In recent years, she hadn't renewed any previous friendships or formed any new ones. Now with a steady career in the reference department at the downtown library, her chances of meeting people slimmed down to those she met going to and coming from work or those at work. Joan shuddered at the lack of hope for her daughter's future relationships. The mystery surrounding these meetings with the Latin men gave Joan some pause, but Janine was sensible, and the Mayor's Ball was a public function.

To receive an invitation, this young man must be a visiting

dignitary of some kind. Maybe he was from one of those sister cities the paper was always writing about. Whatever the case, Janine needed to get out more and socialize. Even if it did get lonely for Joan, this was important for her daughter's future happiness.

"I think that's a marvelous idea," Joan told her as she tossed the mail back onto the table and stood up. "Why don't we go right now and rummage through a few of those old trunks." Joan gave her daughter a quick hug. Tears welled in her eyes. When she looked back on her daughter's life so far there was definitely a dismal pall to the picture.

"This will be fun," she whispered. "How many people do you know who can say they've mingled with the rich and famous from Duluth, Minnesota?"

"Rich and famous?" Janine raised her eyebrows in question. "How many could there possibly be?"

"I guess we'll find out firsthand, won't we?" Joan grasped her hand, and they hurried up the stairs.

Janine again felt that chill of excitement and, for the moment, didn't mind the thought of going to the ball.

6

"Ouch," Janine cried as steam from the iron seared her arm. This was the third time she'd attempted to fix the thick white lace around the collar of the dress she had chosen. Janine had tried every ironing trick she knew, which was quite a few since her maiden aunt had taught her how to iron formal garments many years ago, but nothing could make the stubborn piece of material lay flat like the other side. She slammed the iron down with an angry, but futile, bang.

"Did you try a touch of starch?" Joan asked from the living room where she was lying on the couch resting to get rid of a nagging headache.

"No," Janine sighed. She didn't like to use starch because if you used too much there was nothing that could reverse it. Many a stiff collar had scraped her skin raw because she'd used too much starch. Reluctantly, she reached for the spray can and gently misted the material before she again pressed the iron against it. Amazingly, the collar did what it was supposed to do. Janine lifted the heavy gown from the ironing board and gently shook it several times until the material fell the way it should.

There was no doubt this dress was from a different time, but the regal beauty was still evident. Heavy white lace made out of a material she didn't recognize lay as a shell over a shift of shimmering pearl white satin. When Janine had first lifted it out of the tissue, she'd thought it was a wedding dress.

"More like an old-fashioned bridesmaid dress," Joan had laughed.

Janine looked at her curiously.

"No honey, not mine, your grandmother's."

Janine sighed and began re-folding it.

"What are you doing?" Joan questioned, reaching out to stop her.

"If it's Grandma's dress it would never fit me. She was five feet tall."

"Don't be silly, Jani. If you like it, take it downstairs and try it on. We have no idea what the styles were like or how things fit back then. You won't know for sure unless you try, right?" Joan sighed impatiently at Janine's stubborn expression. "Just do it," she commanded.

Janine did try it on, and the dress fit her. Not like it must have fit her grandmother, but in a way that looked just fine for one night at a ball where she knew not a soul except her caballero. Janine's heart jumped, even if it was unrealistic to hope the man might be as attentive to her as he had been before. She could still hope. Janine hadn't yet figured out what motivated him, but she was sure after tonight everything would become quite clear. He could turn out to be a lecherous foreigner, or he could be as wonderful as she imagined him to be.

In spite of the butterflies in her stomach, Janine continued to carry on with her preparations, fixing her makeup with just a touch of eye shadow, which she rarely used. Her hair, though a mousy brown, was thick and looked nice French braided. The old-fashioned dress and traditional hairstyle lent a touch of whimsy from the past, which seemed to fit her rather nicely. She had hung the dress in the sun all day hoping to bleach out some of the discoloration, but retro was in, so she didn't fret too much about the spots that were still visible. At least it smelled of the fresh air now and not the attic.

She turned slowly, studying her reflection in the mirror, and was pleased with the final product. Not one to dwell on her appearance, she decided she was now prepared to meet Mr. Alberto Casilda, who had come into her life so unexpectedly. If Alberto decided, once he saw her, that he didn't want to spend the evening with her it wouldn't matter with her mother there. Well, it would matter, but at least she wouldn't look like a complete fool.

Janine slipped on the dainty high-heeled shoes and gathered her lipstick, tissues, and money into the small handbag she'd found in the same trunk as the dress. When she left her room, she hurried to her mother's room, anxious to see what she thought.

"How are you doing?" she called out as she walked down the hall to her mother's bedroom. She expected no surprises since her mother was wearing her old "spider web dress," as she referred to the black lace gown Joan wore to all formal occasions, including weddings.

She pushed open the door to find Joan lying in bed. Janine's chest tightened in fear. She hurried to the bedside.

"Mother…mother, what's wrong?" she cried fearfully. She leaned closer to her mother's still figure and gently brushed the hair back from her forehead.

Joan's eyes fluttered open, and she screamed in her face. "What are you doing?" she cried, pushing Janine away.

"I'm trying to see if you're still breathing," Janine shouted back angrily. "You scared me, lying there so still." Janine put her hands on her cheeks and began to laugh in relief. "Why are you still in bed?" she asked, her voice still too loud.

The clock on her mother's bedside table showed it was time to be calling the cab. If her mother hadn't even begun to dress they would never make it. Janine couldn't believe she'd just spent an hour, no, the entire afternoon, getting ready, and it was all for nothing.

"I fell asleep," Joan said, yawning. "At least my headache is finally gone. But now I feel stiff and sore all over. Maybe I have a touch of the flu?"

Janine sighed deeply. "Well, how do I look?" she asked, twirling around in place.

"Oh, Jani, you look absolutely beautiful. That style is so becoming on you."

"Okay, now I can go change," Janine said, trying to inject a note of cheer into her voice though she felt oddly deflated. Funny, in the beginning, she had been so adamant about not attending the ball and now felt bad about missing it.

"What?" Joan cried sitting up in her bed. "Don't be silly! You can't not go just because of me. Please, Janine, you must attend the Mayor's Ball. This is a once in a lifetime chance, and you can't let me ruin it for you."

Janine laughed without amusement. "That is funny. You actually think I would go without you?" she stared at her mother in disbelief. "Remember I was the one who didn't want to go in the first place. I will certainly not go alone."

Joan sat in silence for so long Janine was prepared to just walk out of the room and change without waiting for a response. Then Joan slowly pushed the covers down, wincing as she moved her legs over the side of the bed.

"What do you think you're doing?" Janine asked.

"If you won't go tonight without me, I will get ready, and we will go late," Joan said. Even her voice sounded weak to Janine. Anxiously, she searched her mother's pale face and saw lines of weariness in it. "You can't possibly mother. You still don't look well."

"Thank you very much," Joan declared with asperity. "I hope I can successfully hide that under makeup so nobody else thinks the same."

Janine stood in front of her trying to block her from standing.

"You can't be serious about this?" she challenged her. The bed was so tall the two almost faced each other.

"Really?" Joan asked. "If you doubt for a moment that I would rather faint dead away in that ballroom than give you an excuse not to attend tonight, then you don't know me very well. I will not allow you to remain outside of life any longer, Janine. You are not a widower. Your husband did not die in a shipwreck on Lake Superior, mine did."

She watched Janine's face and saw her confusion. Gently, she smiled at her daughter. The realization it was time to boot her out of the nest had come a bit slow, but it was obvious now and it wasn't going to be easy on either of them.

"Jani, you have worked so hard getting ready, and I've never seen you look more beautiful than you do tonight, or more excited. Please dear, go to the ball and enjoy yourself just by watching the people if need be. But think how disappointed your friend, the ambassador of wherever, will be if both of us don't show up after he took so much trouble to send that invitation."

"I'm not going," Janine said.

Joan hardened her voice and said, "You need to go and thank this man, Janine. If you don't speak to him after that, fine, but he needs to know that Janine Nielsen, American girl, is not a rude and uncaring person."

Janine fiddled with her fingers while she stared at the picture of her father that hung above her mother's bed. It was an oil painting, rather immature in style, but an accurate portrayal of her father just the same. It showed him as the captain of a sailing vessel.

Not an ore boat like he had worked on, but a lovely clipper ship with full sail was in the background. He held the ornate wooden helm with both hands. The wind was blowing his brown hair and beard while he fought the waves. He looked bigger than life—full of bravery and handsome with heroic fortitude. Just as a girl of sixteen might perceive her dead father, the portrait was one Janine had painted in high school. It had won the first prize at the state competition, but it had been the last painting she'd ever completed.

"That's just a bunch of bull, mother," Janine said quietly. "But, I will go tonight, and not because you're blackmailing me, but because I am truly curious about the men I've met in the last couple of days." She paused. "And I've always wanted to meet the mayor," she finished with a shy smile. Her bottom lip trembled. She turned away. "If I don't call for the cab now, I'll be late and have a dramatic entrance, which I don't want."

Joan relaxed against the pillows. "Stop being so hard on yourself young lady, you are an incredibly attractive girl if you give yourself half a chance. Especially in that outfit. You look like someone in a movie."

"Yeah, an outdated movie," Janine said under her breath.

Janine waited on the porch for the cab, feeling more than a little anxious about her decision to continue on by herself. The sky was dark indigo with bright stars glittering in the crisp night air. The air was still, the lake barely moved against the shoreline rocks. She watched the reflections of different lights shimmer across the water.

Headlights disturbed the darkness as the cab turned down the avenue.

"Good night, mother," Janine called out and pulled the heavy front door shut.

As the cab sped away from the house, she knew she would make it downtown in plenty of time. Her pulse raced as she watched out the window, recognizing each building they passed. It brought her closer to an evening she couldn't begin to imagine. Her heart kept time with the speed of the vehicle until she began to feel faint.

"This will never work," she thought. "I will make an utter fool of myself. I know I will."

She leaned forward, ready to ask the driver to turn around,

when he pulled into the hotel's drop-off area and screeched to a halt. It was too late.

"Five bucks," he said, looking over his shoulder.

Janine's hands trembled as she fumbled with her wallet. Her stomach churned when she stepped out onto the sidewalk. Neon lights beat down on her from above. She held the invitation so tight it was becoming damp. There had never been any reason for Janine to go into the grand old-fashioned hotel before tonight, and when she stepped through the front door, she forgot her anxiety as she looked around with interest.

The lobby looked like an old prom movie. The heavy velvet window hangings of deep maroon with gold piping hung from windows that extended from ceiling to floor. A large round velvet settee that was set in the middle of the room was covered with the same material as the window hangings. Ornate cornices of scroll-work seemed to adorn every nook and cranny of the woodwork in the lobby. She craned her neck to look at the old-fashioned light fixtures and saw the ceiling had scrollwork painted in gold.

Slowly, she walked toward the elevators, her high-heeled shoes sinking into the plush carpet. The brightly polished brass doors of the elevator reflected her figure until the door opened. A smartly dressed young man stood inside ready to greet her.

"Your invitation please, ma'am," the freshly shaven youth asked politely.

Janine handed it out to him, and he accepted it with a smile. His eyes quickly scanned the wording, and he handed it back.

"I'll have you upstairs in a few minutes," he told her. "You aren't late," he added softly.

"Thank you," Janine murmured, wondering if she was expected to tip him. She couldn't come to a decision before the elevator stopped and he opened the door.

"Have a nice evening," he said, and the elevator door shut behind her. It was her last means of escape.

"Just to see this place is worth it," Janine reminded herself as she continued to walk as slowly as possible and look around the hallway. The colors used to decorate this floor carried on the rich theme of the lobby. The carpet, the window coverings, and the benches were covered in dark green velvet. She saw stairs leading up either side of the balcony and wondered where they led to. She might explore a little before she left tonight. Her apprehension grew as she approached the ballroom. Soft music drifted from the room. The doors were propped open showing bright lights and people moving around inside. Another young bellman waited in the doorway.

"Invitation please, ma'am."

Janine frowned. Did she really look old enough to be labeled a "ma'am"? How maddening. She found she preferred being called "miss" by the Latin gentlemen.

"Thank you," he said politely. He handed the invitation back to her and asked, "Is there a party you wish to join? I would be more than happy to escort you to where they are seated."

Janine's throat felt dry, and she hoped she could speak without croaking. "I…I'm not quite sure who," she said, casting her eyes anxiously around the room.

The young man smiled. "That isn't a problem. I'm sure I know almost everyone here," he told her boldly, clasping his hands behind his back and rocking slightly forward on his toes.

"Mr. Alberto Casilda," she said, speaking the words slowly so as to pronounce them correctly. Nervously she watched his face to see his reaction to the name. The confident smile faded slightly. Then it returned in full force. "Yes, I think I know where he is sitting. Please take my arm."

Janine slid her hand through his arm. It wasn't comfortable, but it did give her a slight feeling of security. He led her across the room with his shoulders back and his head up. She was almost amused by the amount of pride this young man took in his job.

The room was long and lit by many chandeliers that glimmered like crystal. Janine was aware of people standing in groups and others already seated at tables but couldn't bring herself to focus on any of them. The air buzzed with conversation and the clinking of ice-cubes in glasses. Large floor vases filled with the most beautiful flowers decorated the room, leaving the scent of their freshness as she walked past them. It was somewhat like being in a dream except the glare of the light and the hard pounding of her heart turned it into more of a nighmare.

7

Alberto stopped speaking to the men who stood with him near the windows when he saw her walk into the room. The demure gown matched the modest shyness of her downcast eyes. Her beauty he had not doubted, but watching her across the room he recognized what had caused this incredible infatuation. She was past the fresh youthfulness of immaturity. Her allure had deepened into a promise of lasting desirability, yet she had retained an innocence he could see but couldn't understand. How could this have happened in the fast pace of the modern world?

He felt a stab of jealousy directed at the boy who held her arm.

"She was supposed to be at my side walking next to me," Alberto thought.

He murmured a hasty excuse and walked to the table where Janine was being helped into her seat. With a sure hand, he smoothed his dinner jacket and tie before stopping next to her chair. The boy was assisting her by removing her shawl when Alberto motioned for him to step aside so he could finish the task. His hands moved across the warm flesh of her arms. She abruptly moved away, glancing behind with a startled expression.

"Oh, it's you," she exclaimed softly. A flush swept up her neck into her cheeks.

He draped her shawl over the arm of the doorman before he bowed to her. "I am so delighted to see you," he murmured, his voice low with a tempo unfamiliar to this part of the world. "Your mother is joining us soon?"

"My mother won't be coming," Janine told him. "She isn't feeling well."

Alberto clucked his tongue sympathetically. "I am sorry. Nothing serious I hope?"

"Oh, no," she shook her head. "Nothing serious."

"Then may she return to health swiftly," Alberto replied.

A waiter dressed in black and white, like the doormen, walked up to the table.

"Something to drink?" Alberto asked.

Her eyes, more green than brown tonight, anxiously flitted around to see what other people were drinking. "I'm not sure."

"A glass of wine perhaps?" Alberto said, then shook his head. "Champagne. We would like a bottle of Dom Perignon," he said decisively.

The waiter nodded and left.

"Would you like to sit here for awhile until he returns or take a walk around the room to view it?"

Janine didn't answer, instead she again surveyed the room, avoiding Alberto's dark eyes.

"Of course, you hesitate because we have not been formally introduced, although I believe you have me at a disadvantage. You know my name, yet I do not know yours," Alberto said.

"I do apologize for that," Janine said hastily. "It was terribly rude on my part, and it must have made you're...ah...the man uncomfortable to return unable to tell you who would be coming here tonight."

"His name is Galeno, and I don't know what I would do without him." Alberto explained. "He found you for me, for which I will be eternally grateful." Then he said to Janine, "Have I told you how charming you look tonight?"

Janine fidgeted uncomfortably. "Thank you. And you, too, look very," Janine fished for something more original, but only came up with, "charming."

Alberto laughed out loud. "Come, keep me in suspense no longer, my name is Alberto Casilda, but my friends call me Berto. I hope you will do me the honor of doing the same."

"My name is Janine Nielsen, Mr. Casilda...ah...Berto. Please call me Janine." She swallowed hard. "Oh and thank you for inviting me here tonight."

Alberto smiled. "Thank you for coming. If you were not a part of this evening it would turn into a tedious affair."

Janine vigorously shook her head. "How can you say that?" she protested. "To be invited to this ball is one of the highest honors a Duluthian can receive. Only the high society of Duluth are here tonight." She glanced around the room to confirm.

"Do you know these people?" Alberto asked as he watched her face.

Janine suddenly smiled. "Now I know exactly two people here."

Alberto tensed at the thought of having to share her with anyone. Then he turned and followed the direction she was looking.

"I know you and Galeno," she said, laughter bubbled in her throat.

He, too, smiled when he saw Galeno and Ordando standing next to the wall at the door.

"The man with him is Ordando. They are here with me while I am working on a few business proposals."

Business was a safe subject they could talk about. Janine jumped on the opportunity.

"Tell me what kind of business you are in," she prompted.

He looked surprised at her question. "I am here to examine a herd of cattle," he told her with amusement. "A bull to be exact. We are making an attempt to establish a sturdier breed of cattle to graze in mountain ranges. The weather here equals what the beasts would experience in the mountains, if not the terrain, but it isn't often I am questioned on the subject at a dinner engagement."

"Oh, really," she stopped, then added, "so, you have had success then in finding the breeding stock you were looking for?" What was she saying? She was definitely not comfortable with the topic of breeding stock.

At that moment, the waiter interrupted them. He held a silver bucket filled with ice and a bottle of champagne. The waiter presented the bottle with a flamboyance she found entertaining. When the waiter departed, Alberto handed her a crystal glass with a splash of amber liquid in it.

"Are you familiar with this brand?" he inquired, twirling the glass he held but watching her.

Janine shook her head but didn't add she wasn't familiar with any brand of alcohol.

"Then you might want to sip it first."

"I'm afraid you're wasting it on me," she protested, holding the delicate flute carefully in her hands.

"Then you must try and make an effort not to let me know," he said with a wink.

Janine sipped the drink and found she was unsure what it tasted like. It left a tang as an aftertaste, but she couldn't decide if it was good or bad.

"If you don't like it, just tell me, I will order you something else," he urged her after filling his own glass. "It won't hurt my feelings if you do," he added, smiling.

Janine shook her head and took another small sip, savoring the bubbling liquid across her tongue. "I'll keep this, thank you," she told him, ready to give the champagne another chance.

"Now let us walk around the room," he said, setting his glass down and taking her arm.

Janine glanced at the intimidating array of Duluth's elite.

"I'd prefer not to just yet," she said nervously.

Alberto frowned. "The view is quite picturesque, or am I doing you an injustice? You already are familiar with this place. Of course you are," he answered his own question. "Then I will ask you to humor me. As a visitor, I will not have another opportunity to enjoy this place with you again."

He was so incredibly charming she couldn't resist him. "You've been busy learning about Duluth during your stay," she said, wondering where he lived and why he refrained from mentioning his homeland. She was positive it had to be more exciting than Duluth.

"Yes, I've made time to learn about it," he said. "I found on this visit that I am something of a history buff. Come, when we look around you can tell me what life is like in this city."

Janine decided to relax and enjoy the company of this man. They wandered around as if they were the only people there, and it was their duty to discover everything about the historic hotel. When they paused to look out the windows that faced the lake, Alberto leaned toward her. "Tell me about your family."

She figured he would ask her this question sometime tonight. Why hadn't she rehearsed some witty answer that revealed nothing but filled time?

"I don't really know what would interest you," she said, her voice unsteady as her mind raced. She toyed with the idea of telling him about her father, but that could get complicated. She shrugged her shoulders and turned away from the windows.

"It looks like people are beginning to sit down in the dining room," she covered. The busy atmosphere of the dining room was preferable to revealing her life to this man.

"Then we should return to our seats," he said, leading the way down the hall.

While seated at supper, they barely spoke to each other because of the people sitting with them. Janine didn't remember their names after the introductions because she had no idea who they were or what they did. They didn't seem inclined to enlighten her or add her to their list of acquaintances. Each treated her in an amiable manner that wasn't far from condescending.

When dessert had been cleared and coffee or after dinner liqueurs were being offered, Janine discovered that, despite the attitude of the people at her table, she was having a wonderful time. Alberto had departed to speak with his men, so she had a few minutes alone. In spite of all her fears, she no longer felt a bit uneasy about anything. Her behavior, though far from satisfying her, was at least acceptable. She hadn't done anything awkward like drop her spoon into her soup. Alberto acted like the perfect gentleman, and she found it easy to follow his lead. She'd even laughed at the appropriate times during the speeches whether she understood the joke or not. Soon the evening would come to an end. What could possibly go wrong now?

The microphone squealed interrupting her thoughts.

"Ladies and gentlemen, the orchestra is playing in the Moorish Room. Please join the Mayor and his wife downstairs as the dancing begins."

Her short reprieve ended. The thought of dancing in public made her instantly nauseous. Being held in Alberto's arms was a fantasy full of promise, but she couldn't think about it for too long without breaking out in a cold sweat.

There was a movement throughout the room as the guests prepared to leave the dining room. Soon Alberto would come for her. Janine scrambled to grasp her bag and searched for her shawl. She groaned as she realized it had been taken by the man who had escorted her earlier. She thought of abandoning it and returning for it tomorrow, but it was a family heirloom. She couldn't risk it being stolen. She was still formulating an escape plan when Alberto suddenly appeared next to her.

"You misplaced something?" he inquired.

"No," she exclaimed. "I was wondering what time it is. I don't want to leave my mother alone for too long."

Alberto was silent for so long Janine glanced at him, feeling uncomfortable about the blatant lie she'd come up with.

He took her arm. "Come," he said, his tone almost a command.

Janine followed him out of the dining area into the crowded hallway. Her head felt fuzzy, and it couldn't be from the one glass of champagne she had drunk hours earlier.

Alberto led her into a small unoccupied side room.

She still felt guilty when he abruptly turned to her.

"Are you ready to leave Janine?" he asked. "Or is your mother just an excuse to leave?"

She stared at him. "I think it would be best, you see, I have work tomorrow very early and I…"

"You need to care for your mother."

"Yes, right, my mother." She moved away from him, which wasn't easy in the narrow room. "It has been a wonderful evening, Berto, but…"

"You cannot believe I mean to say goodnight to you in a," he glanced around them doubtfully, "in a closet?"

Janine giggled, "I really must be going."

"Allow me to find your wrap, and then Galeno will drive you to your home." He led her into the hallway and left to find his companions.

Slowly, Janine walked up the stairs that led to the ladies' room. In the bathroom, she combed her hair and reapplied her lipstick. Pausing, she stared at her reflection, the lipstick poised near her full lower lip. Suddenly, a picture of a goodnight kiss flashed through her mind, and the lipstick clattered into the deep bowl of the porcelain sink. She hadn't thought that far ahead.

With shaking hands, she reached for the lipstick and put the cover on. He wouldn't expect a kiss with Galeno and Ordando present. She frowned. That would be awkward for both of them.

Realizing she couldn't stay in the bathroom forever, she walked back downstairs to say good-bye. In only a few days, Alberto had completely destroyed her peace of mind. What would he do to her sanity if he kissed her? She would never forget him, that's what would happen. It was doubtful she could forget about him now.

As she descended the staircase, her gaze fell on the elegant length of Alberto lounging against the brass pillar outside the dining room. This would probably be the last time she'd see him, and she wanted to memorize the sight. His black and white tuxedo was made of the finest material she'd ever seen. His dark hair was thick and it curled around the white collar. He straightened, the pleasure on his face was evident when he saw her. He moved toward her and took her hand in his, cradling it close to the curve of his body as they walked toward the elevator.

"It's still hard for me to believe I'm really here," she told him. "I enjoyed everything, the champagne, the food, watching the people I only hear about on the news. It was all very enlightening."

Alberto nodded. "So you're saying it has given you an insight into what happens in foreign places with different people. That is good, but remember, we are all flesh and blood, Janine. We eat, sleep, and live our lives as best we can. Did you think of that when you watched those people?"

His grip on her hand tightened when he spoke.

The elevator sounded and the doors slid open. The same doorman stood inside waiting. He pressed the floor button.

"Have a pleasant evening," he said as they exited on the ground floor. The lobby was empty except for Ordando, who walked beside them.

"Galeno should be pulling up this very moment," Ordando told them.

Alberto nodded. He paused to drape Janine's shawl across her shoulders, lifting a strand of hair from her neck. His fingers lightly caressed the silky texture before he released it.

Janine turned and grasped his hand, holding it tight with both of hers. The action was impulsive, but she didn't feel like herself at the moment. She was also trying to ignore a twinge of guilt. "Please let me say again thank you, I had a marvelous time."

"Yes, you've already said that," he replied.

"I want you to know what a pleasure it has been to be escorted by you." She bit her lower lip. "I hope you enjoy the remainder of your time in the city," she gushed, her words rushed.

She held tightly to her shawl with one hand as he held her

other hand. She tried to pull away. Alberto frowned and attempted to keep his hold on her, but Janine slipped free.

"I'll just hop in the taxi that's waiting out there. It will save you the drive to my house," she said and hurried to the glass door. She pushed it open and escaped outside.

The cab driver leaned over and opened the passenger door for her. She glanced back before climbing inside. Neither of the men had moved. She slammed the door shut and sank down in the seat. Even though she had escaped without that uncomfortable good-bye kiss, Janine felt terrible.

The cab pulled out and sped down the street. She closed her eyes and took a deep breath.

"Tonight was like a dream," she thought, "a wonderful dream." She sighed. "And this is the end, but not happily ever after."

As the cab disappeared around the corner, the limousine pulled into view. Alberto remained immobile for several minutes, staring out the door before he laughed.

"What was that?" he said to Ordando. "You understand women as well as I," he shook his head, "but who could understand a woman like that?" He spoke out loud but didn't expect a reply.

The young man beside him didn't move a muscle, standing as still as possible with his arms folded behind his back. With a sharp breath, Alberto strode quickly out the door. Ordando silently hurried after him.

8

Janine drifted in and out of daydreams as she sat at her cluttered desk in the back of the huge library room. Tall book shelves were on either side of her desk. The surface was covered with thick leather reference volumes. Sound echoed back in this corner because it hadn't been carpeted when the building was furnished fifteen years ago. The high ceilings and lack of floor coverings made the room cold no matter what time of year it happened to be.

She tapped her pen against the open program book that lay across her desk and stared off into space with an occasional sigh. Footsteps brought her abruptly out of her reverie. She leaned closer to the book flipping through the pages scanning the information.

"Stop acting so busy," a brassy voice said to her. "It's only me."

Janine dropped the pen and stood up. "Is it break already?" she exclaimed, excited at the possibility she might see Alberto out on the boardwalk if she hurried.

"No, in fact, it's practically closing time," Connie said, perching on the corner of Janine's desk. Connie was Janine's supervisor, but also a friend. She had the habit of advising the younger woman and then apologizing afterward before vowing to mind her own business from then on. It was a promise she never kept and Janine didn't want her to keep. She appreciated hearing Connie's point of view, even if she didn't take her advice.

"This package was a special delivery a few minutes ago, and I thought it was important enough to give to you right now."

Janine stared at the silver, foil-wrapped box like it would jump out and bite her. "Delivered?" she asked. "What did he look like?"

"A big man, big and dark, he didn't talk much." She grinned. "I got the feeling he wasn't from around here, especially when he bowed and left."

Janine smiled slightly while her mind raced.

Connie pushed the pretty box closer to Janine when she made no move to touch it.

Janine had no idea what Alberto could be sending her.

"It looks like jewelry. Please open the darn thing," Connie politely demanded.

"I don't know, Connie," Janine hesitated, still unable to touch it. "I shouldn't accept an anonymous gift. Isn't that forbidden in some etiquette book?"

"You don't know if it's anonymous or not until you open it," Connie interrupted. "There could be a card inside."

Janine shook her head. "I can't. Not right now," she said, her expression pleading with her friend to understand.

"Oh, right," Connie jumped off the desk. "I'm such a ninny. I didn't realize how rude I was being. I'm sorry," she said, giving a wave before hurrying away.

Janine jumped to her feet. "No! Connie that's not what I meant," she cried before realizing she'd just yelled in the library. The sound bounced around the walls disturbing everyone.

Several people glared at the two women, shushing them.

Janine was mortified as she sank back into the shadows surrounding her desk. Connie hurried back, giggling at her friend's embarrassment. She'd never seen Janine act like this before.

"I'm afraid to open it," Janine admitted. "I have no idea what it could be or why he would send anything to me."

"You had a date last night," Connie explained. "Why should a gift surprise you? It could've been flowers. Would you feel this way if he'd sent roses?"

"You don't understand," she said softly.

"I'm surprised the guy has manners," her voice hardened. "A first date and he sends a gift? Most guys expect everything a woman has to offer and then walk away without another thought."

Connie broke out in laughter when Janine suspiciously looked her over.

"Oh right, I forgot, I'm a happily married woman, and I don't know about those kind of things anymore. That's why I'm always so nosy about your social life," she added. With a flip of her blond bangs she walked away, her silver bangle bracelets jingling as her slim, brown arm waved good-bye.

Janine could have laughed herself. If Connie, who looked more like a model than a librarian, was waiting for something to happen in her social life, then Janine would be waiting a long time.

Janine picked the package up and turned it over, then hastily set it back down again. After the way she had left him last night, Janine never expected to see Alberto again, much less receive a gift from him. She gave an agonized moan and covered her face with her hands.

Everything had worked out the way she had planned last night. The cab pulled up, and she made it out the door. It seemed the right thing at the time, to leave without any embarrassing good-bye.

But then she turned around to see him standing in the doorway watching her drive away. It had left a horrible feeling in her champagne-filled stomach. What if she'd broken some code of honor by embarrassing him in front of his companions? She felt she could never face him again and never dreamt the opportunity to do so would ever present itself.

Until the little silver box arrived. And there it sat, staring at her as Alberto had stared at her last night as she drove away.

Janine put the box in the bottom drawer of her desk, so she wouldn't have to look at it until she could decide what to do. She felt the proper thing would be to return it unopened, but that seemed unnecessarily cold-hearted. Alberto deserved that as much as he deserved her hasty desertion last night.

"I'll never see him again," she whispered to herself. The words pounded in her head as she made an attempt to finish some of her work.

Alberto acted so differently from other men she knew. But there had to be something wrong with him, some terrible character flaw that he hid from society.

Janine stopped working, laid the pen down, and leaned over to open the bottom drawer. She took the box out and set it on the desk in front of her. After studying the wrap without a clear thought in her mind, she took out her sharp letter opener and slit the tape on the bottom. With that done, it took her no time to do the same to the rest of the tape and let the wrap fall away to reveal a box of rich burgundy but no markings.

Barely breathing, she opened the lid to reveal a watch. She lifted the dainty timepiece and saw precious stones encircling the face. The gold was so delicate she set it back in the case, deciding not to try it on.

There didn't seem to be a card until she lifted the box and taped to the bottom was a piece of paper. Janine pulled it off and slowly opened the many folds. She knew what his handwriting would look like before she even saw it. Dark black ink and boldly flourished letters danced across the paper. Janine rubbed her thumb across where Alberto must have laid his arm while writing.

"Dearest Janine. Please accept this as a thank you for your gracious company last evening and the hope of seeing you again soon. Alberto Casilda."

"No!" she exclaimed as soon as she read the words. She quickly glanced around before realizing she was alone now.

"I can't see him again," she whispered, her cheeks hot. She closed her eyes tightly. "No matter how tempting the thought is I can't give into this. He is already too good to be true, and I don't want to find out the contrary, or worse, find out he is the man of my dreams and watch him walk out of my life." She felt almost desperate at the thought. She felt even more desperate when she realized this man was causing her to talk to herself.

Janine decided she would return the package to his hotel. She didn't know for sure where he was staying but figured it must be Fitger's. That's where she first bumped into him. She'd drop off the watch at the front desk on her way home tonight.

Janine began clearing her desk for the evening. Her nervousness eased with her decision to return the watch and not see the mysterious Alberto again.

Ready at last to leave, she opened the desk drawer and took out the box. For a moment she resisted the urge to open it, but her resolve failed. She flicked the box open and smiled. Her first gift of jewelry from a man was certainly something very special and probably expensive.

"But it doesn't make any difference," she told herself firmly. Even though she must return it, she would always remember the dainty bracelet watch with the thin gold hands pointing at midnight.

Midnight? She didn't ever remember seeing a new watch with the hands pointing straight up the face. They usually were at three o'clock so the hands could be seen.

Midnight. She had left last night at midnight. The big clock in the school tower downtown had been chiming when the taxi passed it. She had a fleeting thought that Alberto had done this on purpose. Janine dismissed the thought. She had never known any man to be as romantic as that. She snapped the box shut, slipped the box into her purse, put on her sweater, and left the otherwise empty room.

The weather had finally decided to remain warm. Even for Duluth, spring had been exceptionally cool. She walked briskly along the Lakewalk until she reached Fitger's and stepped through the doors into a small exclusive shopping mall. Some of the stores were open for business even though the tourists hadn't arrived for the season. The front desk was upstairs on Superior Street, so she hurried past the elevators hoping not to see Alberto or his companions.

When she arrived at the front desk, she asked the clerk if a Mr. Casilda was registered with the hotel. The clerk checked his computer listing and shook his head.

"Perhaps another name?" he suggested.

Janine shook her head. She didn't know his friends complete names, and besides, the room wouldn't be registered to one of them.

"Thank you," said replied, turning away with a perplexed frown.

Leaving the hotel, she hurried to the corner just in time for the bus. As she settled back into her seat she wondered what she should do next. She could call all the downtown hotels, but Casilda might not be the name he uses when he travels. She'd read that businessmen sometimes use other names for privacy.

She could wait for him to contact her, which was doubtful, no matter what the note said. She shuddered at the thought of facing him again, but she didn't see any alternative.

After the bus left her off, she took her time walking down the hill home. It was a lovely night, warm and calm. The shoreline of Wisconsin was hidden in a purple shadow with the coming of night. Maybe instead of fixing dinner tonight she'd sneak off and walk down to the pier. It hadn't been warm enough for the past weeks, and she truly enjoyed the walk. She thought it would be a nice outing for her and her mother, but Joan still hadn't looked well this morning but insisted on going to work.

As she turned the corner, Janine saw a black car parked next to the curb across from her house. The car, with a tapered front end and a shiny hood ornament, looked expensive even from this distance. Janine slowed, her suspicions creeping up her back into her now tense shoulders as she moved closer to the vehicle.

The door opened, glinting with a fresh shine in a shaft of the setting sun, and Galeno exited, rising to his full height. He bowed his head in her direction before he walked around the front to open the back door. Alberto stepped out of the vehicle, straightening his jacket with a shrug of his shoulders before saying something to Galeno. Then he moved away from the car and walked quickly to where Janine had stopped, a smile on his handsome face.

"Hello," she said. Her heart was beating faster just at the sight of him. "You found me again," she said, trying to make her voice sound casual. When he didn't reply, she began to walk again, and Alberto fell into step beside her.

"Are you angry?" she asked tentatively, unsure of his mood after last night.

He stopped abruptly, turning to face her.

"If you do not wish to see me again, please tell me now, and I shall bother you no further," he said. His accent was heavier than she remembered.

Her heart swelled painfully. He was actually asking her permission to see her again.

"Of course I want to see you," she declared at once and knew in her heart the words were true.

Janine stopped at the door of her house. "Please come in, and ask Galeno if he wants to join us."

Alberto glanced over his shoulder at the car and shook his head.

"Galeno would prefer to stay where he is," he told her, holding the door for her to enter. "He is listening to a ballgame on the radio."

Janine stepped inside and called out to see if her mother was home. No answer returned, so she brought Alberto into the living room. He followed closely behind her. She looked around, wondering what he thought of the small, efficient house the two women lived in quite comfortably. There was little extravagance around them, but the house contained all the comforts they needed. She had never been in the position to entertain a man alone in her living room before. She wished her mother would hurry home.

"Would you like something to drink?" she offered, a nervous quiver in her voice. She cast her eyes around the room to be certain everything was in order. "We don't have any liquor on hand, but I make a mean glass of iced tea." She knew she spoke too quickly, but her nerves were jumping.

"I would like to invite you to supper tonight," he said, surprising Janine with his request. "I am not sure where to go, but I'm confident you are familiar with the restaurants."

Janine's pause to answer was a bit too long.

"Perhaps it is too late in the day to ask," he hastily added. "Do you have plans for this evening?" He moved closer to where she stood simply staring at him.

Janine shook her head. "No, I'm not busy," she finally responded. She had to give him back the watch and this was the perfect solution—if only she could control her attraction to him. She was about to explain about the watch when the front door slammed shut with a resounding bang. She let out a relieved sigh.

Alberto turned his back to stare out the window that faced the lake. His broad shoulders almost blocked out the light. He stood like the captain of a ship. Legs apart, hands clasped behind his back. Janine had the oddest feeling when she saw him there.

"Janine," Joan said, "there is the most amazing car parked across the street." She stopped when she caught sight of Alberto in the room.

"Mother!" Janine exclaimed. "I would like to introduce you to Alberto Casilda. He is the man who invited us to the Mayor's Ball last night."

Alberto moved forward with a swift, graceful movement that caught both women by surprise.

"My name is Alberto Ferdinand Casilda," he said. "It is a pleasure to meet Janine's mother." He engulfed Joan's hand in his.

Joan Nielsen smiled. "My name is Joan," she told him, her curious gaze studying his face.

"I have just invited your daughter to dine with me tonight. I would be more than pleased if you would agree to join us."

Joan glanced quickly at Janine to see her reaction to his invitation. Janine didn't meet her eyes. She had moved to the other side of the room.

"I am going to get us some iced tea, mother. Would you like some?"

Joan nodded, anxious for Janine to leave the room.

"Alberto would you please sit for a moment?" Joan asked as soon as Janine was gone.

He did, with an elegant grace, in the only masculine-looking chair in the room, a straightback Windsor style covered in a nondescript, neutral color. At the armrests the material had worn in spots. It was a piece of furniture that was lovingly maintained by the women but never used.

Joan sat across from him and clasped her hands together in front of her. Her gaze was steady and unyielding. He intimidated her, but Joan was concerned about her daughter. Janine was old-fashioned and had little experience with men. To be pursued by this man, who was every bit as Janine had described him and more, would be overwhelming for any woman. Joan half smiled. She was nervous, but there was something about him. He met her gaze with a direct one of his own. She could understand why Janine referred to him as a caballero.

"Where are you from Alberto?" Joan asked him bluntly.

"My family owns the estancia de Casilda. It is a ranch outside a small village near Barcelona, Spain."

"Why are you here?" she asked, trying to keep her tone light. "This certainly isn't a hot spot for the cattle industry."

"I am here as a favor to a friend," he began. "I spent the last week at his family home and moved to town in preparation for our return to Spain. The city interested me, so my companions and myself decided to stay for a few days. I was fortunate to come across some interesting breeding stock nearby, a hearty breed of cattle that might suit my purpose. While I am here, I have been fortunate to be invited to several social events. Which was where I met your daughter for the first time."

Joan nodded. She already knew how he'd met Janine and the rest sounded plausible enough.

"You won't be here long then?" she asked, her meaning clear.

"That I cannot answer at this time, Joan. I am on no time schedule, and right now I am in no hurry to depart."

Joan certainly hadn't expected him to say that. She longed to ask if Janine was involved in his decision to stay but decided against it for now. She studied the faded geometric design on the rug at her feet.

"I think I will see what Janine is doing," she said, her voice quiet with indecision. Slowly she leaned forward to stand, her movements deliberate with weariness.

Alberto stood and waited until she disappeared into the kitchen then walked to the window to stare out at the lake.

Joan walked into the kitchen wondering what she could possibly say to Janine about this man besides the fact that she liked him. His answers sounded honest and he seemed the genuine article, but what couldn't be forgotten was that he would be leaving for Spain sooner or later. She knew her daughter realized this, and if Janine wanted to go with him tonight, Joan had no objections.

"Hi, how is the tea coming along?" Joan asked, entering the kitchen. "I think you can forget it, Alberto is ready to go for supper."

Janine stood at the sink staring out the small window at the neighbor's backyard.

"I have to go, don't I?" Janine said with resignation. "There is really no way to get out of it. I don't want to but I must because...." She stopped, forgetting her mother didn't yet know about the watch.

"Did you enjoy yourself last night? You haven't said." Joan studied Janine's face.

Janine sighed, unable to meet her mother's eyes. "Yes," she said, sounding miserable.

Joan laughed at her. "Then I would think you would want to go," she teased. "He's from Spain," she added.

"How do you know that?" Janine asked, surprised at her mother's knowledge.

"I asked him," Joan said. "You didn't ask him last night?"

Janine shook her head. "It never came up," she snapped. "I'd better go and change," she said, leaving her mother without another look.

Alberto turned from the window when Janine walked into the room.

"What would you like to do?" Janine asked.

"Then you agree to have supper with me." He stated it rather than asked.

Janine nodded. "It'll take me a few minutes to change out of my work clothes," she stated, showing no emotion. She spun on her heel and left to go upstairs.

She could not understand why people enjoyed dating. She thought it was sheer torture. Her heart pounded and sweat formed on her palms as she thought of spending an evening with this man with nothing but the meal to distract them. She knew he would ask her to suggest an activity besides dinner, and she raced through the various options in her mind.

She hadn't come to any decision when she was ready to go downstairs. Her steps were slow to return to her mother and Alberto. She paused to slip the box that held the watch into the pocket of her jacket before she entered the living room.

Joan was listening to Alberto, who had his back to Janine. His hands gestured as he explained his point. From the look on Joan's face, she wasn't immune to the Spanish charm either.

Joan caught sight of Janine as she entered the living room. Their eyes met briefly when Alberto rose and turned to Janine, but not before he took Joan's hand once more.

"Enjoy yourselves," Joan said, standing. "It's a lovely evening. Why not take him on the Lakewalk, honey? There are plenty of restaurants along there, some of them very good." Janine had already come to the same decision moments earlier.

"Thank you for your hospitality, Joan," Alberto said.

"Please return and visit us if you find the time. This house needs to see more company. To see you sitting in Hugh's old chair...well, it's just been too long," she said with a laugh.

Janine stared furiously at the floor. The way her mother put it, it sounded like they lived like hermits. She could feel the heat in her face and glanced at Alberto, wondering what he thought.

Alberto held the door, and Janine walked past him outside.

"I will tell Galeno our plans," he explained and left her on the sidewalk as he strode across the street. Galeno stepped out of the vehicle and listened to Alberto. He nodded and returned to the driver's seat.

She smiled as he rejoined her and said, "If I have learned anything about you, I know Galeno could've told you what our plans will be tonight."

Alberto nodded. "Galeno is very good at anticipating what I have to say."

"If we cut through this field, it's not very far," she began. "We can connect to the Lakewalk on the other side of that bridge. It's the quickest way. Do you mind walking?" Janine asked. She had chosen to wear a long cotton skirt with a matching sweater and white boat shoes, prepared for the walk. Alberto wore leather boots and casual clothes, but she couldn't be sure if he could walk any distance in them.

"No, on the contrary, lead the way. You are the guide for *this* trip," he said, a definite emphasis in his voice.

Janine was wondering what he meant when he suddenly took her hand in his. His skin was warm and rough against her soft flesh. She wanted to rub her thumb against the tough skin on his palm that showed he was used to hard work. She also wanted to pull away from his grasp, but forced herself to do nothing.

"Tell me about your father," he said suddenly.

"My father?" she asked. She was still trying to relax about holding his hand, and he brings up her father. "What do you know about my father?"

"Joan was explaining about what he did for a living, and it sounded interesting. Where I live in Spain we do not have lakes such as yours. Your superior lake intrigues me."

Janine laughed at his description. "It is superior, as you say, but not all things about it are good."

"Yes, a lady of many moods. I know of some and my experience is limited to several days."

"My favorite thing is the foghorn and the bridge when it talks to the boats. When I was young, I would lay awake on stormy nights and listen to their talk. If my father was out of port, I would imagine one of the big boats talking was his. I always hoped that he would blast the horn when he passed our house to tell me he was home."

"And did he?" Alberto questioned her gently.

"No," she said and smiled rather sadly. "He couldn't, regulations and all. They are only allowed to use the horn for business. So, you see, it would have been impossible." She seemed to want to convince herself as well as him.

"But to a small girl waiting anxiously in the dark of her bedroom, very disappointing. Did your father know of your wish?" His question caught her off guard. Her emotions sparked tears in her eyes, and she couldn't look up for a moment.

"I don't know," she replied. "I can't remember if I ever told him or not."

His long fingers caressed her hand. "He should have known."

Janine swallowed the lump in her throat and realized a feeling of peace came from telling him.

"Do you mind if we walk for awhile before dinner?" Alberto asked. "It feels good to stretch my legs. I find little exercise when I travel. It's hard to adjust after being at the ranch. This will be a welcome change."

He held her hand as they walked close beside each other down the path. He could feel the tenseness of her body. She should move with the fluid movements he knew she possessed. He'd watched her walk often enough. He wondered if he may have fallen too fast. Perhaps she wasn't even interested in him the way he was interested in her. Though he'd known of Janine for many days, she'd only known him since last night. He would give it a little more time.

He brushed aside the feelings he'd felt when he first saw her run helter skelter down the boardwalk. The chivalry of duty was bred into him. Since his birth, his parents diligently instructed him on the rights and wrongs and must do's, a part of his heritage. Her need of help and his need to comply didn't explain the surge of emotion the sight of her brought out in him. There was something about her, a characteristic missing from other women he'd known.

His mother would laugh if she could hear his thoughts. Alberto, the eldest son, who remained so cool, always logical, his head always ruling his heart and not the other way around. It was ironic that before he'd left for this trip his mother had taken him aside to reprimand him.

"Alberto Ferdinand Carlos Casilda," she'd begun, and he knew he was in trouble. She only spoke his full name when extremely angry. "Alberto, you have been alone for too long. Enough of this travel and caring only for the hacienda with no commitments to build a family of your own. It is time to choose a woman, settle, and give your father and I a grandchild and an heir with the name Casilda."

Alberto had laughed, as he always did, at his mother's ultimatum.

"I am serious," she snapped. "When you return, you need to give some serious thought to who you would like to see by your side for the remainder of your life. Our family lineage is too long to end with you."

"Mama," Alberto soothed her, his dark eyes defiant. He would not be coerced into marrying until he was ready. "You know when the time comes for me to choose a bride, I will know. Until then, I shall be patient. I think you should do the same. You waste precious time worrying about things you have no control over."

"It isn't like you don't have plenty of women who would be willing to marry you, but I think you are looking for someone who does not exist in this world. You had best change your expectations, and now is the time to do it."

She hadn't been happy with him. Alberto frowned remembering this, but then his eyes rested on Janine and he couldn't help but smile. His mama had been wrong. She did exist, and here she was. With the mass of dark blue water in a frame behind her, he suppressed his sudden desire to take Janine in his arms and kiss her.

They had been walking on the wooden planks for at least half an hour, but neither seemed to notice. Janine was lost in her thoughts, worrying about how she could tactfully return his gift without hurting his feelings, but so far, she couldn't come up with a single idea. When his sure steps faltered, she looked up in surprise.

"What is it?" she asked.

"Would you like to continue walking or begin looking for a place to dine?"

"You must be hungry," she said quickly, worried about him and his stomach. The age-old concern of women for their men.

Her man. The thought warmed her. Then she remembered she had to return the watch yet, and her face shadowed again.

"There's a restaurant around the corner, it's very good if you enjoy pasta. Do you?" she asked.

Alberto seemed indifferent but began walking again.

When the Fitger's building and the patio eatery with a net stretched over the top came into view, Alberto asked, "Why is this netted in?"

"Seagulls are filthy pests," Janine explained. "Restaurateurs found that out quickly once eating outdoors by the lake became popular." She pointed to several gulls gathered at the garbage cans. "Signs were posted everywhere to discourage people from feeding them but it didn't work. They tried the nets, and they must have helped. At least the tables are clean."

Alberto, amused by the story, stopped to read the menu that was posted on a stand outside the eating area.

"If you recommend the food then we shall stay here," he said emphatically.

They were soon seated at a table outside. With the last remnants of the setting sun behind the building, automatic lights began to go on. It was pleasant, but incredibly close quarters for Janine's peace of mind.

A waitress hurried outside, apologizing for making them wait. She wiped off the table with a quick swiping stroke and then opened their menus placing them in their hands.

"Would you like a drink before you order?" she asked.

Alberto turned to Janine, one expressive eyebrow raised in question.

"Champagne, or did you decide you didn't like it after all?" he asked her.

Janine thought for a moment, a bit on guard, because the waitress kept glancing from her to Alberto, like she couldn't believe they were together.

"I did enjoy it, but if you buy it all the time it won't be special. I thought champagne was only for special occasions."

The waitress rolled her eyes.

A smile lit Alberto's face. "I consider each time I am with you to be special, but as you say, we will save it for another time." He turned to the waiting waitress and ordered a bottle of wine so quickly Janine didn't catch the name.

The waitress's eyes widened, leaving Janine to wonder what it was Alberto had ordered.

"Now, what will you recommend?" Alberto asked. He watched her without bothering to look at the menu.

Janine nervously held the menu up to hide her face while she frantically scanned the selections. She'd eaten here before, but she didn't see anything on the menu she remembered.

"I am so sorry. I think they must have changed the entrees. I don't recognize a thing listed here."

Alberto made no comment. Her voice was shaky, and she was more nervous now than ever. His finger appeared on the top of the leather menu cover and firmly pushed it down so she was forced to look at him.

"Something has upset you. Can we discuss what it is?"

Janine breathed a deep sigh of relief.

"Yes," she said, wanting to get it over with. "I didn't know how to bring it up but..." she paused to reach into her pocket. "Thank you for the considerate gift, Berto, but I can't accept it," she told him almost cheerfully.

Alberto looked astounded. "What?"

Janine looked at him, wondering in a flash, rather belatedly, if he hadn't sent her the watch. But she knew he had. There was only one Galeno in Duluth. Slowly, Janine removed the beautiful box to set it carefully on the table.

"This," she told him wearily. She pushed the box toward him, then quickly replaced her hand in her lap to hide its trembling.

Without hesitating he took it, fingering the velvety texture before he slipped it into his pocket.

"That is all?" His eyes remained dark and unreadable, but there was an amused smirk on his firm lips.

"Yes, did you think there would be something else?" she asked innocently.

He frowned, puzzled. "No, I just," he paused briefly, "would you like me to order for us both?"

She gave a nod with a relieved smile, and closed her menu. Now that her ordeal of returning the watch was over without too much ado, she could relax. That is until she remembered there was still the rest of the night.

When the waitress, with all smiles for them, returned to take their order, Alberto gave the selections. He paused, asking Janine with his look to disagree if she didn't approve. Janine nodded in agreement, and the waitress left them with the bottle of wine. Janine timidly tasted it just as she had the champagne last night.

"This is good," she said eagerly, "rather refreshing without that alcohol flavor."

Alberto sipped it and rolled it around his mouth like a true connoisseur. He nodded in agreement. "You're right," he said. "A good choice. I'm glad you approve, Janine." His voice softened.

She loved the way he said her name. The consonants rolled off his tongue in a musical way. She wished she could tape the sound so it wouldn't be lost to her, even after he left for Spain.

Alberto reached for one of his thin cigars several times during the conversation before he took one out. He fingered the smooth texture before taking out a silver monogrammed lighter and flicking it open with a swift motion. The flame flickered in the air catching Janine's attention.

"You smoke!" she exclaimed, surprised.

"Occasionally," he replied, holding the flame away from the tip. "Do you mind?"

Janine shook her head, and he lit the fragrant tobacco. She inhaled the sweet smoky smell and smiled faintly.

"It almost smells like the brand my father smoked, but there is something different."

"It is a Spanish brand unfamiliar in America," he explained.

Janine frowned briefly, suddenly remembering too much. A clear picture of her living room with a man built much the height and width of Alberto standing in the window. She shook her head to clear the image.

"I don't mind cigar smoke at all, but thank you for asking just the same," she added, thinking it was probably rare he had to ask anyone for permission to do anything.

Alberto took another pull from the cigar. "I believe you are still troubled," he speculated solemnly, studying her as he leaned back in his chair.

Janine's eyes widened. She had hoped her thoughts weren't so apparent.

"We haven't known each other long. I really don't understand why..." she fumbled trying to come up with the right words.

"It's the watch, isn't it?" he asked wearily. "A mere trinket, Janine. I bought it more as a joke than anything else."

With Janine's incredulous look he stopped. He took out the box and removed the watch, dangling it in the air between them.

"You see, when you left so abruptly at midnight last night, I was reminded of the mysterious little cinder girl in the fairy tale. That is all." He spread his hands, the movement foreign-looking in its elegance.

Janine smiled faintly to hear this powerful man mention the familiar child's story. She never dared to believe that it was possible that he had deliberately made the connection, but he had.

"When I saw this watch it reminded me of you...dainty and pretty."

Janine swallowed hard, shocked at his description. She considered nothing about herself to be dainty.

"How sweet of you," she said, though her tone implied disbelief. A blush rose in her cheeks, and she lowered her eyes to avoid his.

Alberto studied her face. He couldn't understand this woman. She is pretty, innocent, graceful, and sweet with a figure ripe enough to tempt any man, yet she didn't like his compliments. He had never met a woman who didn't outright appreciate compliments, and there were many who constantly demanded them. But then, he'd also never met a woman who turned down a gift of jewelry before.

"Tell me about your life," he asked with interest, hoping for a glimpse of what created this creature who was fascinating in her simplicity.

Janine thought for a moment, gently chewing her lower lip. She turned and concentrated on the view, wondering what he could possibly want to hear. Again the image of her father standing in their house haunted her.

In a hollow voice she said impulsively, "She loved him enough to accept him as he was. I, however, wasn't so generous." Janine's mouth tightened. "He loved the lake, sometimes I swear more than he loved us, but my mother didn't mind. She never seemed to mind. I resented the time he spent away. Week after week would go by without him. There were few letters and fewer phone calls. When I was young and he did return home, it took me a long time to get used to who he was, my father, for heaven's sake," she declared in exasperation. "By the time I began to enjoy him, he'd leave again. What kind of relationship is that?" Her laugh was bitter.

She never allowed herself to spend too much time reliving the past or her feelings about her father. The coldness that enveloped her whenever she did was so unlike how she usually felt that it concerned her, but she disregarded it tonight.

"It doesn't matter, now he's been gone many years." She shrugged negligently.

"I think it does matter," Alberto said quietly.

His gaze seemed to go deeply into her and touch the intimate places of her soul where she didn't dare tread. Uneasily, she looked away, staring down at her hands.

"Your father did what he needed to do to care for his family. You were young. You could not understand what a man feels when there are people depending on him for their food, shelter, their basic necessities of life."

"Oh, you sound just like my mother, always taking his side." The words hung like daggers in the air.

"Why would I choose sides?" he asked softly.

Janine winced. She couldn't believe what she'd just said.

"How ridiculous of me, I apologize," she flushed. "You're right of course. Inside I've always known that my father did his best, but I can't accept it."

"Can't or won't?"

"Fine then, won't accept it," she admitted reluctantly.

"When you have someone who depends on you in the same way then you will understand," he told her, knowingly nodding his dark head.

"And how would that happen?"

Alberto's eyes widened at her innocence. "When you conceive a child and deliver it into this world. Only then do I think you will fully understand and forgive your father for doing what he thought was right."

"What is this conspiracy between you and my mother?" she demanded, her anger rising.

Alberto's face remained passive. He leaned closer to her. In her opinion, the small table already had them close enough.

"Because you need to look at this from a man's perspective and not a young girl's, at least until you accept it," Alberto told her firmly. "He didn't die in that ship wreck to deprive you of a father."

The words fell like a bomb on her. Janine stared at him, silenced. Her mind raced.

"It wasn't done deliberately to hurt you," he added softly. He reached over and stroked her cheek with one brown finger.

Janine blinked in surprise but didn't move away, her thoughts turning to Alberto. She could see lines around his eyes and mouth, which showed his age and experience. No gray silvered the mass of dark hair, so she remained unsure of how old he could be, but she could see how handsome he was.

She was tempted to lean against the strong hand that touched her skin, close her eyes, and cry. Janine rarely gave into tears. She jumped back, common sense bringing her abruptly back to her senses.

"I find it rather embarrassing to have someone, especially a complete stranger, point out how immature I've been acting for so long," she said. "But I must admit you may be right. Maybe I have been nurturing a grudge against my father all these years."

She gasped as a terrible thought crossed her mind. "I couldn't have allowed this animosity to affect my mother?" she thought out loud, forgetting who she was talking to. "No, I don't believe I have," she murmured quickly to reassure herself.

Alberto, a grim smile on his lips, agreed. "That isn't your mother's concern. Although I am sure it causes Joan pain to have you only remember the negative aspects of your father and her husband."

Janine's eyes narrowed. "I was only out of the living room fifteen minutes to change my clothes, how did you learn all of my family secrets in that amount of time?" she interrogated him. "My mother is usually not so indiscreet."

"Your mother was never indiscreet," Alberto said. "She is only concerned enough to want to hear words of confirmation from a man about the fears she feels are affecting her only daughter." He lifted an eyebrow at her. "And I, Janine, am a man."

Janine inhaled sharply at the low suggestive tone he used. She didn't doubt his masculinity or the power he held over her for a minute.

The conversation was interrupted by the arrival of the food. Steaming plates of pasta and a basket of warm bread with butter that smelled wonderfully of garlic were set before them. The rich wine complemented the entire meal. Janine thoroughly enjoyed it.

"This is delicious," she exclaimed after many minutes of quiet as they tasted the food.

Alberto nodded. "I find I enjoy Italian food in America much more than their beef. If you tasted a steak at my ranch, the flavor of it would amaze you," he said proudly.

Janine laughed at his adamant declaration. "You sound very proud of your home. Why haven't you mentioned it to me before?"

Alberto remained thoughtful for a moment then answered. "I am extremely proud of my home. My family has worked hard to make the ranch a profitable business as well as a family home." A distant smile rested on his lips. "The sky is so blue on the plains it hurts your eyes. The baked earth has its own color, a rusty hue I haven't seen anywhere else I've traveled. Puffs of dust rise from each fall of the horse's hooves as you ride across the countryside. In the distance, the mountains rise majestically from the ground like giants surveying the land, watching it change from purple to rose with the movement of the sun. They are like your lake in a way. The mountains control our weather a lot of the time."

He smiled, falling silent as he pictured Janine on the ranch with him. With him in his family home that was located so many miles away from here. Though he couldn't know for sure, he thought she would like his home. He felt regret thinking he might never know.

Janine watched, waiting for him to continue.

"Janine," he began, "how do you feel about...." He was forced to stop when the waitress returned to clear their plates and ask if they needed anything else. Alberto shook his head. She left the bill on the table before leaving.

Galeno appeared right behind her. "Excuse me," he said.

Alberto hid his impatience and nodded for him to continue.

"There is an urgent wire waiting for you from your father back at the hotel. I thought you should be informed." He bowed and stepped back from the table.

Alberto lit another cigar, leaning back in the chair to stretch his long legs out in front of him. His relaxed manner belied the message he had just received.

Janine sat in silence waiting.

"There are two alternatives for us," he began after a few moments of contemplation. "Our evening together can end right now, so I am free to investigate the urgency of this message. I could return you home and then continue by myself, which I believe would be unsatisfactory for both of us." He smiled thinly when she didn't respond. "Or you could accompany me to the hotel, with Galeno in attendance, while I decide what must be done and then from there we could proceed as planned."

Silence fell between them, though the background noises of people strolling by and children playing were loud enough to fill in quite nicely. Janine didn't give herself time to think too long about his proposal. It was the ticket out of an uncomfortable evening she had wished to end except that she no longer wanted that. There was one thing she knew about this man, she knew he was honest. He and Galeno had proven it more than once. Janine took her time carefully refolding the navy napkin in her lap and smoothed the folds against the table.

"How long will your business take you to complete?" she asked, quite proud of the evenness of her voice.

Alberto narrowed his eyes concentrating for a moment. "That will depend on what it is. Let me say that, if I will not be finished within half an hour, I will bring you home before I begin. Although I have proof that you are quite capable of finding your own passage home, I would prefer if I was allowed to return you there safe and sound. Joan saw you leave with me. I am the one responsible for your safe return." A glimmer of smile touched his lips.

Janine laughed. "I promise I won't repeat what I did last night, for your peace of mind," she said.

“Then you agree to join me?” he asked, covering his surprise.

Janine hesitated but nodded. “Yes, I believe so. I’m hoping we’ll have the chance to walk off some of the wonderful, if rather heavy, food we’ve just eaten. Though right now, I would rather nap.” She caught the suggestiveness of her words and wished she could take them back, but Alberto didn’t seem to notice.

Galeno was waiting in the car out in front of the restaurant. Janine slid into the plush seat of the big black car noticing the people stare at them. She didn’t care right now. Alberto treated her like she was the only woman on the planet. She found that was all that mattered.

9

Ordando was waiting in the lobby of the hotel when they walked through the glass doors. It was one of the oldest hotels in town, but it offered the best view of the canal and the lift bridge. Ordando stood abruptly when he saw them and pressed the elevator button. The doors slid open as they walked over to him. Ordando bowed at Janine. She noticed his demeanor was much more informal than that of Galeno. She thought she saw a glint of masculine appreciation in his eyes. As they rode the elevator up, Janine was mortified by her sudden vanity. She realized that to think two handsome men might find her attractive was ridiculous. She stared mutely at the floor until the elevator doors opened.

Alberto took Janine's hand and led her from the elevator. Ordando fell in right behind them. He was the one who procured the key for the room at the end of the hallway and opened it, holding the door to allow them inside. She glanced around the room with a nervous swallow. There was a wood dining set at the far end. She could faintly see candlesticks in the middle of it. In front of her were a couch and two easy chairs set around an ornate entertainment center. Several table lamps were turned on, contributing more of a romantic atmosphere than actual lighting. An uneasy feeling settled back over her when she spotted the silver bucket and wine bottle. Feeling as if she were in a seduction scene from a movie, Janine wondered if she'd made a terrible misjudgment in coming here.

Alberto slammed the door behind him making her jump. He walked swiftly past her into the room almost as if he had forgotten she was here. He concentrated on a handful of letters. He rapidly flipped through them as he walked to each lamp and turned it up to the highest power throughout the room. Soon they were surrounded by blazing light that showed every nook and cranny of the impressive room. A nervous giggle surfaced in Janine's throat when she looked around.

"So much for any seducing," she thought. She wasn't sure if she should be relieved or if she should be offended that he didn't seem to want to even attempt it.

Slowly, she followed him into the room, looking around with curiosity. She was thoroughly impressed. If she had any doubts of Alberto's financial affairs up to now, she didn't any longer. The suite was the size of her house, probably bigger. She wandered over to the windows that lined one wall. She saw a fantastic view of the bay all the way to the tip of Park Point.

"Would you care for a refreshment?" he asked from behind her. Janine turned to see him standing next to a small bar that looked like it was solid carved mahogany. She shook her head no and walked to the French doors.

"Why don't I give you some peace and wait on the balcony until you've finished," she told him with an assurance she didn't recognize in herself.

Alberto opened the doors before she could reach them, which surprised her since she was closer to them in the first place. He walked outside to inspect the narrow balcony enclosed by ornate wrought iron rails. Two iron chairs were set out with a small table between them.

"Not much more could fit out here," he remarked as they looked together, standing exceedingly close to each other until Janine sat in one of the chairs.

"If I remain seated, then there is room for you and Galeno, but unfortunately, I think Ordando would have to remain inside," she replied lightheartedly. She liked Alberto's constant companion more than the young Ordando. She remembered his look and suspected he had acquired a roving eye since visiting Duluth.

Alberto smiled down at her. He reached over to run his hand across the tendrils of hair that blew across her face. "Please come back inside whenever you like, your presence will not disturb my work."

A pretty smile brightened her face. "Thank you, I will."

Alberto was slow to leave but then spun on his heel and returned to the room, though he left one of the doors open.

Janine watched him until he moved out of sight. "This room is probably equipped with the newest technology," she thought. "Ready for business tycoons that fly in and then fly back out again."

The thought sobered her. With a restless sigh, she stood and leaned her elbows against the cold railing to watch the lights twinkle across the black water of the lake. The air suddenly moved. Her flesh ignited, and she knew Alberto had returned. She kept her gaze fixed on the distant lights. Her breathing quickened with expectation.

He moved to stand next to her, drawing her eyes to his shadowed figure. For a brief instant she could see the bloodline of the Spanish conquistadors. The leanness of his cheeks and the strong jaw line were commanding even in the dark.

"There wasn't bad news I hope," she said, unsure if he would confide his personal business.

Alberto lowered his head. He gripped the handrail tightly for a moment. "Not really, just word I am to finish here and return. Father would prefer I be there for the calving season."

His departure sounded like bad news to her. "Oh," she said faintly, turning away to hide how the news affected her.

He wrapped his fingers loosely around her upper arm. "Come, let us return indoors. I am afraid you aren't dressed for the briskness out here."

Janine shivered, but she didn't think it was from the cold. The warmth of his hand penetrated the material of her jacket, but it wasn't his touch. Alberto's elegant movements in the semi-darkness made his heritage more apparent.

"He's a virtual stranger. What am I doing here in his hotel suite alone?" she thought as dread filled her.

Alberto didn't give her a chance to say anything. He steered her into the room to the couch but didn't pressure her to sit.

Janine wanted to ask when he would leave, but she didn't want him to admit it out loud. She didn't trust her reaction to the news.

"Would you like to continue our walk now?" he asked, though Janine felt his tone implied he'd lost interest.

"It is late," she said gently, "perhaps it would be better if we left it for another time."

"Is there something else you would prefer to do right now?"

Janine stepped back, wondering if he realized how sensual his voice sounded. She lowered her head. Her mouth was suddenly dry.

"Ah…no, I was actually thinking of going home."

She couldn't look at him. If he knew how it unsettled her when he was close to her, she didn't know what would happen.

"Is that what you really want from me, Janine?" he asked her, almost wearily.

Janine looked up uneasily. "I'm not sure what I want," she answered. She knew that wasn't true as she looked at his mouth. "I want you to kiss me" was what she really wanted to say.

Heat rose in her face. Her thoughts shocked her, making her body tense.

"You sound tired," she tried to explain.

The muscle in his cheek tightened as he watched her.

"I know how busy you are, and I'm sure you have plans to make." Janine finally fell silent. She had no idea what he was thinking, and her mindless ramblings weren't helping.

Surprisingly, he smiled at her. "Tired?" he questioned. "Yes, of some things I am tired, but of you, no. I'm beginning to wonder if I shall ever grow tired of being with you."

"Why did you say that?" Janine demanded. It had been painfully apparent to her since the beginning that they could never be a successful match. Even if she could forget that he lived in Spain, there were the obvious differences in their personalities, and he was too vibrantly good-looking for a woman with her quiet personality. But to have him openly say what her own private dream has been was cruel. Reality was cruel, but she preferred not to think about that right now.

"Because it is the truth," he admitted. He spoke slowly, "I know your ways are different from mine." He gave a short laugh. "Before I met you, I had the arrogance to think I understood women," He shook his head. "God heard my rash statement and is still laughing at my vanity while justly humbling me for it."

He paused for a moment and struggled to find the right words. "I am a Spaniard, querida, a foreigner to you and your country. You are so utterly charming and so perfectly American, I do not know the proper way to approach you. There are words I wish to say, endearments in my language I want to whisper to you, yet I do not speak them out loud. I am afraid my ways will frighten you, Janine. You must understand that Spanish people, we touch one another at any time. Whether the touch is meant to be a part of our passion or just to show the depth of our feelings for each other. If

I were to touch you it would not necessarily be meant as a form of seduction. I would never press my attentions if you were unwilling to share in them. I do know the meaning of no," he emphasized.

His dark brow rose expressively. "It is the first word our daughter's are taught when they become the age where attracting men is inevitable, and our sons are schooled to understand when it is spoken by a woman, obey it."

He raked his fingers through his thick hair. "I know it is hard for young women in your situation. Some men, both Americans and visitors, attempt to force a woman into a situation that is beyond her control and then abandon her. I am not one of those men. I am a caballero," he declared, meeting her gaze unflinchingly before continuing. "There is something between us. I cannot explain it, but I feel it every time you are near. Surely, you must have noticed it, too?"

Janine's knees felt weak. She wanted to sit but couldn't move. She'd felt it, too, but didn't recognize the feeling. She knew he spoke from the heart. His fervor emanated from him. She responded to his first show of vulnerability by moving closer to him.

"You are a caballero and take the oath seriously. I do know that about you," Janine said with tenderness in her smile. She reached out and placed her hand on the hard muscle of his forearm. "I don't exactly understand some of what you said, but I don't mind being touched," she said, her voice low. "Touch is comforting. It's just that I'm not used to it," she added quickly. She shook her head and laughed. "How could you ever think to hide being Spanish? It's apparent in everything you do and say. The only thing I didn't know was what Latin American country you came from, and since you didn't bring it up I didn't want to pry."

Alberto visibly relaxed. His hand covered hers. "I've never met a woman such as you before. I feel like a bumbling youth dating for the first time."

Janine laughed softly at his confession wondering if she could believe a word. "No American man would admit that, especially to a woman."

Alberto shook his head. "I do not try to understand American men. They take too much for granted," he said with a touch of contempt in his voice. "And most American woman prance about like pampered show horses, with some wearing too little clothes to veil themselves from view. Then there are the women like you with natural beauty who are unnoticed." His hand moved to her cheek to caress the smooth skin. "Why are you not spoken for and protected by a man? Not that I am complaining. It is my good fortune to find you unattached."

"I'm sure it isn't like you say, though it might look that way," she protested, blushing wildly from his touch and honeyed words. "I certainly can't be called an expert on human behavior. I may work at the library but there aren't many who question me about the philosophy men live by."

"Library, that is where you work. Galeno never told me what your occupation is and yet you work with books." His tone held a note of admiration.

"It's a far cry from the excitement of travel and ranching in Spain," she quipped lightly.

"Yes," he shrugged, "it's true our worlds are very different from each other, but it has nothing to do with our hearts. I feel there is a connection between our hearts." He brought her hand against his chest where she could feel the steady beat through the heat of his flesh.

Janine swallowed hard, fighting the urge to pull away. It would be so easy for her to get lost in his words. They were almost poetic. Spanish men are known to speak more freely about their feelings than American men, but she never imagined it to be like this.

"Berto, I…" she finally spoke.

He slid his arms around her waist and narrowed the space between them. "I like it when you call me that," he murmured. He leaned down to brush his lips against her hair.

Janine's heart skipped a beat. This was getting serious. She couldn't breathe with his arms pressed to either side of her.

Alberto slowly released her. "I think you are right, Janine, our walk will have to wait. Time has run away from us. Joan Nielsen said good-bye easily enough, but I felt her reservations. But, we have spent our time better occupied than with exercise, eh?"

Janine took a deep breath and nodded in agreement. Her mind whirled with emotions she'd never felt before. She had no idea of the time, but she knew her mother would be mortified that she'd gone to his hotel room.

Alberto excused himself to use the phone. Janine waited, rubbing her arms nervously. He spoke in Spanish, and when he hung up, he explained the call. "I asked for the car to be brought around to the front."

"I always wondered why you never spoke your native language, even with Galeno. It is such a beautiful language, I wish I knew it better."

"I speak English whenever possible to practice. It's hard to retain otherwise."

"That makes sense," she said. It explained why she couldn't remember anything but "hola" and "adiós" from high school.

A knot formed in her stomach as they left the hotel and got into the limousine. The evening was ending and what would she do when he kissed her, or worse, what would she do if he didn't try?

Alberto took her arm as they exited the vehicle on the quiet street in front of her house. The exterior light blazed over the door but inside it was dark. He carried on a rather one-sided conversation until they reached the stoop, where he clasped her cold hands in his.

"Will you be free tomorrow after work?" he asked.

Janine nodded. She couldn't speak, she knew her voice would shake.

Alberto stood looking down at her. Moths batted erratically against the bright bulb above them and hit the door with a fluttering sound. He smiled tenderly. He leaned down as she raised her head. His warm lips brushed lightly against hers and then he straightened.

"I will be looking forward to tomorrow night," he murmured before opening the door.

The door closed behind her with a bang. Janine stood in the cramped front hall, her fingertips resting against her lips. It hadn't been a real kiss, but it was something to dream about.

10

Janine walked down the stairs with a dreamy expression on her face. She couldn't help it. Whenever she remembered what Alberto said, she felt a glow spread through her body. She didn't feel the least bit tired, even though the past nights had been unusually busy with Alberto wining and dining her.

She walked into the kitchen, wondering at the empty feeling of the downstairs. She could smell coffee, so she knew her mother was already out of bed. When she opened the kitchen door, it, too, was empty.

"Hmm," she said out loud, "I don't remember Mother mentioning she had anything going on this morning. This is not like her," she said as she walked to the counter to pour a cup of coffee, "running off early without an explanation."

Janine sipped the steaming brew and suddenly smiled, relieved she wouldn't have to explain last night. She couldn't hide many of her feelings from her mother. Joan certainly wouldn't expect a play-by-play action of what happened on the date, but Janine didn't trust her own reaction when talking about it. Whenever snippets of the evening invaded her thoughts, she couldn't stop herself from blushing. An involuntary reflex she despised and couldn't control. Right now she didn't have to worry. Her mother was gone and she had all day to compose herself. By tonight, this feeling of pure joy that seemed to burst out of every pore of her body will have diminished. Satisfied that everything would work out, she set the cup down and returned upstairs to finish getting ready.

As she walked up the sidewalk to the bus stop, she made a mental note to tell her mother that Alberto was returning to Spain soon. Instead of the dread she expected to feel remembering the news, she pictured Alberto in Spain. He had probably started to make plans to depart last night when he returned to the hotel.

A phone call from a distant father and the good son prepares to obey. This image opened a whole new dimension of Alberto Casilda to her. He must be the right-hand man to his father. He took care of the birth of new stock, the future that would keep the ranch prosperous. He'd come here to find a new bloodline for their herd in

Spain. He wasn't just a playboy who wasted his family's money on personal pleasure, expensive limousines, and hotel suites that filled an entire floor. No, Alberto had a purpose. He was responsible for the future of his entire family. All the rest was just a means to reach the end.

"So what if he liked to travel in style?" she thought, enjoying the glowing picture of Alberto as protector of his family. "I'm sure I'd do the same, if I could afford it," she thought, "in fact I know I would."

The bus pulled over to the curb to pick her up. The dust blew into the air and left a grey cloud she was forced to run through to climb aboard. The dust settled everywhere, so brushing her clothes clean occupied her until she exited at work.

The hours passed much too slowly for Janine. She spent the day restlessly moving through the book-lined aisles straightening and dusting volumes of text that hadn't been disturbed by her or anyone else for years.

Losing herself in this section of the library allowed her time to sort through her thoughts. She had to stop herself from reliving Alberto's sweet words that warmed her heart every time they surfaced. Desperately, she wanted to analyze each and every sentence to figure out exactly what he'd meant, but she couldn't. If she did come to the conclusion he actually meant what he said, she'd be devastated when he left. It was better if she waited. Then when he was safely out of the country, she could savor each and every moment spent in his company. She could remember the sound of his voice and the way he looked when he spoke to her. It would still hurt, but she wouldn't have to hide her feelings from him. She brushed aside those depressing thoughts just as she did when their conversation from last night intruded into her thoughts. She had finally promised herself to enjoy this interlude of bittersweet romance in her dull life and worry about the consequences later.

The hours after lunch finally passed away, and Janine felt a surge of excitement as she hurried out the front doors. He had a habit of turning up when she least expected, and she hoped he would do the same now. As she reached into her purse for her bus pass, the rich smell of cigar smoke wafted lightly to her. She paused to inhale deeply and turned with a smile to see Alberto, negligent of his handsome clothes, leaning against the side of the limousine. He had no business looking so casual on Superior Street in Duluth, Minnesota.

"You have quite an impressive building to work in," he said.

He was so handsome her breath caught in her throat. The curious looks from the people on the street didn't stop her from moving into the curve of his offered arm.

"I am afraid I couldn't wait any longer to see you," he murmured close to her ear. "You said last night a touch is comforting. May I kiss you once using this excuse?"

Janine inhaled and nodded slightly, the movement enough to give consent to Alberto.

His dark face was so close to her own that she forgot who she was and where she was. He bent closer as gently he touched her lips with his. The kiss was brief as a second, but enough to send her senses reeling.

He gave a regretful sigh. "It is too bad we do not need kisses to survive, eh?"

Janine, her heart pounding and all coherent thought flown out of her head, slid quickly into the limo, hiding her bright red face in the dim interior. With the other library employees leaving, she had probably been seen and would never hear the end of it tomorrow. For some reason, she didn't care as much as she should. She couldn't have refused him. The way she felt right now, she was glad she hadn't.

He moved into the seat next to her and for a brief ecstatic moment she thought he meant to kiss her again. She wanted more than this fluttering of butterfly wings against her mouth. She wanted the pressure of his mouth moving hard against hers. She wanted to taste the smokiness of his breath.

Abruptly, she stopped her completely wanton thoughts. Just last night she'd been afraid to say goodnight because he might kiss her. Now her body and mind were completely betraying her.

Alberto's eyes searched her face, and she didn't know what he saw. A small smile touched his lips. She looked too long at the firm contours of his handsome mouth. Unknowingly, her tongue moistened her lower lip, parting them. His smile broadened as he recognized where her thoughts had traveled.

"Would you want to go home and freshen up before we dine?" he asked. "Perhaps that would be best." He leaned forward and spoke quickly to Galeno, who pulled out into traffic.

"I would like to invite your mother to join us tonight since she was unable to do so yesterday," he said.

Janine glanced at him and then quickly looked out the window, startled by the thought that she didn't want her mother along tonight. "That would be nice," she murmured, hoping it was a suitable reply.

There was silence in the car, Alberto's attention elsewhere for the moment. "I would like to correspond with you when I return home," he told her abruptly. "I realize it won't be adequate for me, and I hope it won't be for you, but at least it will keep communication open between us."

Janine clasped her hands together and stared down at them. Her first thought was that a long distance relationship would never last, especially with a man like Alberto.

"I'd like to write to you, Berto. I know so little about your family and your country."

"Are you interested in learning more?" he asked. His enthusiasm surprised her.

"Yes, of course I would," she stammered uncertainly.

"Then I will tell you more at supper," Alberto said. "Here we are."

The car pulled to the curb in front of her house, and Alberto followed her to the porch.

"We will wait for Joan if she isn't home yet," he said as Janine unlocked the door.

"She'll be here. Tonight is her early night at work," she explained before going inside.

But Joan wasn't home. Janine searched for a note from her. She might forget to leave one in the morning but not if she was going to be late coming home.

Janine could find no sign that she'd been home at all. She kept a tight rein on her emotions though she could feel the panic building inside. She was happy that she wasn't alone.

"My mother would contact me somehow if she didn't plan on being home. This just isn't like her." Anxiously, she rubbed her hands together as she paced back to the front entryway hoping she'd missed a note left by Joan. "I hope nothing has happened."

"It won't help for you to upset yourself until you have reason," he reassured her. "Can you contact her at work?"

Her heart lightened, until she glanced at the clock. "The answering service begins picking up after five-thirty. It's almost six now."

"Then you must wait to be contacted," Alberto said.

Janine nodded absently, barely hearing his words. "I think I'll fix a pot of tea. I know it's warm outside, but I feel chilled to the bone."

"Perhaps your mother will be here to join us."

The phone rang just as Janine set the tea tray on the coffee table. Curbing her anxious thoughts, she hurried over to it and snatched the receiver from the cradle.

"Yes, yes I am," she said hoarsely. "Of course I will be right there. What is the number?" She listened to the voice at the other end and then set the phone down to stare blankly into space.

Alberto stood silently behind her. "Who was that?" He placed his hand on her shoulder.

Janine flinched at his touch and remained looking down to compose herself.

"My mother has been taken to the hospital. They think she had a stroke." She looked up at him. "They don't know anything for sure, not until the test results come back. I am to report to the office and fill out paper work before I can see her." Her tone was flat while she explained.

He could see the stricken expression on her face.

"I'm sorry but I must go to her at once," she gasped, her face draining of all color. She picked up the receiver again and turned her back on Alberto. "I'll probably have to be there for some time. I'll need to make sure she's settled comfortably. I don't really know what I have to do, I've never done this before," her voice broke.

Alberto took the phone from her hand and replaced it on the cradle. "You are wasting time explaining. Let us go," he told her firmly.

Janine looked at him in confusion. "I'm calling a cab. You go. I'm sure you don't want to spend your time in a hospital."

Frowning severely at her, he gave her a push. "Go and pack some things for your mother. If she must stay, she will need them. Galeno will drive us to the hospital."

Janine remained motionless and stared helplessly around her.

"Go, Janine, and hurry," he commanded.

The trip to the hospital took too long. Janine felt cold icy fingers of fear along her spine. The fact that Alberto sat beside her, silent but close enough that his presence comforted her, was the only thing that kept her grounded. She wouldn't break down in front of him.

He followed her into the hospital once they arrived even though she protested. He remained with her at the front desk and waited patiently outside the business office while she filled out the tedious documents that allowed her mother to be registered. Then the secretary told her she could see her mother, and Janine fled the office.

She raced to the elevator and pushed the number for the Intensive Care Unit. When the doors slid open she was in a hallway. Bright red arrows directed her to follow them until she walked into an open area with no walls to separate the rooms, only glass partitions. People were lying inside, clearly visible to anyone walking by in the hallway. Janine saw a man with a white coat and a stethoscope draped around his neck. She rushed over to him.

"Excuse me, I would like some information about Joan Nielsen."

The doctor shook his head. "You must go to the desk. They'll help you," he directed her.

Janine looked into each bed she passed expecting to see her mother lying there, but they were all strangers. She finally reached the desk and spoke to the woman behind it.

"You will have to wait until the doctor can see you," the nurse told her. The telephone rang and she picked it up. She put her hand over the mouthpiece to finish her instructions to Janine. "The waiting room is down the hall, feel free to have a beverage, they're for the family."

Janine felt helpless, but there was nothing for her to do but obey orders and wait.

She clutched the small overnight bag she'd packed for Joan

tightly as she walked into the waiting room.

"Would you like something to drink?" Alberto asked her.

She glanced up at him, too dazed to wonder where he appeared from and shook her head. "No, but you go ahead if you want."

Each time a doctor walked by she sat up and watched him until a name was called that wasn't hers.

"Miss Nielsen," a soft-spoken man with round wire spectacles said from the doorway, his eyes on Janine. He glanced to Alberto and then back to her. Janine sat poised for a moment then jumped up.

"Yes, that's me. I'm waiting for news of my mother," she cried in relief. "You're her doctor?"

He nodded and stepped into the room then moved to sit next to her.

"I am Doctor Anderson," he started, reaching out to shake Janine's hand. "Your mother's condition has stabilized, so we will be moving her to a different floor within the next hour."

Janine shook her head, still not understanding. "What happened? I haven't heard a word about why she was brought in here."

He paused. "She collapsed at work and was brought here by ambulance. The test results confirm she had a slight stroke. We don't know how much of her mobility has been affected by it yet, but I do feel some physical therapy will be necessary." He pushed his hands into the pockets of his smock. "At least that is usually the case. It's really too early to tell anything at the moment."

"May I see her?"

"Yes, but only immediate family is allowed," he said, glancing again at Alberto. "And it will have to be a short visit. When she has been moved and settled in her new room, then you can have more time with her."

Janine jumped up, completely forgetting about Alberto. She hurried out the door after the doctor and followed him down the hallway. He stopped, opened his file, and then pointed to one of the small glassed-in rooms. Her mother was inside. She was lying on the white pillow with her eyes closed. So still and unmoving, her skin so pallid, she didn't look alive.

Janine stepped closer to her head. "Mother, can you hear me?" she whispered, taking the hand with a plastic tube taped to the wrist carefully into her own.

"Of course I can hear you, I'm not deaf. Well, not yet anyway," Joan said, her eyelids fluttered open. Her lips twitched into a smile. "Did they tell you I couldn't hear anymore?"

Instead of smiling, Janine brushed a stray tear from her cheek. "How do you feel?"

"Tired, sore from all the poking and prodding they've been doing. My, my how modern medicine makes me feel quite dizzy. The amount of information they can find in six vials of blood is frightening."

"I'm sure we don't know the half of it," Janine said ruefully. "I suppose you've already been told they're moving you to another floor. That's a good sign anyway."

"Oh, how would you know?" Joan protested. "You know less about hospitals than I do."

"That's a good thing, mother," Janine admonished her, brushing back her mother's hair from her face. She stopped and stared at her hand wondering what had possessed her to do something like that.

Her mother was too young to be in the hospital, especially the ICU. She was an active woman in excellent health up to this point. Now, she looked like she had aged ten years in one day.

Janine's mind raced. How could something like this happen? Her mother acted so weak, and her color looked gray. What is causing all of this?

The nurse bustled in. "I'm sorry, but you'll have to wait downstairs while she is moved. It will take about an hour before she's settled in her new room. You might want to take her purse with you. A lot of people have had their valuables stolen out of the rooms." The nurse stood looking expectantly at Janine until there was nothing for her to do but stand.

"Will I be able to speak with a doctor at some time?" her voice stiff with indignation.

The nurse gave her a bland stare. "Of course. Once all of the results are in, the doctor will have a consultation with you, but it would be useless before then."

Janine swallowed her impatience and turned back to Joan. "Good-bye, mother, I'll be back as soon as I possibly can."

Tears burned in her eyes as she stumbled out of the room into the hall, oblivious to everything around her. She hurried toward the elevator, driven to put the smell of antiseptic cleaner, the sound of mechanical beeps that meant life and death to people, and the hum of machines that pumped and kept people alive behind her. This was an unfamiliar world and she didn't want to understand it. She spun away on trembling legs and rushed down the shining linoleum. Suddenly, a strong hand firmly grasped her upper arm and stopped her headlong flight.

"Janine, stop!" Alberto said, a commanding tone in his quiet voice. She didn't hesitate to obey. She lifted her lashes to look into Alberto's dark eyes. A surge of anger at the interruption of her thoughts flashed through her, and she actually felt annoyed at his presence. She was not used to sharing her thoughts with anyone but her mother. Suddenly, she found herself resenting him. Resenting the fact that he felt he had the right to ask personal questions. He hadn't said a word, but she knew he planned on it.

"My mother is awake, but she acted terribly weak," Janine blurted out. "She could only speak a few short sentences."

"Is this unusual for the victim of a stroke?"

"I don't know. How would I know?" she snapped bitterly. Not at all willing to hear rational explanations, she had never felt so completely irrational in her life. The elevator opened, and they walked into it together. Janine stared at the floor. They weren't alone, and she hoped Alberto wouldn't ask her anything now.

Janine was informed at the front desk that there were more papers to be filled out. She remembered, this time, that Alberto was with her. She hardened her heart to his concern and turned to say good-bye.

"Thank you so much for all you've done, but I've got do this tedious paperwork and then settle my mother." She shifted her weight from one foot to the other while she avoided looking at him. "There's really no reason for you to stay." She hesitated, then added, "I will be alright." She knew that was why he refused to leave.

"If you are certain I can be of no more use, then I will not distress you with my presence any longer," he said coolly, standing with one hand in his pocket. In the other he held her mother's overnight bag. Without another word he handed it over to her and turned to leave.

Janine didn't look back as she followed the woman down the hall. She could feel a condemning force behind her, but when she paused to glance around there was no sign of Alberto.

"Just my high and mighty conscience," she thought, suppressing the feeling of guilt caused by her rude behavior.

The quiet of the hospital was not the quiet she thought it would be. Janine sat in the chair next to her mother's bed listening to the nurse's station outside the door. The phone rang, plus the call button from each bed on the floor could be heard when they were activated, along with many voices echoing along the hall. Beeps were constantly heard from the machine her mother was hooked up to, and she knew, with her mother sedated, she should go home. Instead, she remained in the uncomfortable chair and allowed her thoughts to wander.

Now, in the dim hospital room, she admitted she had treated Alberto abominably during the entire episode. She didn't even recall if she thanked him or said good-bye before she deserted him. Her behavior was an embarrassment. She had turned into a shrew without an ounce of good manners. And Alberto only wanted to help, not out of obligation, but out of the goodness of his big heart. Of course, she could face this now because she knew her mother was safe and was going to fully recover.

The antiseptic smell of the room and the sight of the monitor connected to her mother's arm made Janine feel lost. Self pity threatened to overtake her. She felt alone and lonely, two emotions she was familiar with but had never been as devastated by them as she was right now. Tears threatened to gather in her eyes again, and she had no good thought of what the future would hold for her besides her mother's return to health. Alberto would be gone by the time this was sorted out, and she would never see him again. Salt stung her skin as tears slid unchecked down her cheeks. Sobs collected in her chest that she wouldn't allow to surface. She would not forget him…not ever.

11

Janine patted makeup to cover the dark circles under her eyes. She hadn't slept well for the past several nights, but it didn't matter, her mother was being released from the hospital today. The house had been so empty with Joan gone. The noises that moaned through the eaves and the wind whistling in the gaps in the old windows sounded much louder and completely different to her when she was alone. It kept the nights filled with faceless fears she couldn't ignore no matter how hard she tried.

Joan wouldn't be allowed to return to work for awhile, but she could maintain the house and the garden and, best of all, she would be at home and out of the hospital. The clock down the hall chimed the hour and Janine gasped. Frantically, she searched the image in the mirror. It was much too pale, with dark grooves around the brown eyes that looked too large for her face. She didn't have time to do anything more about fixing her appearance. The bus would be arriving soon.

If she wanted to leave work early today to meet her mother, she must adjust her work schedule. By arriving earlier than usual and not taking her breaks or lunch, she could clock her full time for the day. She did not want to tire her mother with a crowded bus trip home, so a taxi would be another expense. With a sigh, she rubbed her temples that throbbed slightly from all the plans she'd been making.

When she arrived at the library, Janine stopped at Connie's desk to inform her of what she had planned and why.

Connie brushed her explanations aside. "Don't be ridiculous, Jani, take your lunch and breaks, too. You are entitled to personal days for reasons other than your health, you know."

"I know, but," Janine paused before adding, "I'm afraid I can't do without the pay. With mother taking time off, I'll be the only bread winner." She tried to explain the situation casually, though the loss of income had become another worry for her lately.

Connie frowned. "Is that going to be a real difficulty for you?"

Janine shook her head. "Not right away, but who knows what's up ahead. I've never kept the household accounts. Mother has always done that." She gave a short, humorless laugh. "I can't believe what a fool I've been to never bother asking what the expenditures are, to get down to the nitty gritty," she sighed. "I'm sure now I must get to know the grim details. It's what's expected of me."

When Janine walked up the wide, sweeping stairway to the second floor, it seemed a long walk. Her footsteps were muffled by the dirty carpet, the lights in the high ceiling were still off. It was a cost-cutting effort on management's part. Janine didn't think much of the idea. This part of Minnesota had nine months of winter when the lights had to be on no matter how many people were in the building, including the cleaning service. How much difference could one extra hour without electricity really make for the brief three months of summer? She had made the mistake of saying as much to Connie, who showed her the accountant's figures and efficiently shut her up. Her complaint wasn't thoughtless: the lack of electricity turned the upstairs reference department into a dim gloomy cave, cluttered with high bookcases and many dark, shadow-filled corners where materials were stacked together in unshapely piles. The shadowy places were especially unsettling to her this early in the morning, making her more jumpy than usual.

When she saw the figure of a man sitting at one of the long wooden tables, his dark head bent over, she was startled into immobility. At first, she thought she was imagining him but quickly realized he was real. There must be a legitimate reason he was allowed in here before hours. Indecision held her. She should turn around and go back downstairs to find out why he was here, but she just couldn't find the energy. He was probably some local professor researching a special project. There were times this was allowed, but usually Connie informed her beforehand.

She tiptoed toward her desk, glancing over at him. Something about the dark figure caught her attention. Suddenly, he lifted his head and looked directly at her. His eyes penetrated the shadow she stood in. He moved with a quick, lithe movement and walked around the table toward her. From what she could see, his face showed no emotion. Janine's heart beat hard and slightly erratic when he stood in front of her, close enough for her to see the fresh shave on his cheeks and inhale the masculine scent of him. She didn't know how to react.

"Buenos días, señorita," he said formally, his voice hushed in the hollowness of the empty room.

"Good morning, Berto," she replied hesitantly but met his gaze without flinching.

His black eyes ran swiftly over her face, noticing the circles she had tried unsuccessfully to hide and the strain around her mouth.

"How are you?" he asked in a brusque manner, almost as though they were strangers.

"I've had some excellent news," she began, trying to keep her tone light, though she knew she deserved his censure or worse. Despite her shame, her wayward heart soared because he was here. He hadn't left for Spain without seeing her. If he had, it would have caused her more pain than she could ever admit, even to herself. "My mother's coming home today." She smiled, her face lightening somewhat, but the strain remained visible.

"I am glad for both of you," he said with sincerity.

Janine nodded and then fell silent, her mind filled with things she should say, apologies she should make, but she couldn't find the words. "How did you get in here?" she asked.

"I asked a Miss Ryan if I could speak to you alone before you began to work and she agreed. I didn't see you at first because she assured me you wouldn't be in for some time yet." He glanced at the slim gold watch on his wrist. "You must have arrived earlier than she expected."

Janine frowned, wondering what possessed Connie not to tell her of Alberto's arrival. She couldn't have forgotten he was here. With a stolen glance at him, she smiled. No, not in her wildest imaginings could she ever believe Connie, or any woman, could forget Alberto once she'd seen him. More than likely, Connie had heard the gossip about Alberto when he arrived to pick her up in front of the library several days ago, and her curiosity got the better of her. If Janine knew anything about Connie, she probably couldn't resist letting this man in, knowing his appearance would shake her up. That Irish imp must be dying of laughter downstairs.

"Yes, as a matter of fact, I'm early," she told him. "Connie must have forgotten to mention your arrival to me."

"Your mother must have time to rest completely to recover,"

he said deliberately. His eyes narrowed as he retreated into his thoughts.

Janine smiled more brightly than she was feeling. "For at least a month. She will be able to rest at home, thank goodness. The doctor recommends some physical therapy along with walking and light housework. She'll do fine. She's very anxious to get home. She doesn't think the house will remain standing without her," she laughed.

Alberto was silent for a moment, long enough for Janine to build up her confidence.

"Berto, there is another reason I'm so glad you came by this morning." She nervously twisted her fingers together.

A spark of interest lightened his grim face.

"There is something I want to say, I must say," she declared nervously, chewing her lower lip.

"The other day at the hospital, I was terribly rude to you. I have no excuse for my bad behavior. I know you were being kind and helpful, and I was horribly ungrateful. I want to tell you I don't know what I would've done without you that day." She stopped, breathless, her face flushed with emotion.

"You would have handled everything until it was done," he said matter-of-factly.

"Oh no," Janine protested quickly, "you were so calm during it all. I'm sure it would've taken so much longer if you hadn't been there." She frowned and looked down at her hands. She had wound her fingers so tightly around each other her knuckles showed white. "I know that for a fact, because waiting for the taxi would've taken a full hour longer. I've never regretted not owning a car until that moment."

Alberto waved his hand in the air, flicking his long fingers impatiently. "There is no reason to apologize for something in the midst of a crisis. People act differently. It is human nature. You found you have a spiteful temper in a stressful situation like that."

Janine gasped out loud, her eyes flying to his face in silent protest.

He lifted one dark eyebrow, daring her to refute it. Mischief sparkled in his eyes.

She had the grace to blush and remain silent.

He stepped closer, reaching for her. He grasped her arms and held them firmly in his. His thumb caressed the bare skin below her sleeve. "I would like to thank you for being concerned with my feelings. It more than makes up for any distress you caused."

Janine leaned into the strength of his hands, her stomach muscles quivered. It was such a temptation to give into her weakness and allow his strength to carry the heavy weights she felt. Her palms pressed against the softness of his shirt, into the muscles of his torso. She could feel the steady beat of his heart and knew he would take care of anything she asked of him. It was a temptation she couldn't allow herself to give in to. She flinched, almost stung by the betrayal of her senses.

"I must get to work," she cried in confusion, looking away from him, afraid of what he would read in her face. "People will be coming. I mean, we will be opening to the public soon."

Alberto didn't release her. "I have not yet told you why I am here." His chiseled features relaxed. "You are the most uncurious woman I have ever met, to not even ask."

"Of course, I interrupted you," Janine said, trying to check her frantic pulse.

"My flight to Spain leaves tonight at eight o'clock," he said bluntly. "I want you to know I am free until that time. May I help you return home with your mother this afternoon? My car is at your disposal."

Janine hesitated, masking her distress at his imminent departure. The offer of his limousine was like an answer to her prayers. "Oh yes, Berto, that would be an absolutely perfect way for mother to leave the hospital. You're very generous. Thank you. I'm getting off at three and then going directly to the hospital."

Alberto smiled in return. "I will be here," he reassured her and stepped back, but then took her hand and raised it to his lips. His lips pressed hard against her skin. His eyes, hungry, rested on her mouth, causing her to lick her lips, subconsciously hoping he would kiss her lips instead of her hand.

Footsteps interrupted the warmth of his lips against her cold skin, and briefly the heat in his eyes held her captive. Alberto moved swiftly away, a smile on his lips.

"Until three," he murmured, his accent heavy.

Janine nodded at his retreating figure, still unable to move. The deep tiredness that had controlled her over the past days when she hadn't seen him vanished.

For the rest of the day, she worked the same as she always did, but today the time flew. With a light step, she left the building. Even remembering that Alberto's flight left tonight couldn't dampen her feelings. He was here now. He didn't hate her, and they might be able to carry on a long distance relationship. Even if it did only last for a little while, he would be worth it. Right now, nothing seemed impossible.

The black limousine pulled up alongside the curb in front. Ordando stepped from the passenger side and opened the back door for her. His eyes suitably lowered when he nodded a greeting. He shut the door carefully behind her. Alberto sat forward to take her hand and move her across the seat closer to him.

"Welcome," he said smoothly.

"Thank you." Her eyelashes fluttered at the intensity of his stare.

"Janine," he said hoarsely, "I must confess my plane is leaving earlier than at first was planned."

Janine's breath died in her throat. "I'm so sorry you're leaving, Berto," she whispered.

He took her hand in both of his. "I am glad you feel this way. Then what I am about to suggest will not sound so completely fantastic to you."

Janine looked up into his face with a doleful expression. "What is it, Berto?"

He tightened his grip on her hand. "Come to the Hacienda Casilda," he said in a deep, compelling voice.

Janine's eyes widened in shock. It was the last thing she expected him to say. For a brief moment of total abandon, she almost said yes without another thought.

Alberto went on, his tone persuasive. "Your mother will be able to recuperate there in comfort. She can swim for exercise and walk through the gardens, which are extensive. The weather is temperate, for the most part, with few sudden storms so her routine could be the same, more or less, everyday. You both could have the freedom to do whatever you would like. I know this sounds sudden, but Janine, the circumstances are unusual to begin with. My family and I would enjoy being of assistance to you both." He paused to search her face.

She shielded herself by looking at her hands. Why couldn't she just open her mouth and agree to follow him to his home? She should follow him to the ends of the earth, if that is what he asked of her. The word yes. Such a simple word and yet it stuck in her parched throat. "Oh, Berto," she sighed wistfully, "what a beautiful dream. I wish…" she paused, entwining her fingers with his dark ones.

"It does not have to be a dream," he said. "You do not need to decide this moment. It is too short notice to be able to think about everything such a journey would entail. Ask your mother before you make up your mind," he urged her.

Janine's doubts overwhelmed her affection for this man. "My mother would say she doesn't know you well enough to impose on your family in that way, especially so far from home. What if something happened? She could have a relapse of some kind," her voice rose slightly with her thoughts. "It would be too chancy," she said firmly. This was something she didn't dare bring up to her mother. There were too many risks. Janine must make the decision for them both. It was better for everyone.

"We do have doctors in Spain, Janine," he replied a bit stiffly. "They are quite capable and well-trained. I know. I have dealt with them before."

Janine flushed. She realized how she'd insulted him, albeit not directly, but he had taken offense just the same.

"I know, Berto, of course. You have wonderful doctors. I didn't mean to sound so superior, but this is my mother," she protested, giving him an entreating look. She wished he would understand without her having to come up with an explanation, because she knew the words wouldn't come out right.

"Don't answer," he said, that note of command in his voice again. An imperious expression was on his lean handsome face. "Discuss it with your mother first and then consult her doctors before you make up your mind, Janine." He reached up and grasped her chin with his strong fingers. He turned her face toward his. "Promise me you will do this before you completely reject the idea." The force of his request undeniably swayed her.

Janine couldn't have stopped herself from nodding in agreement if she'd wanted. She didn't want to argue with him only hours before he was to leave the country, and when he touched her like this she could barely think, let alone argue.

"I'll speak to mother," she said with a sigh, "but I must do it when I think it is best, Berto. I'm not sure how she'll be once she's home, so you must let me be the judge," she insisted.

Alberto smiled, lifting her hand to his lips again. "I will be satisfied with that," he said warmly. The tense moment between them was gone. Janine sat back to digest the knowledge that he wanted to take her home with him. Along with her mother, but that was beside the point. A sense of wonder that this powerful man wanted her to meet his family swept through her and gave her a sense of her own power. Never before had she experienced the ability to influence such a man in such a way. It was an astounding feeling to experience for the first time ever, that she could have such an impact on a man.

12

The entrance to the hospital was congested with wheelchairs and orderlies pushing patients to the ramp. The swinging doors leading inside didn't cease to swing with the coming and going of the people. Ordando hastened to open the back door of the limo so she and Alberto could depart, and already several other vehicles waited behind them.

Alberto took her arm and guided her around the crowd into the building. "Galeno will circle the block so you will have time to fill out any paperwork while your mother is being discharged," he told her as they hurried along the bright multi-colored carpeting that led down the main corridor.

"Oh no," she cried in dismay. "You don't really believe there will be more paperwork, do you?"

Alberto shrugged his broad shoulders. "I cannot guarantee there will be, but I also cannot guarantee there won't," he said, lifting a corner of his mouth at her frustrated groan.

"They must have a ward set aside for people with writer's cramp," she muttered, hitting the elevator button with more force than was necessary. "I thought computers were supposed to get rid of all this multiple copy stuff. It seems to have only made it worse."

"Now you sound like my father," Alberto scolded her as he led her into the elevator. "They do not think of these things to personally cause you inconvenience."

"No, they do it to protect themselves against malpractice," Janine muttered under her breath.

He shook his head disapprovingly. "Don't speak so insolent," his tone tolerant. "It's called progress, and it takes time for the bugs to be worked out of a system of this magnitude. You must have come across numerous setbacks when computers were introduced to the library system. Now you must wonder how you did without them."

Janine flashed him a disdainful look. "The computer system was well-established by the time I was hired. Just how old do you think I am?" Her eyes sparkled at the challenge. Let him try to be diplomatic.

Alberto didn't answer when the elevator doors opened and several hospital staff eased past them on their way out with bustling attitudes like they needed to be someplace. Several more people hurried in behind them pressing Janine and Alberto close together to the back of the elevator. He looked down at her. "You think you shall," he paused as if searching, "stump me with the question?"

"I think you haven't any idea what my age is unless my mother already revealed it with the rest of our family secrets," she whispered.

He shook his head. "I know no family secrets. I only know what I have learned from being with you," he said softly. His tone made their conversation sound much more intimate than the content required. The other occupants weren't making a sound and Janine swore they strained to hear what his next words would be as much as she did.

"You choose not to own a car, yet do you drive?"

She nodded yes, watching his face in fascination.

"You are a trained professional, so I would put your age at twenty-six next birthday."

Janine laughed softly, "Good guess. And how will I figure out your age? Since you've made a guess at mine I should at least be given the same chance. You never drive, but I'm certain you can. You give orders and are used to having them obeyed."

Alberto looked amused at her observations but didn't speak.

"Oh yes, I've noticed," she murmured with a knowing smile. "Nobody would do that willingly unless they trusted the man, and who would trust anyone under thirty in that way?" she finished in a rush, having trouble remembering to keep her voice quiet. "Am I right?"

His grin moved slowly across his face. "All in good time," he replied as they arrived at their floor.

Before Janine could protest to him for not answering, he moved forward to open a pathway to the door. Holding her hand, he led her out with little effort on her part. Janine glimpsed a few of the female faces watching her with obvious envy. She took a second to enjoy the courtesies Alberto bestowed on her. Most of them were minor things that she'd never dreamed could make her life more enjoyable, yet they did. He was considerate beyond what a modern American woman would begin to expect from a man, and she was beginning to regret that this art of courtesy didn't belong to their society any longer.

The reception area seemed subdued after the activity they had just left downstairs.

At her mother's room, Janine knocked. A pleasant faced nurse pulled the cloth screen aside and smiled in recognition.

"Your mother is just finishing," she said. "It will be about ten minutes longer." She let the curtain fall back into place blocking their view.

Janine turned to Alberto. The memory of him here in the hospital when she had hastily pushed him aside caused her whole body to stiffen. She wanted to ask for a few minutes alone with her mother, but didn't want to push him away. Indecision clouded her face.

"I will return in ten minutes," he said quietly, seemingly reading her mind.

She nodded with a smile of relief. "Thank you," she murmured as he slipped away into the hall.

Janine took a deep breath and moved the curtain aside.

"How's everything going?" she asked.

The first thing she noticed was a basket of multi-colored tulips and bright yellow daffodils that were packed in a box on the table.

"Oh, how beautiful! When did these arrive?" Janine stepped forward eagerly, her voice filling with excitement. She opened the attached card and saw Alberto's name.

"Mother," she turned to look at Joan, "why didn't you tell me he sent you flowers?"

After the nurse left, pulling the screen closed behind her, Joan moved to stand in front of the mirror and began to brush her short blond hair with slow strokes, a tremor remained in her right hand making the task more difficult than it should be.

"I don't have to tell you everything that happens to me, Jani. If an attractive man wishes to send me flowers, then, I will keep it my little secret for as long as I like."

"Do you realize what this must have cost?" Janine demanded, leaning forward to inhale the delicate floral scent. "They had to be incredibly fresh when they were sent."

"They arrived this morning after my therapy session."

Janine smiled, thinking of the sender. She should be appalled at the extravagant gift but could only feel gratitude at the joy it had given her mother.

"Should I be jealous?" she asked, turning to her mother with a playful smile.

Joan shrugged, "Think what you like." She was struggling to fasten the clips in her hair. The frustrated tension on her face vanished when she saw Janine silently watching her.

Janine stepped forward, their eyes meeting briefly before Joan handed the metal clips over. It took a moment for Janine to secure the thick hair in the style Joan liked.

"It's obvious he's a generous man. The flowers and then his offer to drive us home when he's on such a tight schedule. It's a shame he's leaving," Joan said as she made a few adjustments to her hair. With a sigh, she studied her wan reflection and picked up her lipstick, opening it and holding the tube with two hands to carefully apply the color to her pale lips.

Janine, flustered by her worry for her mother and her sorrow that Alberto was leaving, made herself look busy packing the few personal items left on the counter.

"There now, I don't think my appearance will frighten too many people when we leave," Joan interrupted her thoughts.

"Oh right, as if that could happen," Janine said tartly. "You should see some of the people leaving this place. To be scary, you aren't even in the running."

Joan laughed at the joke, lessening the strain on her face.

A sharp knock at the door interrupted them. Alberto returned and his presence filled the room. Everything seemed to have changed when he arrived. Janine wondered if she was the only one who felt it. Ordando followed Alberto into the room to carry Joan's suitcase and another box of flowers.

When the nurse wheeled in the chair Joan was required to use when leaving the hospital, Joan turned to Alberto.

"I would like you to handle this horrible thing," she said firmly. "I won't feel safe with anyone else."

The nurse, who held the chair steady while Joan sat down,

stepped willingly aside for Alberto to take her place. Janine followed, carrying the tulip basket and wondering what her mother was planning. The brave front Joan had shown during her convalescence in the hospital didn't slip often, but when it did, Janine was dismayed to see how much the stroke had affected her. The velvety blossoms brushed against her as she followed the others, grateful to be leaving this place for the last time. The group moved quickly through the halls and exited outside onto the ramp where the luxurious vehicle Janine had come to associate more with Galeno than Alberto waited.

Joan had never ridden in the comfort Janine had enjoyed on several occasions. Galeno stood straight, looking very professional next to the black limousine. He moved forward to offer assistance whenever the opportunity arose. Alberto gave Joan his hand and made certain she was resting comfortably in the seat. Janine slid in after her, pushing the box of flowers in front of her until she sat across from Joan. She clutched the box in her lap wishing she could hold her mother in the same way and knew Joan would never stand for it.

"This is absolute heaven," Joan said softly, her voice wispy. She closed her eyes and remained completely still. "Much better than the public transportation we're use to," she added with a grin that caused Janine to smile.

"I am pleased you feel comfortable," Alberto told her as he settled his broad shoulders into the backrest next to Janine.

"I'll be glad to get home, but the doctor insists I return for a few more physical therapy sessions," Joan told them as the car sped through traffic.

Janine relaxed at the news and gave a slight smile. Here was the excuse she needed to decline Alberto's invitation. Alberto noticed her movement and asked with a small smile of his own, "What kind of therapy are they using?"

Joan gave a soft laugh. "I stand in a shallow pool and do exercises. It's to increase the strength in my limbs, but my hand still shakes." She raised the offending hand and watched it tremble. "I find this particularly annoying," she said with irritation. "Although the pool would be rather relaxing if the others in there didn't fall about making so much noise. I must sound terribly intolerant, but to be in a pool by oneself would do a lot more good."

Janine shot Alberto a sharp glance, but he shrugged with an innocent look. He couldn't have prompted the confession from her mother, and how inconvenient for her to decide to speak so frankly in front of him. Janine shifted uncomfortably in her seat and noticed Alberto's veiled look and squirmed some more. She might have to be a little devious to avoid his invitation and the thought didn't sit well with her. She always tried to be honest because dishonesty hadn't ever been necessary in her life. To deliberately deceive someone would take an effort on her part. An effort she loathed to make.

The limousine pulled up in front of the house. Janine exited first to unlock the door. As Alberto held Joan's arm, they slowly walked up the front walk. He asked about the garden and quite freely spoke about the gardens in his own home.

"It must be lovely," Janine heard Joan exclaim.

"What's that?" Janine asked as they walked inside. She was ready to have Alberto help Joan upstairs to bed, but Joan wouldn't hear of it.

"Absolutely not. I have just spent the most boring week of my life on my backside in bed. I have no intention of being rushed back into the same position here," she told her daughter firmly. "I will sit and visit in the living room if Berto agrees to stay for a few moments. He was telling me about the flowers and bushes they grow in the gardens at the hacienda. It sounds like a paradise," she glanced at Janine. "Can you imagine geraniums that grow into bushes, Jani?" She laughed. "We work so hard for ours to grow in the three months we have. They must look pathetic to you."

He smiled as he waited beside her until she sank into the chair. Alberto directed Ordando to leave Joan's belongings in the hallway before he returned outside to wait with Galeno in the car.

Joan requested a cup of tea, and Janine left her alone with trepidation. She knew once Alberto returned he would continue regaling Joan with descriptions of his home. Once in the kitchen, she put the kettle on the burner and began to arrange the tray with cups, sugar, and cream. She didn't have any baked goods. She was just plain lucky there was cream in the refrigerator that hadn't yet spoiled. The truth was she had spent as little time as possible at home while her mother was away. She didn't recall eating anything but toast in the morning. When she returned to the living room, Alberto stood and took the tray from her.

Joan leaned forward. "That smells wonderful," she said inhaling. "I could not get a good cup of tea in the hospital. I don't think they boil the water."

Janine poured the tea, adding the amount of sugar her mother used, and handed it to her. The cup rattled, sloshing some tea into the saucer. Joan frowned as she concentrated, but it wasn't until she held it with both hands that the cup stilled.

"Berto was telling me that his home has a swimming pool and a guest cottage right off the back of the house." She smiled and took a sip of the tea before setting her cup down and leaning back against the cushions. "I think I will close my eyes for a few minutes if you two wouldn't mind having your tea in the kitchen. I guess the excitement tired me out more than I expected," Joan said, closing her eyes.

Alberto stood but hesitated when Janine remained motionless staring anxiously at her mother's pale face. He reached down and gently took Janine's arm. "Come, she only wants a few moments," he said.

Janine walked to the kitchen and held the door open while Alberto took the tray from the table and followed her. The door swung shut when they were both inside, and she moved over to the sink to fill the kettle.

"I prefer my tea scalding hot," she explained, her voice muffled as she kept her back to him.

Alberto silently looked around the small immaculate room. The kitchen table with two chairs tucked underneath it was decorated with a vase of simple wildflowers. The countertop was uncluttered except for brightly colored canisters in one corner. The walls were decorated with faded wallpaper of yellow flowers, and the only ornament was a ceramic plaque of a child's handprint hanging above the sink.

"Do you like tea or would you prefer coffee?" Janine asked him.

"Tea is fine," he said briefly.

Janine turned and noticed he was still standing next to the table.

"Please sit down," she said, wondering why she always forgot her manners when he was around.

Alberto first stepped back to the door and pressed it open to see Joan. She lay on the couch flipping through the stack of mail Janine had left on the coffee table. He shut it and moved across to the table.

Janine carried their cups over and looked up at him. He seemed even taller in the confines of the room. She seated herself quickly, hoping he would do the same.

"This is the first American kitchen I have ever been in," he remarked as he pulled his chair next to hers before sitting down.

Janine was surprised. "Well, don't expect many to look like this," she said with a laugh. This was not the usual type of home Alberto Casilda would visit on his travels, and she doubted if he'd ever be in a middle-class American home again. "I could have cooked a meal for you while you were here," she said regretfully. "I never thought of it, and I do enjoy cooking."

"With your busy schedule?" he asked, incredulous.

"Yes, mother and I take turns with the meals, usually something quick and easy, but I do know more than just the rudiments," she explained shyly. It felt like she was applying for the job of his wife. "I don't know any authentic Spanish dishes, just the Americanized versions."

He smiled. "Why would I want Spanish dishes in America? I'd much prefer apple pie and what is it…hot dogs?'

Janine laughed. "You won't eat our beef but you'll eat a hot dog. You're a brave man."

"If you cooked it I wouldn't care what it was, it would taste like ambrosia," he teased, kissing the tips of his fingers. "I will hold you to your offer when I return?"

Janine stopped stirring her tea. The incredulous look on her face caused him to chuckle. "I must return to bring the bull my father purchased back to Spain, to the ranch. It will take several weeks before the testing and shots needed for him to be removed from your country to mine are completed."

Janine couldn't speak. Silence stretched between them. Her mouth fell open at the bombshell he just dropped on her. She never imagined he would return and certainly not in the time frame he just mentioned. Over the days they'd been together, she had steeled herself to his impending departure. Now he speaks of returning thousands of miles as if it meant nothing.

"You have never mentioned this before," she whispered, two bright spots of color in her pale cheeks.

Alberto shrugged. "I have only just found out. The deal was settled minutes before I met you this afternoon." He leaned across the table to take her hand in his. "Are you happy I will be returning?" he asked.

Janine's anxious eyes searched his face. Here was the face of a stranger who had endeared himself to her in such a short time. This must have been what it was like in war time. The woman who met a man, a soldier, who was the most fascinating man ever to walk into her life only to have him leave after a brief time with sincere promises of returning. His words convinced her, making her hopes and dreams of a future together take root, but what if he didn't return? Instead of finding it romantic as she always imagined it would be, she found it unbearably frustrating. To see him again in a few weeks, how could she ever let him go again?

"My news distresses you, Janine. Why?" he asked, keeping hold of her hand when she tried to pull it away.

Janine stared at the hand that held hers, the lean darkness against her pale skin. "I have understood from the first that you would only be here for a few days, a week tops," she sighed, unsure of how to say what she felt, "now you tell me you're coming back." She stopped, unable to go on.

Alberto stiffened. He released her hand and stood up. "I understand," he said abruptly. "This is what's known as a one night stand. I hadn't realized that is what you were looking for from me," he said, his voice suddenly harsh.

Janine's eyes searched his face. "What?" she cried in confusion.

"You were not sincere when you told me you wanted to stay in contact with me once I returned to Spain. Once I am gone, it is for good," he exclaimed haughtily, snapping his fingers. "My returning would be awkward for you?" His black eyes glittered with anger.

"No!" she cried, shaking her head. "I didn't mean that at all.

How could you think such a horrible thing?" she demanded, aghast at his assumptions.

"Then what, Janine? I told you that night in the hotel room how I felt, but you have never let me know how you feel. Now is the time," he declared.

Janine reached for his hand and held it tightly. Her heart pounded heavily and color filled her face as a strange heat pulsated through her.

"I'm afraid," she said honestly, a choke in her words. "I'm afraid of seeing you again. It's so difficult to say good-bye today, what will happen when I have to say good-bye next time?"

Alberto raised her hand to his lips and caressed the fine bones. A flicker of desire rushed through her as she watched him.

He lifted his head, his eyes finding hers. "You will feel as I do and wonder if this is just a dream or something more, something that will last," he said, his tone husky with emotion. "A separation will clear our minds and when we do meet again we will know. Doesn't the anticipation of that moment fill you with excitement of what is to come?"

Alberto moved to kneel next to her chair. The look he gave her made her fears disappear and the hope rekindle. She reached to touch his hair that fell over his strong brow. Thick and vibrant, the strands separated under her fingers. Alberto half closed his eyes, and she leaned closer to kiss him lightly on the mouth. Her eyes widened as his lips pressed hard against hers in immediate response. His hands moved around her waist and grasped her tightly. Alberto turned his head to deepen the kiss, gently exploring her mouth. Janine shyly followed what he was doing in a hesitant way. Her own experience so limited, she was just realizing how quickly passion surfaced. Her pulse, already beating fast, quickened even more. She had to be lightheaded or bewitched to allow a man to kiss her like this with her mother only steps away.

Alberto broke the embrace. His hands moved to either side of her face and held her, forcing her to meet his eyes. His breathing not quite normal, he smiled. "I will have something to keep me company while I am on the long trip home," he said.

Janine blinked as if awakening from a dream. He reclaimed her kiss-swollen lips one last time before rising to his feet. "I am honored to receive such a gift as this before I must go."

Janine snapped back to reality. She jumped up wanting him to hold her and not leave. Alberto looked down at the expression she didn't bother to hide. It was obvious this had been a new experience for her and he knew it by the delight that showed in her face.

"I will treasure your kiss while we are apart," he whispered.

Janine panicked. It wasn't enough. Her body, filled with newly found desire, ached for more, yet she remained silent. It would do no good. The wall clock in the living room chimed the hour.

Alberto glanced at his watch and tensed.

"It is time," he said softly, though he didn't need to say anything.

She nodded, following him out of the kitchen. Her lips were still aflame from his kiss, but her body felt numb. In a daze, she listened to his good-byes to her mother and heard her reply but couldn't remember a word of what was said. She followed him outside into the cloudy afternoon.

"I will write," she choked out through her dry throat. His face remained expressionless as he stared at her before he slid into the limousine and drove away.

13

I can't find my gardening gloves or the tools, mother," Janine called, her voice muffled, though she shouted from the back of the front hall closet. She backed out and stood with a sigh. Absently, she brushed away from her face what she hoped were dust webs but had a sinking feeling their owners had eight legs attached to their bodies.

"Mother, please try to remember where you put that stuff," she said with a touch of exasperation in her tone. She couldn't help it. Her mother's complete change in personality was having a bad effect on their relationship. She found the compassion and fear she felt in the beginning of the trauma slipping into frustrated patience.

"Oh, I don't know, Janine," Joan said from the couch. "I might have left the whole lot outside the last time I was out there."

"When was that?" Janine muttered under her breath. She gave up looking in the closet and opened the front door to investigate. The weeds had just about taken over the front garden, and the side garden looked more like a part of the lawn with the overgrown grass filling in amongst the few flowers. The fall mums stood thick and green in the midst of the chaos but with no buds yet. It was still too early for them to show. Hidden beneath the grass were the gardening tools where her mother left them. It must have rained since then because the tools were now covered with rust. Janine knelt down and gingerly picked them up and stuffed them into her bucket.

Janine began pulling the weeds out of the moist ground. She stuffed the green culprits into a paper grocery sack. She had been so busy working extra hours at the library and taking care of the house as well as fixing her mother's meals, she was unable to keep up with the gardening. Gardening was usually one of her ways to relax but not now. In the quiet of the outdoors, her mind circled a mile a minute, dwelling on her mother and the slowness of her recovery.

Joan's strength had returned but her desire to return to work or resume any of her responsibilities hadn't. Her visits to the physical therapist had ended. She was required by the doctor to continue her workouts on her own, but she refused. Janine encouraged her to begin taking over the duties around the house. If Joan did begin something, it remained unfinished. Janine couldn't continue to ignore what was becoming much too apparent. Her mother's full recovery was impaired by the onset of depression.

Janine found this a much more difficult problem to combat than the stroke. It didn't help that Janine's time away from the house now stretched after five o'clock most days. Working the extra hours was difficult, but they needed the income. In addition, Joan recently began to refuse to leave the house alone. For such an independent person to suddenly remain closeted in the small house for days, and be content with it, was causing Janine to panic. She didn't know what to do. Alone, she wrestled with her fears and worries, unable for the first time in her life to confide in Joan. Her pride kept her from turning to Connie, who was sympathetic with the cursory reports Janine gave her each week.

Today, while at work, she'd come to the conclusion that a new regime of walking would begin at home before they had dinner. She needed to keep a positive attitude. A cheerful demeanor would do much to lift everyone's spirits. If she could only get Joan outside to see the beauty of the evening, it would be much easier for Janine to convince her how inspiring such a walk could be.

"Mother," Janine called, forcing cheerfulness into her voice as she walked in the front door, "I've found the tools."

The living room was empty, and as she wiped the worst of the muddy soil from her hands with a tattered tissue found in her pocket, she heard laughter coming from the kitchen. Thinking her mother was listening to talk radio, Janine opened the kitchen door and glanced expectantly around the room. Joan looked up with a smile that Janine hadn't seen for the past month. Sitting across from Joan, Alberto stood immediately at her appearance and stepped forward with a smile.

At the sight of him, an instant rush of pure physical pleasure raced through her as her eyes slowly drank in his appearance. His face was lean and his skin much darker than when he left. It accentuated the masculine aura he possessed, making it more potent. She had to admit, "absence makes the heart grow fonder" proved to have more truth than "out of sight out of mind" in her case. She eagerly moved toward him.

"Berto," she whispered before she averted her eyes to hide how deeply she felt at seeing him. She looked at her mother, who remained seated, beaming at her daughter.

Joan laughed gaily at Janine's reaction. "I knew this would be a fantastic surprise for you," she said as the tea whistle blew. "He just walked in a few minutes ago right from the airport." Joan stood and hurried over to the stove to lift the steaming kettle off the electric burner.

Alberto had been watching Janine, and when she met his eyes, she knew he wasn't pleased with what he saw. She had lost weight since he'd left. Deep shadows marred her eyes and worry lines that hadn't been present before caused her to look haggard.

"Janine," he said, "please sit down." He held out the chair he had occupied.

She hesitated. She should help her mother fix the tea tray, but Joan was already busy gathering the cups and saucers. Janine swallowed the resentment that surfaced as she watched her mother. Joan hadn't done a thing around the house for weeks, and now she was perfectly happy entertaining Alberto. Janine did as he suggested and sat down.

"No, not in here, Jani," Joan protested, "let's go into the living room. It's much cooler there. Berto, do you mind carrying the tray?"

When Alberto picked up the tea tray and left the room, Joan hurried after him until Janine stopped her.

"Mother," she gasped out, leaping to her feet. "Couldn't you have given me some kind of warning that he was here?"

Joan turned to fix her eyes on her daughter. "Why, dear, I didn't have the opportunity to tell you when he arrived."

Janine looked down the front of her. "Look at me!" she cried and noticed every stain on the wash-worn shorts and t-shirt she wore for gardening. "I look like a complete wreck." She was truly angry at her mother's insensitivity. "I have to change." She spun on her heel and pushed open the door.

When she met Alberto on the other side, she looked down at the floor. "Excuse me, Berto, while I go and clean up. It'll only take a few minutes," she said, then tried to hurry past him.

"You always wish to run away," he said softly.

Janine attempted a light-hearted laugh for his benefit but failed. The sound caught in her throat.

"Only long enough to shower and change into something decent without Mother Earth all over it."

"It doesn't matter to me what you wear, Janine," he said as he leaned closer to her. "What does concern me is how tired you look. I cannot believe the library has extended its hours to cause you to lose sleep, so that means there is something else keeping you awake."

Her eyes flew to his face. "Please," she whispered, "let me go freshen up."

Alberto frowned. "Of course," he said abruptly and stepped back.

Janine jumped toward the stairs. It frightened her how desperately she wanted to talk with him. How she wanted to cry out her worries about her mother and about money. Even if he couldn't help her at least he was here to offer comfort.

As she hurried into the bathroom, stripping off her shirt while kicking the door shut behind her, Janine recognized why she couldn't tell him. She already felt too dependent on him to fill this aching loneliness that had become a part of her life since he had left, and she didn't want to give him any extra leverage if he should bring up the trip to Spain again. She knew they couldn't afford such a trip right now.

Janine spent more time getting ready than she usually did. The tea dishes had already been cleared away and spread across the coffee table were photographs and sheets of stationary. Joan and Alberto were gone.

Janine wondered what was going on when she picked up one of the photographs from the table and saw a man and woman standing in front of a huge jacaranda tree. They were laughing with their arms clasped around each other.

"Berto was showing me some photographs of his family," Joan said as she walked up behind her. She leaned over Janine's shoulder to see which picture she held. "Those are his parents. There are several that show more of the house and are simply breathtaking. You look tired, honey, sit down, I've fixed you some hot tea." Joan was holding a cup of steaming tea in her hands.

Janine stared in astonishment at Joan's hands. They weren't trembling.

"It's such a relief, that shaking is finally gone from my hands," Joan said.

"I didn't realize it was completely gone, why didn't you tell me?" Janine asked. "How long?"

Joan shrugged. "I'm not sure. For awhile. You haven't had much time for visiting lately, and I've usually forgotten everything I had to say by the time you get home from work."

"Thank you, mother," she said, taking the cup of tea, "and I'm sorry." Janine was filled with remorse that she hadn't paid more attention.

Joan looked at her in surprise. "Whatever for?"

"For not noticing how much better you are and…for a lot of things," she muttered and began to shift through the photos.

There was a picture of several young men of various ages standing together. Janine recognized a younger Alberto in the group and those with him had such a close resemblance to each other.

"He has brothers?" she said, glancing at Joan.

"Yes, I do," Alberto said, walking out of the kitchen in time to hear her question. He stopped next to her and leaned closer to see the picture. Janine stared at his profile and noticed the thickness of his eyelashes that surrounded his night-dark eyes.

He didn't look at the photograph when he answered, instead he looked at her. "There are also some of my cousins pictured as well. We are a close family. My relatives visit often, especially in the summer months."

"Really," she said, feeling breathless. She moved the picture closer to hide her face from him, hoping he would think she wanted to study the picture.

He pointed out two in the group. "These are my brothers, Frederico and Juan. They, of course, are older now by about three years. I also have two sisters, one is five and the other is married. She lives in Buenos Aires with her husband's family."

"How fun a big family must be," Janine said as she looked at the faces looking back at her. They each had such a cheerful expression for the camera lens. "They are all very handsome," she murmured.

"You must take a moment to read this letter Janine," Alberto said, handing her an envelope. "It is from my father."

Janine guessed what the contents would be as she slid her fingernail under the flap and took out the single sheet of paper.

"He wants us to come and stay at the hacienda with his family," Janine announced. There wasn't anything else she could do. She certainly couldn't conceal the contents from Joan when she was standing right there.

"What!" Joan exclaimed. She turned to Alberto. "Your family wants us to come to Spain. I don't believe it," she grabbed Janine's arm. "Spain, Jani," her voice rose. "It's been so long since I've traveled anywhere."

At Janine's lack of response, Joan paused.

"Don't you think that's an extremely generous offer? It rather overwhelms me," Joan explained.

"Janine knows the reason my parents have extended their invitation already, Joan," Alberto offered. "We spoke of it before I left for Spain."

His voice wasn't condemning Janine like she deserved, instead it held no emotion. This made her distinctly uneasy. Why didn't the man ever react like she expected?

Joan didn't allow the uncomfortable silence in the room to last too long.

"Do you know what an experience it would be to stay on an honest to goodness cattle ranch in the interior of Spain?" Joan said to her.

Janine felt so ashamed she could have hidden in the corner. She knew he thought she'd kept his offer a secret from her mother on purpose. And she had at first, but then the subject seemed to become irrelevant.

"Do you think your doctor will allow you to travel?" Janine heard him ask. "I know that traveling tends to tire some more than others. Once you arrived at the hacienda your schedule would be your own to plan as you like, but the traveling is what can cause problems."

"I've always been a good traveler. I especially enjoy flying," Joan smiled, a far-off look on her face. "Or at least I used to be a good traveler. It's been so long since I've done anything like that

I'm not sure, especially after what's happened." She frowned, remembering how much her life had changed since her stroke.

"I'm sure it won't take you too long to adjust to traveling again if that is what you would like to do," Alberto said to her.

Joan looked up with a smile. "You are very gallant, Alberto, and I'm still young enough to appreciate it. Thank you, or should I say 'gracias'?" She crossed her arms and stared at Janine for a moment with a puzzled frown before walking away to stand by the window.

Janine was astounded that even the mere possibility of a trip to Spain could revitalize her mother so. Her hope that Joan's depression would pass by itself now seemed trivial beside the cure that Alberto was offering. It was obvious that Joan was going to need something more to get herself back on track and from what she was saying, it sounded like travel might be a possibility. Janine hadn't even been aware that her mother liked to travel.

"Look at you, Janine, you look so lovely in that dress," Joan said, interrupting Janine's thoughts and successfully changing the subject. "Thank goodness Alberto is here to take you out and show you off. I'm extremely grateful you've returned right now, Berto. It gives Janine an excuse to get away from the house. She's been so considerate of me that she hasn't had a moment to herself."

"I will only be here for two days," Alberto said quietly. "Would you like to walk, Janine?"

"Perhaps, mother," Janine said with an anxious glance at Alberto, "you'd like to join us?

Joan brushed off the suggestion. "I'll stay here and think about all that Alberto has so kindly suggested." She nodded with satisfaction. "Thank you, Alberto, for bringing so much excitement with you. I'm as giddy as a school girl just thinking about it."

Janine listened to her mother, distressed that she was thinking of accepting his invitation without consulting her. Janine would never make such a momentous decision like traveling to Spain without first discussing it with Joan. She suddenly didn't know her mother at all.

After bidding Joan good-bye, Alberto and Janine walked for quite some time without speaking a word to each other. Alberto knew the path to the Lakewalk and didn't ask if that was the destination she had in mind. Janine followed him, lost in her thoughts.

"Did your companions come with you again?" Janine asked him suddenly, her tone more stilted than she would have liked.

"Galeno returned with me, but Ordando is busy helping Frederico on the ranch."

"Oh," she said, her eyes on the dark water of the lake.

The sun had already dipped behind the horizon, so it looked darker than it should for July.

"I'm glad you're here," she told him.

Alberto remained silent.

She had the distinct feeling he doubted his return was all that welcomed.

"My mother hasn't been this excited about anything since you invited her to the Mayor's Ball last month, thank you."

"I did nothing. Save your gratitude for when it's deserving."

Janine stopped and faced him. She reached out and touched his arm. His expression remained stern.

"Berto?" she said softly, pleading for understanding.

He sighed and reached over with gentle fingers to brush her light brown hair away from her face.

"I have thought of this moment many times," he said. "It did not happen as I expected but, then…this is America," he shrugged. "You never spoke to your mother about a visit to the hacienda."

Janine shook her head. She couldn't make up an excuse, and she didn't have one.

"I suspect something distressing has occurred since I left."

Janine felt her throat tighten as her thoughts turned to her mother. She controlled her emotions with difficulty.

"It's been awful," she exclaimed. "The doctor says there is nothing physically wrong with her, yet she's not the same person. She has no energy and no attention span. She'll begin a project and then just wander off like a child. She spends way too much time on the couch, not watching television or reading, just sitting there, or else she falls into a dead sleep." Janine couldn't believe she was telling him all of this, but once she started she didn't want to stop. "Today is the first day that she's acted like herself," she said, fear in her hushed tone.

"Something must be done Janine," he said quickly. "What about different doctors or a different medical facility? Do you believe that her condition has been misdiagnosed?"

Janine was shocked at first. The doctors had accused her of being overly sensitive about Joan's condition. Alberto actually believed her.

"They've diagnosed it," she said. "It's depression, Berto," she admitted the awful fact in a whisper. It didn't sound as bad as she thought it would. She couldn't control the tears on her cheeks, but at least she hadn't fallen apart. "She's recovered in every other way, so why am I crying?" she laughed at herself.

Alberto took her hand and led her off the wooden walkway to a bench that faced the lake. The walk was crowded with people, and she appreciated not having an audience.

"Health is body, mind, and soul," he said as they sat down. "When the mind remains unhealed, it can cause other problems. You are perfectly justified to be anxious about this."

A feeling of relief rushed over her just from hearing Alberto's sympathetic response. "I don't want them to put her on medication," she explained.

"Medication, I would think, would be a last resort. There are other things that can be tried, aren't there?" Alberto asked.

"Drug therapy has already been suggested. The effects of any drug are so difficult to judge, and I know she won't want to take pills. She hates taking even a little aspirin. How do you think she'd react if they tried to put her on an anti-depressant?

"The only problem is I can't get her to cooperate with any alternative treatment. You saw how she reacted when I suggested going for a walk tonight. The story about me staying at home is more like her own decision not to leave the house, ever. She won't even do the gardening anymore, and she used to love gardening."

They silently stared at the water. An ore boat moved toward the bridge causing white-tipped waves to tumble in front of the rusty bow. Seagulls wheeled through the sky in front of them. Their raucous cries filled the air. The ground fell away at their feet and beneath them was the rocky shore.

"Let me ask about you, Janine," he said, still holding her hand. "Your mother mentioned that you've been gone more than usual," he probed in a quiet voice. "I can tell that you are close to exhaustion. What is the cause of this, if I may ask?"

Janine glanced at him and saw him frown before he looked away. "You have every right to ask, but it's something you might not understand," she began.

Alberto inhaled sharply, his nostrils dilated for a moment.

"It's money, Berto," Janine blurted. "With my mother unable to work, I've been picking up extra hours. I don't get home sometimes until seven o'clock. I'm afraid my absence is affecting her recovery, and I haven't been able to spend the time I need figuring out our finances. I've never paid monthly bills before. All this time I'd just hand over whatever money she asked for from my check. I'm just beginning to realize I haven't been contributing nearly enough."

Alberto shook his head. "This is what you assume I will not understand?" he demanded.

"You have to admit money doesn't seem to be a problem for you."

"Money is a problem for everyone in one way or another. Finances or budgeting happens to be something I can work with," he told her.

"No," she cried. "There might not be any reason to be concerned, and I don't want my mother to start worrying about it." She laughed. "Really, Berto, it's my mother that's causing me the sleepless nights."

Alberto stood and slipped his hand under her arm. "Come, we should start back to the house. It will be dark soon," he ended the conversation abruptly.

Janine couldn't tell if he was angry or not. She began to feel miserable for once again rejecting his offer to help. There was little conversation between them during the walk home. The limousine was parked next to the curb, and Galeno stepped out of the driver's seat when he saw them approach.

"You've returned with Señor Casilda, Galeno," Janine called cheerfully to the hulking man. "Welcome once more. I'm so glad to see you again."

Galeno nodded. "Señorita, it is a pleasure to see you again."

"Are you able to come in for something cold to drink?" she said, including them both with a look to see how Alberto reacted to the invitation. "Do you have the time?" she asked.

Alberto gave a short nod. They walked to the house.

"If your mother is resting already we will not stay," Alberto told her when she opened the front door.

Janine nodded in agreement hoping her mother had stayed awake tonight.

On the front table, when they walked inside, was a pitcher of lemonade and several glasses. Joan bustled into view a few seconds later carrying a plate of cheese and crackers.

"You're back," she said with surprise. "I was hoping you wouldn't stay out much past dark, the weather is supposed to change and a storm's coming in off the lake. I wouldn't want you caught in a downpour."

Janine searched her mother's face for any sign of fatigue, but she looked like her old self.

"Don't fret," she reassured them, "I took a little catnap while you were away and feel quite refreshed now. I was going to see if I could convince Galeno to come in and play a hand or two of cards while we waited for you two." She caught sight of Galeno behind them. "Good, I see you already invited him in. Well, don't just stand there, come in and find a seat."

Her voice held a joy that gave Janine hope. Maybe the visitors could pull her mother out of her depression without having to drag them both halfway around the world to a foreign country.

The next hour passed pleasantly with the conversation centering on Spain and the hacienda. Alberto did most of the talking. Galeno spoke only when Janine or Joan asked him a direct question. He spoke slowly, not as comfortable with the complexities of the English language as his boss. When the clock struck ten, the two men stood to leave. When they were alone in the hallway, Alberto took Janine into his arms.

"I will see you tomorrow," he said. His lips slowly brushed against hers.

14

When Janine walked out of the double glass doors of the library, the familiar black limousine was parked in the bus stop. Galeno stood next to it and leaned to open the door.

Instead of climbing immediately into the vehicle, she stood beside him and waited. Galeno, with an unhurried manner, lowered his chin so his dark brown eyes rested briefly on her face. Then he looked away.

She noticed that his eyes weren't the obsidian black of Alberto's. The wide flatness of his features and the furrow of his broad brow were daunting, but Janine had never felt that he was anything but a big gentle bear of a man. A faint smile touched his lips softening the hard angle of his chin.

"Buenas tardes, señorita," he said.

Janine, her face alight with mischief, still didn't move

"Good afternoon," she returned. "I do believe, Galeno, we've known each other long enough for you to call me Janine. Would you please call me Janine?"

Galeno nodded. "If that is what you want me to do."

"It would make me feel a whole lot better, especially when you have to drive me around town."

"Very well, Janine."

Satisfied, she climbed inside. The backseat was empty. Alberto wasn't waiting for her. Undecided if she should ask his whereabouts, she waited long enough for Galeno to slam her door shut. If he had left a message, Galeno would have already told her.

All the way home, she fretted. When Galeno helped her out of the car in front of her house, she again debated whether she should ask about Alberto but decided she shouldn't. As Galeno got back into the limo, she didn't know if she should say good-bye or not. After all, Alberto had bought his precious bull. Now there was no reason for him to return. She walked away from the limousine with mixed feelings. She swallowed hard unable to face the thought of missing Alberto.

As she stepped onto the porch she noticed the stoop looked

freshly swept. Inside the front hallway she could smell something cooking. Janine set her purse on the entry table and smiled. Her mother had fixed dinner. She was truly surprised and a bit relieved that her mother must be feeling better.

Eagerly she hurried toward the kitchen. She passed the dining room table, which was next to the kitchen door, heard voices, and stopped. So this new energy was the result of having Alberto Casilda visit. He was the only man who had stepped foot in the house except for repairmen in eleven years.

Janine felt a thrill of anticipation flash through her that Alberto was here. She hurriedly brushed her hair into place with a belated thought on what her appearance might be. After his surprise visit yesterday, she could never look worse.

She opened the door, the disappointment of his absence gone, now that she knew he was near. The sight that greeted her stopped her dead in her tracks. She gasped deeply. Familiar images she had hidden away from the world mocked her in the bright room. In horror, she looked around and felt her very soul was on display.

To see the childish paintings spread out in an array in front of her was too cruel. The canvases leaned lazily against kitchen cupboards or were set haphazardly on the countertops. Each one glared at her, each looking more amateurish than the one before it. She cringed in embarrassment and clenched her eyes shut.

"This has to be a nightmare. It can't really be happening," she thought.

When she opened her eyes again, the sight of the large cumbersome frame of her father's portrait greeted her. His features looked out of proportion to the body. He resembled a demon instead of the man he'd been.

"What have you done?" she choked out, whirling to face her mother with blazing eyes. "I can't believe you would do this," her voice faltered. "How could you bring these down without asking me first?"

"They were a mess, covered with dust and spider webs," Joan declared, ignoring her outburst. With her hands on her hips, she looked the pictures over. "I'm surprised they're in such good shape after being neglected for so many years." She walked to where Janine stood unmoving in the doorway and patted her arm. "Alberto asked me if he could see them," she said, unperturbed by Janine's obvious discomfort. "After I showed him the one of the Captain, he wanted to see more of your work." She paused to study her daughter's stricken face. "Don't fret, Jani, that's a compliment. Now I've cleaned them, and they look wonderful." She returned to the stove leaving Janine stunned.

Alberto stood in the corner out of Janine's line of vision. His broad shoulders leaned against the basement door. He had his arms crossed over his chest. With hooded eyes, he watched Janine from the moment she opened the door until now. He saw the ashen whiteness of her face when she first entered and then the deep flush that quickly replaced it. He knew Joan had no idea how devastated Janine was.

Janine glanced around and caught sight of him. He could see the change in her when she saw him. Her hazel eyes widened as they stared at each other across the room. Janine's breathing was visibly erratic. Alberto felt composed, though his thoughts raced. He couldn't come to a decision about what he should do.

This woman was driving him to distraction. He wanted her, both physically and emotionally. He could still feel the curves of her body that he'd held only long enough to make him hungry for more. A magnetic force emanated from her since the first time their paths crossed. It continued to hold him in a way he couldn't ignore. Even after his absence and the complications of her mother's stroke, he had to admit to himself that she was an exceptional woman. He knew it. Her mother knew it. But Janine might never allow *herself* to know it. That was the danger.

While he was prepared to spend the rest of his life with the stunned woman in the kitchen, he didn't know if she believed in herself enough to make a similar commitment.

Janine couldn't control the thudding beat of her heart. Alberto could probably see it throbbing in her chest. She blushed under his scrutiny. She couldn't read his thoughts. He couldn't possibly know how difficult it was for her to stand here and meet his eyes. Her first instinct was to gather each one of the canvases and hide them and the deep agony she was feeling.

She broke the silence with a strained laugh. "I'm sure Alberto didn't realize how juvenile my paintings would be when he asked you that, mother," she said, trying to salvage some part of her composure. "Painting is just a hobby from my past and from the look of it, it deserves to stay there. I'm surprised at you, mom, venturing into the very back corner of the attic underneath the eave to dig these out." She shot her mother a withering glance. "Are you positive the extra activity wasn't too much for you?"

Joan, with a look of understanding shook her head. "The paintings are quite good, Jani. Alberto even said so. He also said your instructors were right when they told you to continue your art lessons. You show signs of great promise."

Janine flushed again but for a different reason. If Alberto had been impressed he certainly didn't look that way any longer. She was afraid he would find it easy to wash his hands of her when he left Duluth, Minnesota, tonight.

"I will help you return the canvases to the attic, Janine," he said quietly. He reached for the nearest canvas.

"Wait," she cried. Her body coiled tightly enough to unbalance her as she jumped toward him, or toward the painting, she didn't know which.

Alberto stepped forward to steady her before she fell. He held her around the waist to stop the headlong rush. She could feel his palms and the width of his fingers pressed into the flesh of her back. Prickles of heat flooded through her body from the warmth of his touch until he released her and stepped away.

She looked up at him. This physical reaction she felt whenever he touched her could become a problem. She was alarmed at how strange she felt. It seemed to become more persistent each time it happened. Especially after he'd kissed her, she found herself longing for those kisses constantly. The thought brought her eyes to his mouth.

"I'm sorry," she said softly. "I'm clumsy because I was wrong. I don't care about these old things. It's just…I was so surprised. I…." A movement from her mother reminded her they weren't alone. She stopped and turned her face away.

"Janine studied with local artists when she was in high school. They were sorry when she decided to quit," Joan told him, looking down at the paintings. Her hand rested on the frame of the portrait of her husband. "This one has comforted me on many occasions."

Her voice held a whisper of melancholy.

Janine glanced at Alberto to see if he remembered their conversation about the Captain. The larger-than-life man on the canvas seemed to look more like a young daughter's ideal than a man she didn't like. Joan rambled on as if Janine wasn't in the room. Janine didn't care. It gave her a chance to catch her breath.

Joan turned to look where Alberto had retreated against the wall. There was a shine in her cornflower blue eyes. "So you see, Berto, you are joined by some of the top teachers from the Northland when you say she has promise."

"Had," Janine corrected her. "It's been years, too many years to begin reflecting on what might have been."

"Janine painted from her heart. That is what I see in these," Alberto said.

For the first time since walking through the door, Janine moved closer to look at the work she'd done so many years in the past.

Painted from the heart. It sounded poetic. At one time the paintings had meant something to her, but now she faced the fact that the depth of those feelings had faded.

"The colors of the lake in this one have captured nature quite admirably," Alberto said as he picked up a painting of an intense summer storm over Lake Superior. In the distance, the Aerial Lift Bridge was a silhouette, almost a shadow. It blended in with the gray cloud-ridden sky and the tempestuous waves of the lake. "It's a rather stark portrayal, but convincing. It looks like you mixed something with the oils to add an intensity to the colors of the water. "

Janine looked at the canvas and then at Alberto, undecided if he was being honest or condescending.

"I could have," she said, trying to remember what she'd done to this particular painting. "If I did, I can't remember what it was." She studied the paint and saw he was right. The oils for the water did contain a slightly different depth than the rest of the painting. A rich hue she hadn't re-created in any of the other oil paintings she'd completed. She found she wanted to hear more and listened attentively when Alberto pointed to the next painting.

"In this one you caught the motion of your father and the movement of the sail behind him." He glanced at her before looking again at the painting. "That isn't an easy accomplishment, especially for a beginner."

Joan moved forward. "Excuse me, Alberto. I hate to interrupt, but might we continue this conversation at the supper table? Everything is ready, and I don't think Janine's had the chance to wash up after being at work all day."

"Oh, you're right, I completely forgot," Janine exclaimed. "I'll only be a minute." She whirled around to hurry out the door.

Janine surprised herself. She was impatient to get back and discuss the art of painting with Alberto. Perhaps it was something they had in common. Preferably they need not discuss her paintings. His comments had given her new insight, and she felt in the pit of her stomach a small stir of the old enthusiasm she had for painting.

His knowledge of art critique should have surprised her, but it didn't. He seemed to be proficient in many things. Janine thought it would be impossible for her to learn everything that makes up Alberto, but she could certainly enjoy trying.

15

Janine raced up the stairs, quietly closed the door to her bed room and sank onto the downy comforter that covered her bed. She leaned her head forward and covered her face with her hands.

Painting was another part of her past that she had turned her back on. As a required course in high school it had added a nice change to her rather uninteresting life. It made her something more than just an ordinary teenager. Her talent had been a complete and pleasant surprise to her, but she had always held a suspicion that the people who were most profuse in their praise of her work merely pitied her—the poor teen who had lost her father in such a tragic way.

The public sensation that surrounded the wreck of the Edmund Fitzgerald caused a commotion to the residents surrounding the Great Lakes but especially to the families of the crew. The media was everywhere. They wanted to delve into the heart of the tragedy and those affected by it. When the facts surrounding the ore boat's disappearance weren't intriguing enough, they began to create a mystery of their own.

In the quiet life the Nielsen's led, the rush of attention fell like a bomb into their midst. Even before the reality of her father's death had set in, the media explosion destroyed the well-ordered world in which the two women lived. They had no privacy. Janine's schoolwork suffered, and her mother's life at work and at home became unbearable. Then, just as suddenly, the prying eyes and the demands from reporters stopped. The hype simply disappeared into nothing. Just like her interest in painting.

The summer after their lives had become total mayhem, Janine immersed herself in painting. She had spent hours hidden in the attic. She practiced and experimented with colors and different kinds of paints. Creating different subject matter came easily for her, so she painted landscapes, flowers, and various animals. Whatever caught her eye. The one exception, the only human she'd ever attempted to paint, had been her father, and she didn't start the project until his death. Now, after all this time, a stranger had brought the forgotten piece of her past back into the light.

Janine threw herself back onto the mattress to stare up at the ceiling. She couldn't understand why her mother had decided to open up and reveal everything about her to a man who lives on another continent. A man whose entire existence was revealed to them only because of a misunderstanding in the fog.

She brushed her hair out of her face impatiently. Her mother's behavior was only one part of the chaos Janine's life had become.

"Dinner's ready," Joan called up the stairs.

After washing up, Janine walked down the stairs and could see the dining room table was set. Alberto was helping Joan carry dinner plates already filled with food out of the kitchen.

"It's too hot in the kitchen to eat there," Joan told Janine when she appeared. "Jani, would you get the pitcher of iced tea, it's in the refrigerator."

"Sure," she said. "The food looks great, mom. You must've worked all day on this."

Joan smiled as she set down one of the plates. "I enjoyed it. With the table set like this, I feel like it's the holidays and we're celebrating."

"Celebrating?" Janine questioned.

"Yes, Alberto's invitation and hopefully a passing review on my health from the doctor."

Janine met Alberto's intent gaze unflinchingly. She then turned and went to the kitchen to get the iced tea. When Janine returned, the conversation between Joan and Alberto ended abruptly. She glanced from one to the other.

"What's going on?"

Joan looked uncomfortable. "I have something to tell you, and I know it's going to upset you."

"What do you mean?" Janine asked guardedly. She quickly set the heavy pitcher down on the table.

"There's nothing else to do but just come right out and say it," Joan said. "I've decided to accept the invitation. I'm going to visit the family's ranch in Spain."

Anger boiled inside of Janine, but for some reason the news didn't surprise her as much as it should. Her mother was putting her in an awkward situation, and she didn't even seem to know it.

"It's a rather sudden decision," Janine said, keeping her voice deliberately quiet.

"It didn't have to be," Joan reminded her. "You've known about Alberto's invitation for a month. When did you think you'd get around to asking me if I wanted to go? I hadn't heard one word before Alberto mentioned it in the kitchen yesterday afternoon."

Silence fell. The clock ticked loudly in the front hall for several strokes before Janine could answer.

"You haven't been in the best spirits lately," she declared. "I had no idea what your reaction to an invitation like this would be." A flush crept into her cheeks as her eyes furtively returned to Alberto's face and then back to the table.

Joan stared at her daughter until she laughed. "I thought you were playing nursemaid and didn't feel I was capable of traveling all the way to Spain. You weren't?"

Janine shrugged. She spoke frankly. "In a way. Of course I was worried about your health. Your recovery wasn't going well and you didn't seem to care. How do I know you'll decide what's best for you?" she burst out. If Joan didn't care that Alberto was watching and listening to this personal conversation, then Janine didn't care either. "You have no interest in anything. Not even returning to the things that you liked before your..." she paused, unable to voice it, even in anger.

"My stroke," Joan supplied coldly. "Do you blame me? After what happened I thought everything in my life was pointless. I suppose I was going through the steps of grieving because something had been lost—my health. I wasn't going to continue blithely through life hoping the next time it happened wouldn't bring my death. I needed to make changes, and I wasn't sure how to start."

Janine glared at her. "Well, did it ever occur to you that I might have needed some reassurance that you weren't wallowing in a pool of depression that you couldn't get yourself out of?"

"It did at times, but I didn't have any answers for myself. How could I know what to say to you? You're always so full of questions about everything. I just didn't feel up to answering them."

The two glared at each other across the room until Joan sat down. "The food is getting cold."

Janine took a deep breath, undecided about what to do. Alberto continued to stand next to his chair waiting for her to take her seat before he would. She was filled with indignation about her mother's lack of consideration but decided to sit down and join in the meal.

"I've already called the doctor to explain about the trip," Joan said, breaking the silence. "He probably won't be able to return my call until after the office closes so that should be any time now."

Again her mother was being totally unpredictable. Without bothering to put a forkful of food in her mouth, Janine concentrated on separating the vegetables in the salad and then pushing them back together again. She listened to the conversation between her mother and Alberto with little enthusiasm.

"You realize I can't go with you," Janine said, her voice suddenly sullen.

Joan sighed impatiently. "What is it now?"

"You haven't given a thought to the expense or the kind of planning that a trip like this takes, and yet you've already accepted."

"How do you know that I haven't given it a thought? I've been on the phone with a travel agent all day. She was very helpful, and whatever she doesn't know I'm sure Alberto can help me with."

Janine, half-rising from her seat, faced Joan. "Who are you and what have you done with my mother?" she demanded. Then she turned to Alberto and declared, "It has to be your influence."

Alberto smirked at her accusation. "Calm down, Janine. This isn't a conspiracy against you. Your mother needs a vacation after eleven years. I cannot understand why you want to begrudge her this opportunity."

"Because we can't afford it!" Janine shouted at him. "I thought I made that perfectly clear to you yesterday."

Joan burst out laughing. "What are you talking about, girl?"

Janine turned in disbelief. "I'm not kidding. We honestly can't afford for you to go on this trip," she said. "Ever since your stroke I've been trying to figure out the finances. From what I saw in your budget book, I can't understand how you've managed to make ends meet all these years."

"You were never interested in the family finances," Joan said, still amused. "It's quite simple, really." She paused. "I'm glad you brought this up. With me going to Spain, we have to do something we should have done years ago, talk about our finances and my will."

Janine sank back into her seat feeling deflated. She crossed her arms in defiance. "Well, are you going to explain?"

Alberto interrupted. "Perhaps you would prefer to discuss this when I'm not here."

"Of course not, Berto," declared Joan. "Especially when it's so simple. I'm not using our monthly income for the trip, Jani. The expense can quite easily come from your father's death settlement. I've been rolling it over in government treasury bonds for just such an occasion. I had originally planned for it to go for your college education, but with your scholarships, there wasn't any need. The bonds have done well over the years. And, our paychecks were always sufficient to maintain us month to month. You would have known all this if you had shown any interest." Joan looked pleased with her well-laid plans.

Janine simply stared at her dumbfounded.

"I will go, with or without you," Joan glanced at her, a frown on her face. "If you feel your job will suffer, then by all means stay, but it will do me a world of good to get away. Especially with the life changes I need to contemplate." She reached across the table for her daughter's hand, but Janine moved swiftly to avoid the contact. Joan reached for the pitcher instead and said nothing.

When she spoke again, Joan's voice was determinedly cheerful.

"Please, Alberto, thank your family for their generosity and tell them to expect one visitor. I'm certain everything will be okayed by Doctor Larry."

She looked at Janine's stubborn expression and shrugged. "Hopefully two. If you won't come for the entire month, Janine, maybe you'll consider joining me for a week or two. You will, won't you, Jani? It will be such fun," she urged.

Janine focused her eyes on the plate. It felt like her world was crumbling down around her. She was falling into a deep chasm without any means to save herself, but she nodded, not for her mother's benefit, but for Alberto who sat silently watching them.

Joan breathed a loud sigh of relief. "Thank goodness. I was beginning to despair that you wouldn't even agree to that. Talk to

Connie, I'm certain she could give you some time off."

Janine grimaced, but nodded stiffly in agreement, only to acknowledge that she was listening.

The uncomfortable meal seemed like it would never end. Joan was determined to make the most of it and continued to ply Alberto with questions until Janine felt like screaming. Finally, Joan stood to go get the dessert and coffee. Janine, relieved that it was finally over, began to clear the table. She didn't want dessert, so she could escape into the kitchen.

Alberto pushed his chair from the table and she thought he was going to offer his help. She stiffened, ready to refuse, but instead he wandered out into the hallway. She heard the door slam. Soon she smelled familiar cigar smoke through the open window. Her hands full of dishes, she pushed open the kitchen door with her elbow.

"Thank you, dear, that was helpful," Joan said as she moved past her daughter.

"I'm going to start cleaning up," Janine said. She didn't think she was capable of carrying on a civil conversation. She was still so angry with her mother for making all these decisions without her. "If I don't start now I'll be up until midnight," she complained.

Joan smiled. "That's so considerate of you, thank you. I'll admit I'm feeling washed out after all the excitement." Joan pushed the door shut on Janine before she could say anything else.

Janine, in a huff, prepared the hot dishwater and began scraping the leftovers into plastic containers when Alberto opened the kitchen door.

"Joan has agreed to relax for the remainder of the evening and left the kitchen clean-up to us."

Janine faced him. She felt nervous, anxious. She was filled with guilt and excitement all wrapped into one. She wondered how he would react, now that they were alone, to her not telling Joan about the invitation. Her back dug into the hard porcelain of the sink as she watched him.

Alberto reached for the dishtowel she had draped over the back of the chair. He walked past her and picked up one of the dripping plates.

"You handle that dish towel like you really know how to use

it," Janine said, watching him out of the corner of her eye. Her heart hammered in her chest as she slowly returned her hands to the wash water.

"I am a bachelor, do you find it odd that I should do dishes?" he asked, a cutting tone in his voice.

She tried to forget what a disaster the entire night had been. In a very short time he would be boarding a plane for Spain. So far tonight she'd managed to alienate both her mother and Alberto and felt completely awful about it. But her remorse was too little, too late.

"I find it difficult to picture you without plenty of help in the kitchen. Didn't you say you live at home with your family?"

"Yes, but I haven't always lived there. I went away to the university, and after that I traveled with my uncle to learn the family business. Only two years ago did I return home to help my father with the ranch."

"I thought the family business was the ranch and what university?"

"The University of Madrid for awhile and then I studied in Paris, France," his explanation cursory.

"Wow, to study in Madrid and Paris," she murmured, the thought itself inspiring awe.

"Ranching is my father's business, but it isn't the only enterprise the Casilda's are involved in. But you are right. Now that I'm living at home, there are very few times I must fend for myself in the kitchen. My mother closes the kitchen at the same time each evening. If I am detained, then I am expected to care for myself and clean up any mess."

The kitchen clock chimed the hour and Alberto frowned.

"When does your plane leave?" Janine asked, lifting a soapy pan from the steaming water. She envied his ability to handle the preparation for travel with such ease.

"Galeno will be here in about twenty minutes." He shook the damp towel. "We are driving to the Minneapolis Airport to catch a late flight from there."

"That's inconvenient. Why didn't you take a connector flight from Duluth?"

Alberto scowled before answering her. "I wanted to spend as

much time here as I possibly could."

Janine hated herself all over again. Shame washed through her, making her shoulders sag. "Oh, Berto," she whispered. "You must feel like you've completely wasted your time."

"The invitation from my family is a genuine one," he told her, bringing up the subject she had tried to avoid. His voice remained impersonal. He continued working without looking at her. "My parents were delighted when I told them an American family had been so kind to me. They expressed a wish to meet you and return your generosity. My father has known about you since the Mayor's Ball and his desire to meet you is sincere."

Janine sighed, turning to face him. "But Berto, they are too kind. We have done so little when you are the one who has extended so many gifts to my mother and myself that we could never repay you. I just feel this is too much generosity on their part."

Alberto's jaw muscles tensed. "You are basing this assumption on American custom, not mine. Su casa es mi casa. That is the motto of my country, my culture." His steady gaze remained on Janine. "It is something we believe in. It is not such a big deal as you say in America. Our home is somewhat isolated, so when we do have visitors they are expected to stay for a month, many times two. Traveling is not as convenient in Spain as it is here. We move at a slower pace than Americans do."

Janine rubbed her forehead distractedly. Right now she didn't know what to think. It was all too unreal. Her nerves were raw from the turmoil with her mother, and it would be horrible if he left with this anger hanging between them.

"There must be another reason you are unwilling to accept my family's invitation," he said coolly. His dark eyes moved over her with chill in their depth.

Her head jerked at his perception. His gaze held her for a moment, and she stopped breathing, wondering if he could tell what she was thinking. The thought frightened her. It would be so much easier if he knew that whenever he was near he blotted out everything in her life—every fear, every doubt, every other man she'd ever known. He was all she thought about. Saying good-bye to him wrenched her insides into a knot of pain. How could she even contemplate going through this kind of pain again? That is exactly what would happen if she went to Spain.

She could feel his impatience at her continued silence, but she was afraid. Whatever she said right now would come out wrong, but she must say something.

"I will leave you in peace, señorita. I have said enough." He set the towel on the table and turned to give her a short bow. "Adiós," he said with a regal turn and strode swiftly from the room. Janine heard the front door slam and dissolved into a heap on the cold tile floor. Sobs wracked her body as she finally gave in to the anguish she'd kept at bay through the entire night.

Joan heard the car door slam from her open window as she sat on her bed. For all her bravado in front of Janine and Alberto, she was terrified. Not for herself but for her daughter. She shivered and pulled the sweater closer around her body, wrapping her arms tightly around her waist.

For a long time, she had lived with loneliness. It had become a constant companion. When she had first met Hugh Nielsen, she had known the rest of her life would be spent with him. There had never been a doubt in her mind, and once Hugh was convinced, they were married. She traveled with him on the big boats for six months of the year. To have spouses travel with them was one of the perks offered to the officers. The rest of the time was spent in their cozy house in Duluth. But once the baby was on the way, she decided not to travel the lakes any longer and stayed at home. The long days and even longer nights she spent alone crept by until Hugh returned.

Joan never regretted the decision to stay home and raise her child. Her only regret was that Janine was an only child. The little girl with blond pigtails and chubby pink cheeks filled her life with such joy, she found it easier to accept Hugh's long absences. He loved the water, the big boats, and his family—in that order. He was a good husband and father, but the very best sailor. Joan knew Janine couldn't be happy married to a man like Hugh. To live on a ranch with a man like Alberto Casilda and his family was exactly the opposite of what Janine had here. The hustle and bustle of the ranch lifestyle would be so much more compatible to Janine's temperament than living out her days in this house with her mother.

Janine was already on the road to living life alone, and suddenly, she was presented with the opportunity to be with the man she loved. Joan had no doubt in her mind that Janine was in love with Alberto and would remain in love with him for the rest of her life, whether she married him or not. Joan wasn't absolutely certain of how Alberto felt, but he certainly wouldn't be hanging around and offering invitations to Spain if he didn't want to get to know her better. It was obvious that this trip to Spain was important to him. He wanted Janine to know his way of life. The time in Spain would be just what the young couple needed. If only Janine would get the better of her stubborn nature and her fear to take a chance and simply visit the Casilda's.

16

Janine." Her name echoed in her mind and brought her straight up in her seat. The safety belt wrapped securely around her waist cut into her. Dazed, she looked around the airplane to see if someone had actually spoken to her. All she saw was the other passengers putting their magazines away and getting ready for landing. She must have been dreaming.

A voice in Spanish spoke quickly over the intercom and then the message was translated into English. "Once we have stopped at the gate, please remember to check the upper compartment and under your seat for personal belongings," the flight attendant announced.

Janine brushed at the strands of hair that had strayed into her face. She looked out the window as the ground flashed past. The landscape looked brown and flat. She took a deep breath and leaned back against the seat. The first leg of her adventure was almost a thing of the past. The next step would be when the real excitement began. She couldn't believe she was actually there. She leaned forward to look out the window again. Suddenly the jetliner lurched as the wheels touched down.

A warm wind swept briskly across the landing strip easing the midday heat. Patches of wetness steamed under the sun as the clouds scudded over the azure blue of the immense sky. As she stepped out of the exit, she realized the plane wasn't in a terminal. It was stopped on the edge of a runway in the middle of a field. Janine, with dismay in her eyes, looked around. She could see the airport terminal about a block away, across the blacktop.

"This can't possibly be right," she thought.

Her stomach grumbled, and she felt waves of dizziness. The plane's landing had left her feeling shaken. She paused, taking a deep breath to steady herself before she felt able to walk down the steep metal staircase. She was following the other passengers across the tarmac when the brim of her straw hat, bought for the trip to keep the Spanish sun at bay, was caught by the wind. The stiff breeze lifted it off her head and sailed it away. With a desperate lunge, she attempted to grab it.

The hat was the most stylish purchase she made for this trip and had, with its wide brim, constantly gotten in her way. The thought to just let it go and walk away crossed her mind until she remembered the price tag. It cost more than she ever wanted to spend on an accessory again in her lifetime. She began to run after it.

The hat fell to rest very nicely on the blacktop and was probably filthy. She reached down to retrieve it while battling to keep her handbag and the small travel bag she carried from falling off her shoulders. Before her very eyes, a pair of scuffed cowboy boots appeared, and a dark hand swooped down and lifted the straw hat from the blacktop. Pushing her sunglasses straight on her face, she looked up into a tall Spanish man's face. With a wide smile, he handed it to Janine and then bowed.

Flushed and out of breath, she thanked him in Spanish.

"Gracias, señor," she said and replaced the hat, pulling it securely around the crown of her head before tying it at her throat.

"Señorita Nielsen!" the Spaniard exclaimed with obvious delight. His eyes moved slowly over her and with his hand outstretched offered to take her bag.

Astounded the stranger knew her name, Janine held tightly to the straps of her bag, unsure of how to react.

"You know me?" she asked with suspicion, clutching her possessions tightly against her.

His grin widened impossibly. His two front teeth were slightly crossed at the bottom but it detracted very little from his good looks.

"Of course!" he said with an easy laugh. "Berto described you to me, and he was very thorough." An amused frown creased his high brow. "I am surprised at this from him," he told her, removing her bag from her hands with an air of assurance. "He also told me you would now be speaking Spanish like a native so I should not be surprised by it."

Janine felt pleased at the unexpected compliment. "A native?" she questioned. "Hardly."

"No, not exactly as we do," he agreed. "Your accent is off, but it won't take any time for you to pick up the right inflection. You will learn just by listening to all of us."

Gallantly he held out his arm to her, and Janine took it. The feeling she already knew this man became strong as she watched his gestures and the movement of his mouth when he spoke.

"You must be one of Alberto's brothers," she said, proud of herself for making the observation. They strolled out of the heat of the sun into the cool air conditioning of the terminal.

"Si, si," he replied. He paused and turned soulful eyes to her. "I am without manners. Mi mama would be furious for not introducing myself right away. It is like we are…how do you say it…like we are already acquainted with each other. This is possible because I have listened to Berto's stories about America since he returned."

Holding her hand lightly, he bowed over it.

"I am Frederico, the brother in the middle of the boys; Alberto first in line and Juan Carlos third. But then you must already know this. Berto wished with all his heart to be here to meet your plane himself." He grinned at her sudden attentiveness. "Unfortunately a mishap at the ranch did not allow him to leave in time. I am to give my deepest and most sincere of apologies for my brother."

Janine couldn't help smiling at the dramatic words Alberto's brother inserted into his conversation. She couldn't see Alberto actually reacting with the enthusiasm his brother related so eloquently for him.

"I hope it was nothing serious," Janine said.

"No, no, a stubborn calf who did not wish to be born during the regular season and now has become too large for the cow to deliver by herself. Berto is el doctor during these difficult deliveries."

Janine could barely murmur a suitable response. The images such a description brought were vivid.

When the two emerged into the parking lot much later, they had become better acquainted. Frederico chatted endlessly as they went through customs and waited for the luggage. Janine was totally charmed by Frederico's frankness. Where Alberto seemed to be in control of every situation, Frederico was impulsive and tended to be a chatterbox. He took delight in revealing whatever came into his head. Frederico carried her two suitcases while she held the smaller partner to the matching set and had to hurry after his quick stride. An expensive black town car was waiting at the curb.

"We will stop for a meal on the way home," he told her, glancing at his watch. "We should be at the restaurant in about an hour. Will that suit you, señorita?" he asked as he deposited the suitcases in the trunk and then followed her to open the car door. "There you will have an opportunity to freshen up."

"When will we reach the hacienda?" Janine asked, feeling a quiver at the thought of seeing Alberto again.

"After supper, but before nightfall. It is not too far," he said, unconcerned. He tucked the fold of her dress inside the car before he slammed the door shut and hurried around to the driver's side.

The traffic in front of them looked like a snarl of cars when they merged with a squeal of the tires into the fast moving flow. She quickly fastened her seatbelt and sat back, clinging to the armrest.

"We will make excellent time," Frederico told her as they sped along. "For Barcelona, there is hardly any traffic today."

Janine glanced around at the mass of cars surrounding them. Car horns blasted at each other nonstop, and she slid lower in her seat wondering briefly what he would consider a traffic jam.

Once they were out of the city, traffic did lighten, and Frederico's high speed didn't seem so reckless. Without warning, Frederico veered off the road into the parking lot of a charming inn on the side of the road.

"Come, I will secure a room for you where you will be able to freshen up. We will meet in the restaurant in half an hour. Will that be sufficient time?" he asked before jumping from the driver's seat.

Janine nodded, lost in the rush of being bustled into the lobby of the inn. A maid led her up the stairs, and she was alone. The peaceful atmosphere of the small quaint bedroom was a great relief after the jet engine noise, the traffic, and Frederico's reckless driving. Janine dumped her bag on the chair and crossed the room to where a porcelain basin and a pitcher were set up. Splashing water into the basin, she soaped the washcloth with lavender scented soap and wiped her face. She wiped off the grime of thousands of miles. Her head ached, but if she could lay down for a few minutes in the stillness of the room, it might go away.

A knock on the door brought her awake. Slowly, she looked around, not recognizing where she was until a soft voice called from the other side of the door.

"Señorita, please, your dinner is waiting downstairs."

Janine flew from the bed and opened the door to find the little maid waiting outside with a flustered expression on her face.

"I am so sorry," Janine exclaimed. "Tell Señor Casilda I'll be right down." The girl nodded and left.

Janine looked at her watch. "Good heavens, I fell asleep for an hour." She smoothed her hair back into place and then grabbed her bag, hurrying out the door.

Alberto's brother sat at a table chatting with a man who was at the table next to him. When he saw Janine in the doorway, he jumped to his feet and hurried over to her.

"You had a pleasant rest?" he asked cheerfully.

Janine's apology almost died on her lips she was so surprised at his greeting.

"I didn't mean to be so long," she said quickly.

He shrugged. "You look rested, that is good. Come, I've ordered a light meal because we will be traveling for some time yet." He held her arm and led her to the table.

The food was delivered as soon as they were seated, and Janine was hungry. She hadn't eaten much on the plane, and the pastries and cheese were warm and smelled delicious.

They didn't speak while eating, but once in the car and on the road again, Frederico told her about his family and the ranch. For Janine, to carry on a conversation with him took little effort. She was able to look out the window while he prattled on.

The countryside turned out to be nothing like she had imagined. It was beautiful. Fields filled with golden crops and a ridge in the distance of blue and purple that must be the mountains Alberto had spoken about. They were driving toward the purple ridge yet never seemed to get any closer to it.

Dusk began to settle like a dark blue blanket of velvet. Well away from the remaining light on the horizon, stars appeared bright white in the sky. Janine could see them as clearly as when they were across the dark water of Lake Superior.

Silence had fallen for several miles when suddenly, Frederico's voice cut through it.

"We have arrived on the boundary of the hacienda," he told her. There were no lights, no signs of civilization.

"Where?" she asked, squinting as she stared out the windshield.

"This is the front pasture. There are not any buildings here. It will be awhile before we reach the house."

"It's quite a distance from the city," Janine said, her voice hushed. "You have driven most of the day because of me."

Frederico laughed. The sound, loud and boisterous in the enclosed area, was incredibly infectious. She couldn't help joining in, though she hadn't a clue what was so funny.

"No, no, señorita," he said sincerely, "this has been a vacation for me. If I had had to stay for the day of work Berto planned for me, I would only now be returning to the casa for a bit of rest."

Janine smiled in the darkness. "Surely, it's your father who is in charge as the true head of the ranch."

Frederico shook his head.

"Oh no, Berto has taken over for a couple of years now. He is the boss of the ranch hands, of which I am one. You see, señorita, I am but a poor lowly vaquero. Berto is in command of all we do. Of course Papa advises him. Berto asks his advice on most decisions, except the last purchase he made. That was a decision Alberto made all on his own." Frederico's tone held a strong note of humor in it, but he didn't explain any further.

Janine's cheeks heated under the glance Frederico gave her, realizing that she might have had something to do with his decision to buy that darn bull.

"What happens when Alberto travels like he did to America?" she asked in order to change the subject.

He shrugged indifferently. "Berto is the head of the ranch now, but we all know what makes it tick from the inside to the outside. It has always been our life, the heart of our family. Of course, only after the church," he added quickly.

The prideful tone in Frederico's voice reminded her of his older brother, and Janine suddenly felt a chill raise bumps on her flesh. This land was a part of him, and he was a part of this land. There wasn't room for any outsiders.

As he drove the final distance to the ranch house, Janine lapsed into her thoughts. There had been letters from her mother after her departure for the Hacienda Casilda. She relayed so thoroughly her activities and plans from the distant land that Janine felt she already knew the place and some of the people who lived there.

Once she had written and agreed to join her mother in Spain, Alberto had written to her at once. A very unsatisfactory letter of a single page, it was written in his bold hand with sweeping strokes. She studied each line, looking for any innuendo that set her apart as more than a mere acquaintance. But there was nothing. She stared unseeing out the blackened window wondering what her welcome in person would be like.

Frederico slowed the car as a metal gate loomed into view. The strong beam of the headlights made it impossible for Janine to see beyond.

"The animals are not free in this pasture," Frederico explained to her. "Berto saw this in your country and thought it a smart precaution in case the animals did break free. He had them installed when he returned from your country."

Frederico put the car in park, jumped out, opened the gate, and returned to drive the car through. He then stopped again to shut and lock the gate. When they encountered a second gate, Janine protested.

"This is hard work for one person. I'm perfectly capable of helping you," she told him.

Frederico shot her a look of shock and shook his head. "I could never allow you to do that," he said. "The gates are heavy and dirty. It is better if I take care of it." He didn't need to add the words "This is man's work," but the condescension in his tone said it quite clearly.

Janine nodded, wondering if she had insulted the young man. It didn't seem to offset his good humor when he returned to the car.

"That is the last one so we can relax."

Janine leaned forward and searched for some sign of civilization in the vastness.

"There… there!" Frederico cried in the silence.

Janine looked in the direction he pointed and saw something shimmer in the darkness. It looked like a firefly, only she knew it wasn't. It must be a light, which meant a building.

Janine felt her pulse quicken as the hacienda appeared ahead of them. The darkness no longer surrounded them. Along both sides of the driveway torches with open flames licked toward the sky with hungry movements. Alberto was in there. She was in his homeland now. She felt a rush of apprehension when she remembered how she had behaved during his last visit to her home. On the plane, she'd vowed to herself no matter what happened here, she was going to enjoy every moment of this vacation even if it killed her.

17

Frederico pulled in front of the house and hit the brakes, bringing the car to a skidding stop on the gravel. He threw the gearshift into park and announced, "This is Hacienda Casilda." He leaned closer to look at the house as did Janine.

Slowly, Janine's gaze swept over the front of the ranch house. She didn't know what expectations she had of the ancestral home of the Casilda's, but the lit torches that led the way were pretty spectacular. It didn't look like an exceptionally large home considering how many people lived here. Set amongst mammoth bushes was a wide arch that gracefully encircled the doorway. The porch glowed yellow from an ornate iron light fixture hanging in front of a dark wooden door. She could feel Frederico's breath on her neck.

"Well, what do you think, señorita? Is it how Berto described it to you?"

Flustered by his closeness, she leaned even closer to the side window.

"I'm at a loss for words. It's magnificent."

Frederico laughed. "I do not see this because I am here everyday, but I do enjoy listening to other people when they first arrive. Your mother was very excited, but she saw the house for the first time in the daylight. The front is especially lovely when the jacaranda trees are in bloom, but now the blossoms have withered and died so they are not beautiful anymore."

In the next moment, he was gone. He exited the vehicle then slammed the door. Janine slumped back in her seat. Thank goodness he hadn't questioned her further on what Alberto had told her about the house and his family. How could she explain that she'd never allowed his older brother to tell her a thing about any of this? He'd described it in detail to her mother, but, at the time, Janine had been too filled with anxiety to pay attention. Until this very moment, when it was actually happening to her, she had never thought to find herself about to enter the actual Hacienda Casilda.

Frederico opened the passenger door and said, "Welcome to my home."

Janine stepped out of the car and, there, stretching away beyond the jacaranda, was a verandah unlike any she had ever seen before. Supporting the white arches that lined the porch were large round pillars, also white, draped with hanging baskets of flowers whose dewdrop shaped leaves hung in long tendrils all the way to the ground. Patio chairs of different shapes and sizes lined the stone wall and disappeared into the gloom beyond. Along the wall were small windows that shed scant light into the darkness, doing little to illuminate the porch.

"Come, Señorita Janine," Frederico said, "I am certain everyone will be waiting to see how you fared the long journey. I will return later for your baggage."

Janine's stomach jumped worse than when the plane landed hours before. To meet Alberto's family after a long car drive and the exhausting day she had just experienced, how could she possibly get through it without collapsing?

"Perhaps I could…may I see my mother first?" she pleaded.

He paused and frowned. Then a smile brightened his face. "Si," Frederico agreed with excitement. "She will already be here in the main house with the family waiting for supper. Let us hurry."

Janine draped her handbags over her shoulders and attempted to brush some of the wrinkles from her skirt, but it was hopeless. There was nothing else to do but follow his quick step across the flagstone entryway through the front door. She didn't even want to think of what she must look like and, anticipating the worst, she took a deep breath and stepped through the door. But the hallway was empty. "Oh, thank goodness," she murmured out loud. The smile she'd plastered on her face faded.

Frederico looked around before he led her through the hall into another room where a wide staircase curved around one wall and led upstairs. Thick jungle-like ferns fanned out along the pale cream stucco walls. The ceramic tile on the floor was a bright coral color that was just becoming popular back home. It swirled into a beautiful array of colors—teal, purple, and orange—that looked like a southwestern sunset. Janine hated to walk across it. Other than the plants, there was little decoration in the high-ceilinged room, but it didn't need decoration. Light and color filled the space.

The sound of heels clicking against the ceramic tile announced the arrival of someone long before they came into sight.

"Ah, Señor Frederico," a small Spanish woman in a white apron said with approval. "You have arrived just at the right moment."

"Why is that, Marisol?" Frederico asked. "Is supper served already?"

Marisol shook her head and looked pointedly at Janine.

Frederico gestured with a flourish of his hand. "This is Señorita Nielsen. But, señorita, perhaps you would prefer to converse in Spanish with Marisol?"

Janine gulped. She hadn't taken the time to explain to Frederico that her Spanish was not the same as what she'd heard being spoken.

"No, please, I tried to follow the Spanish conversations spoken by the people on the airplane, and I couldn't do it. They spoke so quickly. I found I lost track of the words right after the first greeting."

Frederico smiled. "Like I told you before, once you are listening to it spoken, the words will fall into place, and it will become easier for you. You'll be surprised how little time it will take for this to happen."

Marisol nodded and, with a slight smile, said, "Bienvenida, señorita. Por favor, er… please follow me. Since Frederico has made such a speedy return from the city, the señorita will have time to see the guest house and become settled before supper."

Frederico grinned at the older, authoritative woman. "Of course, Marisol, surely you of all people would know that this is how I planned it." He turned to go back outside.

"Señorita, I will send your luggage to the cottage," he called after the two women who had already almost disappeared down the narrow hallway.

Janine followed the quick-footed little woman, barely able to glance at the different rooms hidden in shadows. Suddenly, they exited the house. Back outside, they were on a terrace that was surrounded by six-foot flowering bushes sculpted into walls. They hurried along a path that widened into a garden walkway. The night air felt warm after the coolness in the house and the car. The flowers on both sides exuded an overpowering scent, a mixture of sweetness and citrus. This place looked like the Garden of Eden to Janine.

She smiled when she remembered how, back in Duluth, Alberto had admired the small beds of flowers she and Joan cared for so diligently.

After a long walk, there appeared, nestled among shrubs and shade trees, a house that looked like a miniature of the main house. A terraced area led to French doors, which Marisol opened. They stepped into the kitchen. A light was on over the stove. Janine paused to catch her breath and wipe her brow. She wasn't used to the humidity or altitude. Janine looked at Marisol who hadn't broken a sweat and didn't look winded from the half-mile trek they had just taken.

"You'll find the elevation takes awhile to adjust to," Marisol explained. "This is the kitchen, your mother has eaten most of her suppers at the main house, but if you prefer to eat here, it is fully equipped."

Janine glanced around and found it neat and tidy. Nothing out of place except sitting on the white countertop was her mother's handbag. The small part of her mother's presence gave her a sense of welcome. She missed her mother and hoped she might be here waiting for her even though Frederico said she would be at the main house.

"The Señora Nielsen is having cocktails in the lounge with the family," Marisol explained and began moving again. "The bathroom and the bedrooms are upstairs," she said, waiting at the door to lead Janine in that direction.

Janine set her bags on the counter. "Gracias, Marisol," she said, not quite certain what Marisol wanted of her.

"I will show you the rooms," Marisol patiently explained.

Janine laughed and shook her head no. Now she understood. "Oh no, please. I'm sure I can find my own way. Thank you so much for your help."

Marisol hesitated, giving her an odd look. "If that is what you want, señorita," Marisol said with a glance around the immaculate room. "Señor Alberto wished me to explain supper is not served on the hacienda until nine-thirty. There is plenty of time for you to freshen up from your journey. An escort will be sent from the main house ten minutes before supper."

Janine felt a thrill race through when she heard Alberto had specifically mentioned her. Marisol still waited, an expectant look on her face.

Janine suspected Marisol doubted she could find the upstairs by herself. "Thank you again, Marisol," Janine said.

Marisol nodded and finally left the house, closing the door behind her.

"People here move so fast, not the slow, easy pace I expected at all," Janine thought. She was ready to drop. Her journey had been long enough that day. The hike to the guest house was almost too much. She lifted her hair off the stickiness on the back of her neck and stretched. She hoped she adjusted to the altitude quickly, otherwise she would not be able to keep up this hectic pace for the next two weeks.

18

The deep silence that settled over the empty, unfamiliar house began to unnerve Janine. She stood listening where Marisol left her. She heard nothing but the electrical whir of the appliances. With a sigh at her foolish apprehension, she pulled her bags from the counter, ready to venture further into the house when the delicate chiming of a clock stopped her. She waited until the last note of the musical sound faded before she remembered time was wasting. She left the kitchen with no idea of which direction she should take.

"Why didn't I let Marisol show me?" she moaned out loud. It was obvious Marisol had expected to show her the rest of the house, but the whole idea of servants made Janine uncomfortable.

When she walked into the hallway she recognized that it was a replica of the hacienda. The polished wood stairs were smaller but matched what she'd seen and were in the same position, so she walked up to the second floor. She paused at the narrow landing to admire a smaller version of the tiled sunset on the gleaming floor below her.

"How absolutely gorgeous," she exclaimed. "The original must be magnificent from this vantage point." Janine continued upward and thought with pleasure that she would, for the next two weeks, be able to enjoy this one.

At the top of the stairs she found the second story laid out in a simple floor plan. It included a small foyer in the middle with doors branching off in four directions. Janine opened the nearest door and found a bedroom that obviously was vacant. Inside the room was a bed and a dresser with a small ornate secretary tucked cozily under the windows in the corner. Two doors led to a closet and an attached bathroom. The closed door on the other side of the bathroom led into the next bedroom. She peeked inside the other bedroom and found it was identical to the one she had chosen. This one too was unoccupied. Janine walked back through the small but quite modern bathroom and into her bedroom.

A mirror above the dresser allowed her, for the first time in hours, to see her reflection. "I'm not too frightening," she thought, "but a shower would do wonders to help me cope with the night ahead." It was rather daunting to face the prospect of meeting Alberto again while in the midst of his entire family.

The clothes she wore looked travel-worn, but they would have to do. Without her luggage, she had nothing to change into. At least in her carry-on she packed the basic toiletries.

Fifteen minutes later, when she pulled back the shower curtain, she reached for the fluffy towels conveniently hanging on the wall. Janine wrapped one of the yellow bath towels around her body and wiped the steam from the mirror so she could brush out her hair. She twisted the thick strands together and secured it in her usual French braid at the base of her neck.

She dreaded the thought of putting her dirty clothes back on now that she felt clean. When she walked back into the bedroom, she saw her luggage placed neatly next to the bed. "I don't believe it," she cried. Eagerly she reached for the largest case.

Several weeks ago, when she had made the final decision to take this trip, she was determined to have a new wardrobe. It took many visits to the shops at the mall before this was accomplished. Janine was hopeless at judging what she liked and disliked when it came to new clothes, especially the type needed for an airplane trip and a visit to a Spanish ranch. The store clerks had been helpful, giving their advice on what looked good on her. But now that she was actually in Spain, how they would look remained to be seen. After she finished dressing in the outfit she had bought to wear for this night in particular, without realizing she was doing it, Janine held her breath. She closed her eyes and faced the mirror, then opened them. The woman looking back at her, unfortunately, was exactly the same, but the outfit did add a new dimension. The material clung to her curves accentuating them far more than she had realized. She didn't remember the outfit fitting this tight in the dressing room.

"Too late for me to return the darn thing now," she thought, twirling around as she watched herself in the mirror. The silky skirt swayed with the movement of her hips. Quickly, before she allowed the coward in her to change her outfit, she put on her lipstick and switched off the light as she left the room.

Instead of exploring, she decided to wait downstairs for her escort as she had been instructed. The smell of wet ground and leaves became strong as she walked down the stairs. The front door stood open. It hadn't been open earlier. Hesitating on the last step, she looked suspiciously around the hallway. Whoever had delivered the baggage must have forgotten to pull it shut. With a nervous glance at the floor, she briefly wondered if there were any creepy crawly things hiding in the shadows around the furniture. She shuddered before hurrying out the door onto the porch. It was identical to the front verandah of the main house. The heat and humidity, after the coolness of the guest house, struck her.

The heavy scent of gardenias met her as she walked to the railing and leaned against it. Through the foliage she could see the shadows of the flickering torches along the drive in front of the main hacienda. There was an immense stretch of lawn between the guest house and the driveway. She was shocked at the distance. Suddenly, the perfume of the flowers became mixed with the familiar scent of cigar smoke.

"Señorita," a deep voice spoke to her from the shadows.

Janine spun around. "Señor," she replied just as formally.

It was dark on the verandah. Alberto's form was a denser shadow of gray in the gloom. He stepped toward her in an unhurried movement. Could he be feeling the same hot and cold flashes that raced through her? When he reached her, he flicked his cigar into the bushes and slowly exhaled the fragrant smoke. The two faced each other silently. Janine anxiously waited for some indication of what his greeting would be. Every nerve in her body waited for the next impulse that could lead to either ecstatic joy or dismal depression.

Janine realized that, even after their month-long separation, she didn't need her eyes to remember each detail of the man. The warmth of his skin, the smell of his shirt, the thick silky hair that fell over his strong brow with a definite curl in its depths, all of this she could picture in the light or the darkness. With her eyes closed or open, he was burned into her memory. She took several deep breaths to slow her racing pulse. The need to feel his touch, to have some reassurance from him that his feelings for her hadn't changed, almost brought tears to her eyes.

"Your journey has fatigued you," he observed, his voice remaining cool.

"No," she denied quickly. "Well, a little, but I'm feeling much better now. I took a shower. It felt wonderful, and now I'm fully refreshed."

"A shower and a change of clothes does wonders to revive your spirits when traveling. I, too, appreciate it."

Janine's cheeks heated. "You are the one who brought my luggage…thank you." She trembled at the thought of him in her bedroom while she was in the shower. A shiver ran through her.

"You are cold? In this heat?" he questioned.

A giggle escaped her. "No, how could I be?"

"You trembled. Perhaps from the dampness," Alberto said. "Sometimes it chills. We live so close to the mountains it rains most nights and can remain quite humid." He wasted no time in changing the topic of the conversation to something much more heavy on his mind. "Do you find my home acceptable?"

She heard the change in his tone and realized her response must be important to him.

"Señor, you put me in a difficult position. How, after such a brief time, can I give credit to the beauty I've seen without sounding overwhelmed or insincere?" she murmured as she searched for the right words. "I'm afraid to admit it, but I believe I'm in danger of falling captive to all I see." She wished her words were not so utterly true. She wished desperately that she would not lose her heart to this place. "What I've seen is more magnificent than I could ever have imagined. Now I understand where the pride and love when you speak of the hacienda comes from. It's your soul." She sensed he was pleased with her reply.

Alberto's smile flashed pale in the night. He moved closer to her and placed warm hands on her arms to run his palms gently on the soft exposed flesh to the slender curve of her shoulders.

"It is the soul of not just me, but my family," he spoke softly as he corrected her. "But it is I who would like to welcome you to Spain and the hacienda." He leaned down. His lips hovered near her mouth.

The roughness of his palms against her skin and the strength in his touch made her knees weak. The warmth of the night, the seclusion of the porch, and the rhythmic hum of insects in the leaves all combined to shatter Janine's determination to remain uninvolved. She did not want to fall in love with this man and then have to leave. Her body melted into him. Her arms slid across the cotton of his shirt and moved up the muscles of his back to cling to him. She tilted her head to look at his face.

The little encouragement was all it took. Alberto's lips touched hers. His arms tightened around her shoulders cradling her into his chest.

Janine wasn't afraid. She remembered his mouth, remembered how he tasted. A sigh rose in her throat. She had been so lonely without him. He made her body burn with his touch. Her first taste of desire had sharpened over the long separation and with each kiss it surged to the surface becoming more powerful until it swept her away.

Alberto lifted his head. He rested his forehead against her hair. "A month," he said, his voice ragged, his strong arms around her shoulders holding her close, "is a long time."

Sense returned to Janine in an alarming rush. Her arms dropped to her sides. She could barely breathe in his embrace. "A month without you," she thought, shifting her body to move away, "is a lifetime." But she couldn't say it out loud.

Alberto took her hand and pressed it hard to his lips. "You will not admit it, but I believe you feel the same way."

Janine looked at the ground, shy now because of her impulsive actions. Her self control disappeared whenever he touched her.

At her continued silence Alberto said softly, "I am afraid the others will be waiting for us."

Janine could only nod and compress her trembling lips together. "Then we must go," she managed to say. "I would hate to begin causing problems the very first night I'm in your home."

Alberto chuckled. "We will take the path. It is lighted, but right here the ground is a little tricky. I will lead the way." He continued to hold her hand close to his chest as they began to walk across the porch.

Janine's heart sang, filled with joy as they walked down the path hand in hand.

19

Janine was surprised she felt giddy and light-headed instead of exhausted. She couldn't believe she was standing on the balcony of the hacienda sipping a cup of Spanish coffee, let alone sipping from a cup over one hundred years old, a treasured family heirloom. She listened to the voices inside the house on the enclosed porch. They were fewer now. Right after the late supper, Alberto's darling three-year-old sister and younger brother had gone to bed with the parents leading the way. That left the two brothers, Frederico and Alberto, with Joan and Janine to visit over coffee and drinks.

Janine cradled the delicate china cup in her palm. She stared at the garden that spread out beneath the balcony. The glowing moonlight of the pale half-moon illuminated the bushes. The shadows of different flowers formed lacy images on the ground. The effect was beautiful. It was especially lovely from where she stood. A slight shift of movement in the night told her she was no longer alone.

"Your mother is ready to go home," Alberto said. His voice blended perfectly with the exotic feeling of the night.

To her, home meant Duluth. She turned to him in confusion. "What?" She didn't want to leave Alberto so soon after being away from him for so long.

"She does not wish to walk to the guest house alone," he explained, "and you, too, must be tired after your busy day."

Janine smiled. "It has been quite a day," she agreed shyly. "A day full of surprises, and it was rather wonderful."

"In what way wonderful?"

Janine shook her head, becoming tongue-tied at his directness. "I'm not exactly sure what made it wonderful, just everything. I made it here to Spain, by myself, all in one piece and you…you're family is so wonderful,"

"Hmm, wonderful again," he teased her gently. "I guess I must believe you."

Janine gave a soft laugh, "I'm not very articulate when I try to describe my feelings. But it's true. *Everything* is wonderful."

Alberto leaned against the wrought iron railing next to her. "I should have apologized before now. I was so sorry to miss the opportunity of meeting your plane this afternoon, but, calves come into this world on their schedule, not the airline's."

The moon touched his striking features making him look like a stranger, but she was now well aware of the comfort she found in his presence. "Please, Berto, there is no need to apologize. Frederico was an excellent substitute guide," she grinned. "He was actually quite entertaining."

Alberto glanced at her. "Frederico can be very entertaining especially where beautiful women are concerned. They seem to bring out his dramatic instincts as well as his charm."

Janine laughed. "You can't be seriously implying me?" She held tight to the coffee cup. "I'm so much older than he is."

Alberto turned to her. He crossed his arms, and the muscle in his jaw was flexed tight. "Really, señorita, and this great age that you boast of. How do you know Rico is the younger one? Did he confide this to you on the journey to the hacienda this afternoon?"

Janine realized that he had become irritated.

"Your age has nothing to do with it. You are innocent to many aspects of life...deny it?" he taunted her.

Janine stared up at him, her breath caught in her throat at the glitter of his dark eyes.

He moved his hand toward her face, and his finger lightly caressed the curve of her cheek. He moved it down her jaw to tap her bottom lip with his fingertip. "Age is irrelevant, but, Frederico turned twenty-seven this year. Anyway, he is a decade older than you in experience."

Janine was relieved when he removed his hand. She shook her head and frowned. "I don't believe it. He acts like a college kid."

Alberto turned to face the garden. "Yes, he does that well," Alberto said brusquely. "He becomes carried away by his audience. Like I said, especially when a lovely woman is involved."

Janine turned away in confusion. For a moment she thought he sounded jealous, but that was ridiculous. Frederico was his brother. Nervously, she took a sip from the cup and grimaced. The coffee had gone cold. Only moments before they had been getting along so well. She didn't know what had gone wrong.

"How are the patients in the barn doing?" She paused, waiting for an answer, when a sudden wave of exhaustion swept over her. The heavy scent of flowers overpowered her and blackness moved in front of her eyes.

"Patients?" Alberto asked. His voice sounded hollow and distant as Janine reached out to grab the railing.

"Oh, the calf!" he realized. "When I left the barn he was already giving his mother trouble, acting his age, unlike Rico."

Her knees seemed weak, so weak. "Berto," Janine whispered, she held the cup toward him. "Please take this, I think I might…."

Without a word, Alberto slipped his arm around her waist and pulled her against his body. Swiftly, he removed the cup from her fingers.

"Do be careful of that," she exclaimed in a shaky voice, worried about the precious heirloom.

"Who cares about that?" Alberto's voice was fierce. "Are you alright? What happened?"

"Janine?" Joan called from inside the house.

"My mother," Janine whispered, and tried to move away, hating that she felt so weak. "I think I'll be all right now."

"Poor thing, you are completely worn out," he murmured.

"Ah, here they are, Mother Joan," said Frederico, who appeared in the doorway. Joan was right behind him. He held a tumbler of ice with a half-finished drink. He watched them with a wide smile on his generous mouth. "They are just out here in the beautiful night together."

Janine slowly moved away from Alberto's side with a quiet, "Goodnight."

Frederico turned and snapped a short bow to Joan. "Buenas noches, señora," he said and then turned to Janine. "Buenas noches, señorita." His words were spoken slowly as his eyes lingered.

Janine kept her eyes lowered, unable to look at anyone. Her lashes looked very dark against her pale cheeks. Her lower lip trembled slightly as she felt the two men watching her. Her nerves were strung so taut she felt sure they were going to snap right this minute. She needed to leave, but she couldn't move.

"Janine is falling asleep on her feet," Joan declared. She took her daughter's arm. "I'd better hurry and get her moving before she faints at our feet."

Janine glanced through her lashes at Alberto. He stood watching her. Concern was etched on his striking features. She wanted to tell him she was all right but couldn't speak. At her mother's tugging, she turned away and they walked out.

With an impatient look at his brother, Frederico called after them. "Señora, if you or Janine find you need anything during the night, please call the main house."

"I already know that, Rico," Joan returned with a laugh as they continued down the hallway.

20

When silence fell over the room, Frederico turned to Alberto with exasperation. "Do you see what is happening? You are always the one who remembers to be the perfect host. Now you are leaving the task to me and I am bound to fail. I haven't the manners that you have. Or so Mama tells me often enough."

Alberto didn't answer. He stood, as if made from stone, his face an unreadable mask as he stared at the doorway.

Frederico drained his drink in one swallow. "She is very like a Spanish girl, Berto," he said with a twist to his mouth. "I am surprised you are attracted to her. Perhaps it is her fairness of skin. Fresh peaches from the north must be the perfect ripeness for the sweetest taste," he said slyly. When Alberto didn't react, Frederico gave an exaggerated sigh. "Maybe it is those lips of hers. I must admit they do beckon to be kissed. I noticed when you two arrived for supper, there was something different about her. Perhaps it was, I don't know. She looked, I don't know, different."

Alberto interrupted him coldly. "Don't, Rico."

Frederico chuckled. "I do admire you, brother. How do you control yourself so well?"

Alberto said, "It is most fortunate that you are not in a position of responsibility. Control over emotions is an important part of business," he paused, "and pleasure."

"When I am as old as you I will call upon this control as you have, until then I have no reason not to be impulsive."

"I suggest you do not give in to impulsive actions where the American señorita is concerned. She frightens more easily than most."

Frederico chuckled. "I don't recall you ever before seeking the attention of a woman such as this. You've always avoided the debutante innocents that Mama tried to introduce. What makes her, how should I say it, more appealing than these women and all the women you have known before?"

"I'm not sure," Alberto admitted. "She has something the others didn't." He fell silent in his thought. "I may never know."

Frederico shrugged his shoulders and left.

Alberto stared at a cleared area of the garden where he could see the path to the guest cottage. Several minutes passed and he wondered if he had missed seeing Janine and Joan, when a movement in the bushes caught his attention. Soon, two figures came into view. Between the branches of the trees he could see the women walking leisurely arm in arm. He could see by the movement of her head that Joan was talking, but it was Janine he was worried about. As he watched them move down the path she seemed steady enough. He pictured her features in his mind. She acted so cool at times. Until he kissed her, he began to doubt she felt any softening in her heart for him. A smile softened his stern features as his thoughts drifted back to the kiss. He hadn't imagined those petal-soft lips had clung to his. She was physically attracted to him, but for the first time in his adult life, he was worried about a woman loving him. Loving him enough to spend the rest of her life with him in a strange country.

"Then there's mama," he thought. "If she has the same opinions as Frederico, I will be having a confrontation with mama in the very near future."

Behind him, Alberto heard, "I was hoping to gain some insight into this change in you and what Janine Nielsen has to do with it. And you have nothing to say?"

Alberto groaned out loud. "Save your words, Rico. I will tell you nothing more about Janine. By now you must know this."

Frederico moved to the railing and stood next to Alberto. "If that is the way you want it. I am simply trying to be sympathetic."

Alberto turned and snorted his skepticism. "Sympathetic? I've been a victim of your sympathy before. I remember several occasions, my dear brother, when you sabotaged me with a woman because of something I had confided to your sympathetic ear."

"All for my own benefit," Frederico said smugly. "I don't always like to be treated as the second son in the Casilda lineage. If I find an opportunity to be one step ahead of you, then I feel I must take it."

Alberto tensed. "It would be best for you to choose not to act that way with this señorita, Rico," he warned softly.

Frederico laughed and held up his hands as if in surrender. "I always at least make the attempt to act the gentleman, Berto, and you are usually close by to make certain I do." He paused to look intently at his brother. "Just remember, brother, when something becomes precious to us, it is easy to miss the opportunity to claim it," Frederico snapped his fingers in the air, "and then the chance is lost."

Alberto frowned. "Since when have you become a philosopher, Rico?"

"Just say my limited experience and impulsive ways have taught me that lesson," Frederico said indifferently. "That, and mama has embroidered a pillow with much the same words. I merely rearranged a few of them. When I fell in love for the first time, the pillow reminded me heartbreak awaits he who does not act." Frederico moved closer to Alberto and patted his shoulder before he bid him goodnight. He chuckled and, whistling a familiar Spanish love song under his breath, he left.

Alberto remained in the moonlight silently reflecting on what his brother had said. "It isn't often Rico plays any kind of prophet, but this time many of his words ring with honesty." Alberto turned his mother's saying over in his mind. *Two with the same love must overcome to become two hearts that beat as one.* He knew exactly what it was Rico had described. The small rectangular pillow had sat on his mother's rocking chair ever since he could remember. He, too, had mulled over the cryptic words when he first learned to read, but he'd never put any meaning to them, especially not the idealistic one about first love that his brother chose.

A silent hulking figure emerged from the hacienda to join Alberto at the railing. "Rico is right about one thing," he said to Galeno, "Janine has somehow remained protected from the world just as we protect ours. The quality in a woman I have never in my life found to be attractive has caught me to her." He sighed and raked his fingers through his hair. "Why?"

"Maybe it is you who has changed?"

Alberto chuckled. "That makes sense, but it's not something I care to admit." The two men stared into the darkness. "So old friend, what are your thoughts of my fool-hearted actions in bringing the Americans into the center of my family? Do you have any insights to help me through this dilemma I've brought upon myself?"

Galeno's big chest moved with his laughter. "It can't be that bad. And since when do you care what Rico says."

"You heard all of it?"

"No, just his words of wisdom to you about love," Galeno laughed low.

"I might listen to him this time," Alberto declared. "Nothing I do seems to have any influence on her. The short time he spent with her driving and she already speaks of him with more feeling than she does of me."

"Has she kissed you?" Galeno asked bluntly.

Alberto shot him a sharp look then nodded his head. "Yes."

"Since she has been here?" he clarified.

"Yes," Alberto said again.

Galeno shrugged. "She has been here less than a day and she kissed you, not Rico. That answers your question."

Alberto laughed. "You make it sound so simple." He looked at Galeno with a grin. "You cannot hide the smugness you feel at my uncertainty with this woman. You're enjoying the whole thing. Could it be you are remembering our visit to Madrid last month? I'm sure you think my anxiety is just a payback after the abuse you were subjected to then."

"You must be talking about the time you kept a certain señorita waiting for more than an hour while you were bargaining for a bull? I admit it does sound familiar," Galeno said. "I do remember that it was I who took the whipping from her tongue because you weren't available."

Alberto laughed. "What the tempestuous señorita didn't bother to share with you is that she arrived at the townhouse uninvited and unannounced. I had no idea she was coming and didn't want her there at all."

Galeno grimaced. "Knowing this now did little to help when she was screeching at me."

Alberto lit a cigar. "Even then, as that pest was buzzing about, I couldn't get Janine out of my mind. Janine is an angel," he said softly.

Galeno smiled. "What did the family say when they met her?"

"They think, or at least I hope they think, she is an acquaintance who was kind to us when we were in Duluth. At least that's how they treated her tonight."

"All except Rico," Galeno shook his head. "I've never known him to be overly observant before this."

Alberto frowned. "Neither have I."

"His wit is more like yours than you suspected?"

Alberto remained silent a moment. "Yes, it is, and I will keep that in mind. He has been playing games with me by not taking his share of the responsibilities and duties where the ranch is concerned. I believe the time has come for change, and the first change will be for Frederico to manage the round-up next month without any help from me."

"That will make it easier for you to be away from the hacienda," Galeno's voice held a note of shrewdness. "If the need should arise."

Alberto laughed out loud. "I think you are much more clever than even Rico. I had better start guarding my thoughts more closely when you're around or is this just a lucky guess on your part?"

"I believe your thoughts are well occupied, thinking and planning about your future," Galeno said carefully. "Every unmarried man with responsibilities to consider should have many decisions to occupy his thoughts. Thus he will make fewer mistakes."

"Yes, the continuation of the family line. I suppose this is your sneaky way of taking me to task," Alberto broke in. "Well, Galeno, you can save whatever it is you want to say. I've heard enough of it from my mother," he said impatiently. "I suppose you have come to plead my father's case for settling down?"

Galeno shook his head. "I wouldn't think of it. If your father has something to say to you he will say it himself," he said indignantly. "I think enough time has been spent brooding over things we have little or no control over. Let's go inside and have a drink to end the night."

Alberto shot him a quizzical look. "You know better than to try and get me drunk." He walked inside with Galeno but wondered why Galeno dropped the subject. "Father has to be looking for answers now that he has seen Janine. He usually sends Galeno to ask questions first. Galeno had worked with his father since the two men had gotten out of the army.

Galeno asked, "Was I ever with you when you were drunk?"

Alberto laughed, "It's been many years since I've been drunk. I won't be unwittingly ensnared into explaining my future plans…by you or anyone else."

Galeno gave a heavy sigh. "I believe your father said the same thing to me when he was your age and he had recently met your mother."

Alberto stopped him. "I have heard the story from you and my mother. I'm still not quite sure which one of you is telling the entire truth. If this is your sneaky way of warning me about marriage, then forget it."

"If you don't want to talk then we will have our drinks in silence," Galeno said agreeably. He reached for the glasses and Alberto poured the rich amber liquid from the crystal decanter.

21

"I spoke to Berto earlier about what plans we should make for after your arrival," Joan told Janine. They were sitting at the breakfast counter over their first breakfast in Spain together. "He suggested that we remain on the hacienda for a few days, so you can get over your jet lag. It's so relaxing here, Jani. I've had plenty of time to wander around the grounds by myself. The family village is only about a mile from here if you walk through the gardens, and I've been there many times to meet the people. I've never seen such beautiful children. Each and every one has nut brown skin, and their eyes are so dark they remind me of licorice snaps, and such sweet faces," Joan paused. "Are you listening to me?"

"Yes," Janine said, hiding a yawn behind her hand.

"Then we'll drive through the countryside to Madrid. We can sightsee or shop, whatever you want. I haven't been there either so there'll be plenty to do. He warned me at this time of year it's a lot hotter in Madrid than it is here."

Janine was now concentrating on pulling the dry toast left on her plate into small pieces and yawning again.

Joan let out an exasperated sigh. "How does that sound?"

"Madrid sounds exciting. Where will we stay?" Janine asked, though she did not really care. Right now, she did not want to carry on a conversation.

Last night the two of them had stayed up into the early hours of the morning to catch up on each other's news. She was tired and her head hurt. It might be because she was thinking too much—about Alberto, about her mother, about this magnificent place.

After listening to her mother explain life on the hacienda, Joan seemed to be included in everything the family did. After meeting the aloof Constancia Casilda, Alberto's mother, Janine had a hard time understanding why Joan had been so warmly received. It was apparent to Janine that Constancia Casilda took her position as the matriarch of the old Spanish family quite seriously. Her manners were courteous to the point of coolness, and Janine had the distinct feeling that was just as far as she wanted the American friendships to go. If a friendship had developed between her mother and Constancia, Joan had never mentioned it.

"The Casilda's have a house in Madrid they use when they visit the city. We will be staying there."

"How nice for them. Two houses, they must be rich."

"Alright Jani, what's wrong?" Joan demanded. "Don't you feel well? Is the cottage not what you expected or Spain or the family? You've made it quite obvious that you're tired, but there must be something else."

Janine looked up in surprise and laughed. "I feel fine. What are you talking about?"

"I'm not sure, but your attitude is beginning to rain on my day, and I won't stand for it."

Janine looked at her mother in surprise and felt hurt. "How can you say that to me after all I've done the past few weeks? I've been in a nervous stupor about this trip since I bought my ticket. I haven't been able to sleep or eat for weeks and now you're accusing me of being a party-pooper? After all I've suffered? You are…you are, so…ungrateful."

Joan held up her hand. "Wait a minute. Why would you call me ungrateful?" She paused and bit her lower lip. "If you came all this way just because of me or some misguided notion that you were needed to keep me company, then you, young lady, can get right back on that plane and go home. In case you didn't notice last night, I have plenty of company when I want it. I also had peace and quiet when I wanted it too. I'm a big girl and don't need a babysitter."

Joan shook her head.

Janine looked close to exploding into tears.

"I didn't mean to be harsh, honey, I just wanted to remind you, in case you forgot, that I'm fully recuperated now and able to take care of myself."

Janine glared down at the marbled white countertop. She was in a strange house, in a strange country, and her mother was talking like it would have been better if she hadn't come at all.

Joan continued, "I don't pretend to know exactly what is going on in that head of yours," her voice gentle, "but I'll take a guess at some of it. Please, please stop using that brain of your's, girl, and listen to your heart. Take advantage of the beauty of this place, let it soothe your soul with its peace, and then everything will look clear. Just give this place a chance."

Janine sniffed. Her eyes burned from unshed tears. When she saw her mother studying her, she stood and walked over to the sliding glass door that overlooked the garden. "Where were you so early?" she asked, hoping to change the subject.

"I do my exercises before the sun becomes too intense," Joan told her. "During the noon hours, when it becomes stifling, I stay put in here and read or take a nap. It's nice in the morning to keep the doors open, but when it gets too hot, the air conditioning needs to be turned on. Right now, I have to change out of this damp suit, and then I'll look into making something more substantial than toast for breakfast. Is there anything you prefer, since you didn't touch the toast?"

"Do you think it's too hot for me to swim right now?" Janine asked.

"Swim?" Joan repeated.

"Yes, I assume you meant you do your exercises in the pool."

"Of course I do, you cheeky young woman," Joan admonished her. "After the Casilda children's respectful behavior I can see it's too late for me to try and change you. Yes, you still have time to swim as long as you don't stay in the sun too long and use waterproof sun block."

"Is the pool nice? I've always enjoyed swimming in an outdoor pool. We don't often get the chance at home. It would be a shame to waste it." Janine stood up and began to clear off the counter.

Joan took a quick look at her watch. "Of course. It's a beautiful pool. You'd better leave those dishes, though. Go and change. We have all afternoon to pick up around here, but swimming is done in the early morning or the evening."

Janine set the plates in the sink and wondered briefly at the excitement in her mother's voice about something as ordinary as her wanting to go swimming.

22

Juan Carlos Casilda eyed the food on his plate. He felt a storm brewing across the table from him.

"Why is it sons always make the most disappointing choices when it comes to a woman?" Constancia Casilda demanded from her husband at the breakfast table. With the younger children already off playing with their cousins in the village, the couple was enjoying their breakfast alone. Alberto hadn't yet returned from the barn, and Frederico hadn't gotten up for the day. "I'm not quite certain what's going on with this American woman, but I do know my son, and with her around, he's acting very strange."

Juan Carlos lifted an eyebrow, recognizing his wife's petulant tone, but remained silent. He knew from experience it was best to wait until he heard what his wife was upset about before he opened his mouth. He continued to eat while he listened.

"I find nothing about her attractive. Her coloring is insipid, her style non-existent, and I did not detect any superior knowledge in her, though she does work in a library," Constancia mused out loud as she liberally doctored her coffee with cream and sugar. "Alberto is accustomed to beautiful Spanish flamingos, not an insignificant little brown sparrow from some god-forsaken place called Minnesota."

Juan Carlos controlled his laughter. "Come, come, my dear. Aren't you being rather hasty in passing judgment on this señorita after meeting her only once. Alberto has had more time. He knows these women." He paused before adding, "It isn't often he invites anyone to stay with us."

"He has never invited anyone from America here," she snapped back.

Juan Carlos nodded. He gave his still-beautiful wife a knowing look. "Then that should tell us something. It would be best for us to wait and hear from our son about the señorita before coming to any conclusions."

Constancia dropped her spoon onto the plate. "Alberto has too many obligations to even think of bringing a complete stranger into this family. An American with no Spanish blood! Berto knows this is completely unacceptable. It won't do, Carlos. It just won't do."

Her husband turned his attention to his plate, staring at what remained. He knew Constancia was impossible to reason with in this mood.

"Carlos," Constancia said. Still holding her cup in her hand, she pushed her chair back and stood walking slowly around the table. He looked up, narrowing his dark eyes to watch her. Her hips swayed in a brightly patterned skirt, her waist slender as a willow. She was a woman he still desired but a woman with a turbulent nature he had never learned to deal with to his satisfaction. She pushed his plate aside and sat on the table facing him.

"Berto has proven himself," Carlos said softly. "He is level-headed when making important decisions. Didn't he set aside his work with Uncle Armand and return home when we asked him?"

Constancia laughed. "Oh yes, like the purchase of two pedigreed bulls within months of each other. Even you were shocked by his purchases," she scoffed.

Carlos frowned. "You and I both know his plans for the cattle. I'm willing to give him the chance to improve our stock and the ranch." He read the stubborn look on her face and shook his head.

A flush filled her cheeks as she stared at him. "I can't understand why you insist on allowing him to behave so carelessly when what is at stake here is the future of the Casilda family name." Her words began to fall quickly from her red lips. "You know Berto has never been as responsible with affairs of his heart as he has with every other aspect of his life. For the past two years since he returned home, he has continuously refused to allow me to introduce him in the proper way to suitable young women, and now he brings this, this girl into our midst. He doesn't explain what his intentions are, and you, his father, the head of this household, expect me to be patient with him and wait. I can't do that, because how will I know he won't make the wrong choice, and then it will be too late. No, it's best to confront him now before any real damage has been done. The girl can stay for her vacation and then she and her mother will return to Duluth, Minnesota," she sneered the names. "They will be gone, and Alberto can choose a nice local girl to take as his wife."

Carlos hid a smile behind his cup and looked away so as not to betray his own feelings. He, like Frederico, recognized the change in Alberto the moment the girl came into the room.

"If you refuse to remind him of his responsibilities, Carlos, then you only force me to do it myself." Constancia declared. She looked at her husband who shrugged.

"Alberto is aware of his responsibilities, Constancia, and if I remember the conversation you had with him on the telephone when he was in America, all you said was, 'you need to marry.'" Carlos gave a brief smile. "I believe it is this responsibility he plans on taking care of very soon."

Constancia flew to her feet and audibly gasped. "Not with the American! You're wrong!" Coffee splashed into the saucers when she unsettled the table. "Has he asked your permission?"

Carlos pushed his chair away from the table and stood. He wasn't a tall man, five feet ten inches, but his wife topped five feet two inches in the heels she wore. "You will rein him in too tightly, Constancia. You know Berto's temperament is much like Juanita's." He grasped his wife's slim arm and pulled her close. "Even though Berto is the oldest son, it is still possible for him to do as Juanita did and leave so that he may live his life as he chooses."

Constancia tightened her lips and tossed her head. "Don't be foolish, Carlos. That wasn't Juanita's decision. As a wife, Juanita had to follow her husband. He was the one who chose to move their family to Argentina."

Carlos released her. Sadness etched his words. "Constancia, it broke Juanita's heart to leave her family."

"Someday they will return," she murmured, "I know they will. Just like Alberto did."

23

The lush plants and trees around the house kept the area cool, but Janine didn't realize how much of a difference it really made until she walked away from the cottage. She felt moisture forming on her face and realized it was hot. She understood the schedule Joan had described earlier. She had fallen into the pattern of life necessary for living in this part of the world.

Janine was dressed in her new swimsuit with a filmy swim cover over it. Her skin was sticky with tropical smelling sunscreen, and, carrying her white towel, she set off along the path toward the main house.

Janine paused for a moment when the path split. She took the pathway that led sharply to the left. The path gradually became narrower and narrower. With both hands Janine had to push aside wide deep green leaves the size dinner plates until she walked into a clearing. Under a white canvas canopy sparkled blue-green water in an Olympic size swimming pool. White rock paved the patio surrounding the pool. It looked like a hotel with padded lounging chairs that matched the umbrellas atop the tables that encircled the area. On the nearest chair, she sat down to discard her sandals and slip off her cover. Her long pale limbs would be on fire if she stayed too long. At the far end, the shallow area of the pool was protected by the canopy but the deep end was open. She walked eagerly toward the pool stepping onto the hot patio stones.

"Ow…ow…ow," she exclaimed, dancing over the few feet to the pool's edge before leaping awkwardly into the water. She sank quickly, and the sunglasses she'd forgotten to take off floated off her face. She grabbed at them, but they slipped through her fingers and disappeared into the shadows of the pool.

Janine, with her lungs aching, swam to the surface. "I don't believe it," she muttered blinded by the sunshine. She couldn't see a thing under the water with the brightness of the sun.

A sudden splash at the other end of the pool brought her around. Along the bottom of the pool a long distorted shadow of a man came closer to where she treaded water. A moment of panic gripped her when he burst through the surface.

"Berto," she gasped out, half thrilled, half embarrassed at seeing him.

Water droplets slid on his dark brown face dropping onto the muscular chest that dipped in and out of the water. He swiped the water from his face with a large hand and grinned at her. "Hello."

She sank lower in the water and studied his face, thinking how young he looked right now with water droplets clinging to his ears and his thick eyelashes clumped together. Janine opened her mouth to return the greeting when pool water splashed her in the mouth. Sputtering and gasping to catch her breath, she paddled over to the side of the pool and clutched the edge.

"What are you doing?" she gasped, wheezing as fresh air filled her lungs. "Trying to drown me?"

Alberto laughed. "That small splash will hardly drown you. I just wanted to wake you up. Why wouldn't you answer me?"

"You surprised me. I didn't expect to see you this morning. I thought you'd be working."

He gave her a puzzled glance. "What do you mean? This is where I work."

"I thought you'd be busy doing…well…doing ranch things. My mother seems to think everyone on the ranch is up and busy at work early."

With a glint of amusement in his eyes, he said, "I see, I surprised you when you thought you were alone with no one watching."

Janine hastily looked away. He was right. She did feel caught. But why? She wasn't doing anything wrong. Alberto himself was the first to tell her to use the pool whenever she wanted. "Mother told me I wouldn't bother anyone if I swam now."

Alberto took a few swift strokes to the edge of the pool and rested his muscular arm on the wall beside her. "Your mother is correct, but your presence here doesn't make any difference. I enjoy company. Unfortunately, Joan is always leaving the pool when I arrive."

Janine frowned. Now she knew why her mother was in such a hurry to get her to the pool.

"But Frederico and my mother both told me you are insatiable where work is concerned. You know what I mean. Up at dawn to work at the barns and that sort of thing…" Under his steady gaze, her words faded as she gulped uncomfortably. She had the feeling she said something that annoyed him again.

"Compared to Frederico, I am," he slowly studied her face, his eyes resting on her mouth. "Insatiable? What an unusual word for you to use."

Janine had shocked herself when the word slipped out. She hoped he might not notice. Looking around she frantically tried to think of something else to say.

"I do start my day in the barn, but now is the time I return to the house for an hour or so. I exercise, relax, and eat breakfast and have coffee with my mother and my sister before I must return to the ranch office to work on the books."

"Oh, how wonderful. You get to make your own schedule," she cried. "I quite envy you. To have the freedom to be your own boss, though I'm sure the demands must go way beyond a union workday."

Alberto shrugged. "There is more than just myself who are considered the boss. My father and my brothers also have duties. There are many vaqueros, too many to name, who work with us. They are mostly cousins and uncles of the family."

The clear blue water lapped against them and reminded Janine of how little she wore and that he was right next to her and that he too was almost naked. She gave a shaky laugh. "I must be keeping you from your exercise. Please don't let me ruin your routine."

"Exercising can wait," he said with a lazy smile.

Janine felt her heart melt. Why was he so different? She'd always thought of him as a no-nonsense, man-in-charge kind of guy. Now she wasn't sure. He looked lighthearted and carefree as if he had no duties to keep him from carrying on a conversation in the swimming pool for as long as he liked. Her heart was beating much too fast. She could swear her palms were sweating in the pool water. Slowly, she backed away from him while saying, "My mother has grown very fond of your lovely home, Berto. I'm afraid Duluth will be lonely with just me for company."

Alberto pulled himself through the water as Janine retreated. "Has Joan said this to you or are you merely being kind?"

Janine stared into his eyes. She felt the power of his presence pulsate through her body. Joan may love this paradise, but it was this man that electrified Janine.

"Alberto," a female voice intruded on them.

Janine splashed away from him so fast she slipped and could barely keep her head above the water.

Alberto reached out to grasp her arm and hold her until she clasped the side again. He smiled at Janine before he looked up. "Yes, mother?"

"Oh, señorita, you are here, too," Constancia said with obviously feigned surprise. "How nice for Alberto to have company during his morning swim." A thin smile stretched her lovely mouth. "Oh, my dear," she clucked with mock concern, her quick dark eyes sweeping over Janine's face. "The sun has become too much for you. Your face is so flushed. It takes awhile for strangers to become used to it. A hat would help and, of course, sunshades. The sun can cause terrible headaches, especially when it shines on the water like this."

"Goodness," Janine exclaimed. "I completely forgot about my glasses." She swam with sure strokes to the middle of the pool. "My sunglasses fell off here."

"You wore your sunglasses into the pool?" Constancia asked with a wicked laugh.

"Didn't you just say the sun can cause headaches when it shines on the water?" Alberto interjected. "If you will excuse me, mother," he saw his mother's expression fall as he turned his attention to Janine, "I must help the señorita."

"Berto," Constancia said quickly, "I would like to speak with you…alone." She impatiently tapped the stone patio with her high-heeled foot.

Alberto pushed away from the edge of the pool and flipped onto his back. "Of course, mama. As soon as I find a spare moment, we will talk." He blew her a kiss and dove cleanly under the water before Constancia could say another word.

Constancia huffed in derision and walked away.

24

The bright sun blasted against the water as Janine broke the surface gasping for air. She choked and sputtered, a consequence of laughing underwater. She and Alberto had taken several dives trying to find the lost sunglasses. The search had become a competition. Alberto was a stronger swimmer, but she was fast. She had caught sight of the glasses' outline against the underwater drain but couldn't reach them before she needed to surface for air. Alberto had been right behind her, so when a dark hand holding the sunglasses appeared next to her she wasn't surprised.

When his entire body surfaced, almost bumping her, Janine raced away as fast as she could to avoid any contact. She didn't trust herself to actually touch his bare skin in the water. She reached the poolside and pulled herself out onto the gritty stone. With a quick glance behind her, to see what he was doing, she hastened to stand and jump away from the pool.

Alberto leisurely swam toward her. From his hooded look, she had the oddest feeling he could see right through her and knew why she had fled his nearness. Crossing her arms to cover herself, she hid her anxiety behind laugher. "Truce! You've won. You're a much better swimmer than I, so give me back my sunglasses."

Alberto held the plastic frames by one finger out over the water. With a grin, he dangled them loosely. "Here they are, señorita, all you need do is take them from me. I will not resist."

His tone raised goose bumps on her flesh.

"I'm not foolish enough to think I can take those away from you. I will not come back in there. I know when I've been beaten."

He chuckled. "It wasn't I who was stubborn and refused to come up for air. I had plenty of time to reach the glasses and then swim to the surface."

Janine burst out laughing at his mischievousness. She found this Alberto easy to tease. "Alright, señor, I concede. It is true you have better lungs than me, now return my glasses."

Constancia's high heels clicked loudly on the patio. Her voice was icy in the humid heat. "You really should return to the cottage. I'm sure your mother must be looking forward to having you to herself for a time." She paused then added, "You and your mother will be joining us for lunch at the main house. It's a rather special occasion. We have a guest." She turned away from Janine to smile at Alberto who had left the pool when his mother showed up. He was toweling himself off.

"We have a guest, Berto," she repeated, her voice changing from chilly to cheerful when she spoke to Alberto.

Alberto didn't look up.

Constancia, undaunted, continued. "It's Esme. She has ridden a most wild stallion all the way over here for a visit. This would be a perfect opportunity for you to introduce your American friend."

At the mention of Esme, Alberto instantly froze.

Constancia eagerly turned to Janine. "Doesn't visiting over lunch sound like an enjoyable way to spend the afternoon?"

Janine swallowed hard and wished she was anywhere but here with the sharp black eyes of Señora Casilda dissecting her. She already felt defenseless with her wet hair plastered to her head, wearing a swimsuit, and standing in bare feet.

Even in the revealing light of the sun, Constancia Casilda remained a beautiful woman. Because of Alberto's age Janine knew she must be in her fifties, but time had given her features a depth of character a younger woman wouldn't have. The shiny black hair of the elegant woman was youthful-looking. It was all pulled back tightly in the traditional Spanish style and woven around a black lace ribbon. Fine wrinkles spread across pale skin the color of porcelain. A striking white blouse was bunched dramatically low on her arms accenting perfectly the delicacy of her shapely shoulders. The peacock blue peasant skirt that looked designed for her petite figure combined to make Constancia a real Spanish beauty.

As Janine looked at her, she knew Constancia would fit into Duluth's upper society in an instant. Constancia possessed a quality that Janine had never seen before she'd met Alberto. It was old world elegance, and Janine decided that a person had to be born with it.

"Esmeralda is the daughter of our nearest neighbor," Constancia explained. "Her family, the de Martés, are old friends of ours. The children have all grown up together so they know each other very well. It will be good for you to know her and for her to know you."

Janine forced a smile. "Thank you, señora, I am looking forward to it," she murmured before moving away to where she'd left her swimming things. Under the umbrella, she pushed her feet into sandals and jerked the swimming cover over her head wishing for more protection than the flimsy robe offered. She hoped to sneak off when, with a glance over her shoulder, she saw Constancia walking toward her

"Tell me, Janeene," Constancia said, her tongue catching on the pronunciation. "You have only been here a short time, but how are you adjusting? Is the isolation of the ranch too difficult for you after the busy life of the city? You do live in the city?"

Janine nervously clutched her wet towel with her hands. "Yes, we do, but we're quiet people, my mother and myself. We spend most of our free time at home," she admitted. "As a matter of fact, señora, the most exciting times I've ever experienced in Duluth, my home town, were when your son re-introduced me to all the amazing attractions we have. I never appreciated the sights as much as when he was with me."

Constancia frowned. She glanced sharply at Alberto and then back at Janine with her eyes narrowed.

Alberto, with a towel draped around his shoulders and a plain white cotton shirt unbuttoned, walked to where they were talking. He smiled at the two women but spoke to Janine. "I would like to compliment you on your swimming," he said. "I must say, you caught me by surprise. I didn't expect you to keep up with me."

"Really?" Janine said with a laugh. "I guess that's a compliment, so, thank you. I mean, gracias. That would explain why you knocked me aside when I saw the glasses first." She hesitated and expected his mother to interrupt them again. She had already found that Constancia didn't allow the conversation to be long out of her control. When she turned, Constancia was gone. "Your mother…where?"

Alberto glanced around to see if his mother was still outside, but except for the two of them, the patio area was empty. "She has company. Perhaps she returned to entertain them," he said, unconcerned about her abrupt departure. He handed Janine the glasses.

"You'd better put these on," he instructed.

Janine took them and put them on. "Your mother's right, the sun is bright."

Alberto nodded. "It is, but you will become used to it. I will walk you back to the cottage now."

Janine panicked. "No! Please," she protested. "Your mother will be so disappointed if you miss having your morning coffee. I've already interrupted your swim. I don't want to mess up your breakfast plans, too. I can find my way back."

"Yes, I am sure you can find your way, but I would like to show you some of the garden," he said. "The paths in the garden can confuse people at first, so I would prefer to point out the main ones in case you wish to explore the less traveled areas on your own afterward."

"Won't your old family friend be waiting?" Janine asked, as casually as she could manage.

"No."

"Oh," she replied. His one syllable response cut off the conversation. She said what first popped into her head. "Your mother is a beautiful woman. I have never known anyone with looks like hers before."

"Si, mama's pure Spanish line comes from many generations. I believe it has been traced back to the Conquistadors. She is quite proud of it."

Janine stopped abruptly. "As well she should be, Berto," she exclaimed excitedly. "I'm not sure how many people could claim such a historical fact. The Conquistadors, unbelievable. It would be important to try and preserve such a remarkable lineage."

Alberto looked at her with amusement. "You are correct, but then my father's line is not so pristine." He took her hand. "Your fingers, they are pruney," he teased, holding it tight when she made a feeble attempt to pull away.

"Yes, they are. And so are my feet."

A deep laugh rumbled in his chest as they walked away from the pool area.

"I bet you are just as pruney as I am," she retorted.

They reached the secluded section of the flagstone path. The stones were unique, instead of the blue-gray of northern Minnesota slate, they were pink, ivory, and almost a peachy color.

"How long has your family ranched here?" she asked dreamily. She didn't want to interrupt their walk with conversation, but the questions about him, his heritage, and the ranch flew rapidly around inside her head.

"For almost 300 years we have been working this land. At first, they were squatters, but then the land was deeded to my great great great grandfather who fought with King Ferdinand, the reigning king of Spain at the time."

She knew a little of Spain's history. After meeting Alberto, she looked it up on the Internet.

"The dictatorship stifled our country for many years, too many years," Alberto explained. "We could not expand or make any changes during that time. Once it ended, the country came back to life. We are still way behind in many ways, but the Spanish people are working hard to join the modern world. We on the hacienda have begun to use modern equipment and, in the process, are working on improving the bloodlines of our herds."

"Which explains your visit to Duluth," she finished for him. "But tell me more about your grandfather, three times removed."

They walked leisurely in the magnificent garden. "You are hoping for a romantic story," he said smiling. "After great great great grandfather met his bride, he moved her and her family here to live alongside his own. They quickly populated the area and as the family grew, more land was added until the settlement spread out for a thousand miles."

Janine stopped abruptly and turned to look up at the house behind them. "This building is 300 years old?"

"No," Alberto said abruptly. "Not this building. It was my father's father who re-built this house after a fire destroyed the family home." He paused briefly, his lean fingers tightened on hers.

"Something else happened," she said softly. "You don't have to tell me."

"Yes, I want to tell you. He lost his wife, my grandmother, and a child, my father's oldest brother, in that fire."

They stood side-by-side, hand-in-hand, studying the pale pink stucco of the Hacienda Casilda's ornately designed pillars, graceful archways, and the delicate scrollwork of the balconies. The windows looked like happy eyes, and the doorways smiled in welcome. Janine thought it was a most beautiful home and an ideal subject for a watercolor.

"It was designed with love," she said. "It looks like your grandfather took great care in rebuilding."

"I think near the end it became like a memorial for him. Every step of the process needed to be perfection in order to please him. I am afraid he turned into quite a tyrant at the end." Alberto frowned briefly, but his expression lightened when he looked at her. "It's that memory of my grandfather that most people remember, but my father remembers the happy times before grief scarred him."

Janine lowered her face. She felt close to tears. "With that kind of tragedy how could people blame him? He was brokenhearted."

"It happened a long time ago, chica," Alberto said gently.

"But still, Berto, that one incident changed his whole life."

"Yes, the fire changed his life, and my father's life, and consequently mine. My father was the second son," he explained. "A second son only inherits the family estate if the firstborn dies or decides to join the monastery. If my uncle had never died I would never have been able to invite you to Hacienda Casilda. Is the thought of your never coming here good or bad for you?"

25

Janine found she could not look at Alberto. She wanted to hide her face. She had been thinking the same thing. What if she had never come here? She would never have had this time with Alberto. She was afraid her expression might reveal the emptiness she felt at the thoughts.

How quickly things changed. She had fought visiting here and now dreaded the loneliness she knew awaited her when she returned home. Would her life have been better off if she had never seen Alberto's home and the life he led? A worse thought was, what if she had never met him? A bleak picture of what her life had been like before Alberto filled her mind. Her future didn't hold much hope of ever improving. Her time in Spain was going to pass too quickly, and the end of the trip loomed blackly ahead.

Janine glanced at Alberto. They had traveled off the main path that led to the guest house and into an area with huge magnolia trees that canopied over the path blocking out the sky. The thick, gnarled branches reclined almost to the ground and were covered with wide rubbery leaves that looked ancient. Each branch held a profusion of beautiful blossoms, some flowers were pink with white centers and others white with bright yellow centers. The drone of many bees flitting from flower to flower caught Janine's attention.

She glanced nervously around. "How big are those bees I'm hearing?" she asked.

Alberto reached down to pick one of the fallen blossoms off the path and held it out to her. "Not too big, although probably larger than the bees in Minnesota. Don't worry. They won't bother us."

Janine reached out to touch a petal with her fingertip. The petal didn't feel anything like she expected. It was thick and sticky. "They look pretty," she said wiping her fingers on her towel. "It's a shame they have to wither and die."

"Full many a flower is born to blush unseen, and waste its sweetness on the desert air," Alberto said.

"What's that supposed to mean?" Janine asked.

Alberto shook his head. "It is a quote from Thomas Gray. It

means there is no waste where beauty is concerned."

"Oh?"

He chuckled. "It does not matter." He threw the flower over the hedge. "I was trying to be ambiguous."

"Ambiguous has several different meanings. Are you sure it's the word you wanted to use?" Janine asked.

"An ambiguous meaning for an ambiguous word. Yes it is the right word," he laughed. "As a matter of fact, I would say our relationship has had an ambiguous existence."

"What?" Now Janine was completely lost.

"Yes, I think I would be fair saying that," he said with a grin. "The first night we met out in that desolate fog on the boardwalk, you almost fought me with your handbag and now here you are walking in the gardens of my home an entire continent away."

Janine laughed. "You're right. Who could ever have known what the future held?" She paused, then added awkwardly, "But I have this feeling that I still don't know you. I know about your relatives and your home and your family but… it's you. You're so different. I mean you're not at all like you were in Duluth, of course in a good way. You're so relaxed here."

As they walked along in silence, Janine grew nervous because she was asking him to explain himself. She concentrated not on the man next to her, but on studying the different kinds of flowers that ornamented this new part of the path.

"Such questions," he said. "If there is anything you wish to know about my family or our history you have only to ask it. I will answer as honestly as my knowledge allows." With a smile he added, "But if you think I have suddenly acquired a mysterious side to my nature because of this change you imagine, I am afraid you will be disappointed.

"In my heart, I am very much a simple rancher. All I wish to achieve in this life is to have my business prosper enough to maintain this home and to watch my children, when I am blessed with them, grow.

"If I judge what to expect in the future by what my father has lived then I know if I lead his kind of life, it will hold enough excitement for me."

Alberto looked at his watch. "I am afraid we will only have

enough time today to make it to the first grotto of the garden. I must be in the village before siesta."

"We should go back now. I don't want to delay you," Janine offered.

Alberto shook his head. "No, we have the time. The first grotto is just around the corner, but it is not where I wanted to take you today. We will start earlier tomorrow, that is, if you will agree to join me again for a swim and then a walk."

Janine nodded happily. "I would enjoy that very much." She allowed him to lead her along the path at a much quicker pace.

"When are you going to ask me your questions?" he asked after a few minutes.

Janine was carefully watching the uneven stepping-stones that layered the path. She didn't want to trip. "Not right now," she said. She was quickly becoming short of breath.

"I thought they were important."

"They are, or will be when I've thought of them."

He laughed softly as they ducked under a low hanging branch startling a small bird hiding there. It frantically fluttered away into the upper branches. "So you were merely baiting the hook and now wish to leave me in suspense wondering what it is exactly you want to know."

"No, not at all. I just want to be certain to ask the right questions."

Alberto reached down to brush a small insect from the damp skin of her arm. "So you're planning on taking full advantage of my offer?"

"Of course. There are many things I don't know about you even though you say you haven't any secrets. I'm not sure if you're being modest or cautious."

"Cautious? I have been far from cautious when dealing with you, but I will not explain anything until you have made the first move by asking your questions."

Alberto's fast pace left Janine breathless, her mouth was dry, and sweat collected on her nose making her sunglasses slide. She reached up to drag the towel across her forehead. "That will have to wait until after our walk because right now I haven't the breath to say anything."

"It must be the altitude."

"The altitude or this sprinter's pace," she declared, stopping dead.

Alberto looked down at her. "Don't worry, chica, there is a bench to rest on right over there. We will take a moment so you can recover."

Janine mopped her face and took off her sunglasses to wipe them dry while she looked around the small clearing they had stopped in. It was another part of the garden and just as lovely, but here there was something different. In the middle of two flowering bushes was a stone grotto. Protected under a wide protruding arch were two statues; one of an exquisitely beautiful Lady whose expression was of the deepest grief. She was dressed in black and gray with her eyes raised. One hand covered her heart while the other was held out like she was reaching for something. The other was unmistakably the Infant Jesus, but of a likeness Janine had never seen before. The Christ-child's face was that of a child, but the eyes were filled with great knowledge beyond his age. On his head was a crown of gold. A flowing scarlet cloak spangled with golden stars fell elegantly from his shoulders.

"This is the grotto my grandfather built after the fire," Alberto explained. "Here is the plaque where he dedicated it to his wife and son." He led her across a blanket of tiny pink flowers to a stone bench set before the grotto. Janine crouched down to look at the metal plaque attached to the bench. It was green with moss. She squinted to read the inscription, but the letters were almost entirely worn away.

Disappointed, she stood up to see Alberto standing near the grotto with his arms behind his back and his head bent. She didn't want to interrupt him and sat to wait on the corner of the bench. After a moment he came and sat with her. They both were silent while they looked at the grotto. Freshly cut flowers filled several vases at the base of the statues.

"Your grandfather never met anyone else?" she asked, reaching down to rub at the mold on the cool metal of the plaque. It bothered her that the words had been allowed to fade.

"No, he never tried," Alberto said. He watched not only the movements of her hand but saw the frown on her face. "The inscription is not lost," he explained, pointing at the stones of the grotto. "The words have been carved deep into the rock on the back."

Janine jumped to her feet. She rushed behind the grotto. It took only a few minutes to read the simple dedication of names, birth dates and death date before she returned to the bench. "Your grandfather was a man of few words."

Alberto shrugged. "The poignancy of his grief is apparent in other ways. My grandfather explained the significance of the flowers and statues to all of the children in the family many times. The flowers he had planted around the statues are fire flowers and represent the flames of grief." Gesturing toward the Madonna, Alberto said, "This is our Lady of Sorrows, who stood at the foot of the Cross to watch Her Son die, and the Infant of Prague is for my uncle. Grandfather was not familiar with the Infant of Prague statue, but it was the only statue of the Christ Child available at the time. Grandfather found out many years later the Infant is known for healing, and always claimed the Infant is the one who healed the destructive grief of his loss."

A chill crept over Janine's skin at the story. She wasn't sorry when Alberto stood up.

"I believe that is enough of my family's history for today. Shall we go back?"

She jumped up and, taking the hand he held out for her, followed him down a path that was behind the grotto and led off into the garden.

26

Janine opened the door and walked into the air conditioned kitchen with a smile that was slow to fade. She stood leaning against the door daydreaming until the same feeling of exhaustion she'd had the night before returned. The heat or the jet lag or whatever that caused her to be so tired made her desperately want to lie down. Her stomach growled and with a glance at the clock she saw lunch was two hours away. She fixed a snack of cheese and bread.

When she walked up the stairs, eating the last of her sandwich, she saw her mother's bedroom door was closed. Quietly, Janine closed her own door so she wouldn't disturb Joan. After a refreshing shower, she wondered if she needed to get dressed right away but decided to give in to the urge to crawl under the covers. The sheets were so crisp and clean. She pulled the light blanket around her and fell immediately to sleep.

"Janine," a hand pushed on her shoulder.

Janine lifted her head out from under the pillow. "What?" she mumbled.

"We have to be at lunch in fifteen minutes. Hurry!" Joan exclaimed as she shut the door.

It only took a second for Janine's head to clear. She glanced at the bedside clock and flew out of bed.

The two women met in the kitchen hastily rushing over their last minute preparations. Janine dragged a brush through her hair. She had to leave it loose because there just wasn't enough time to plait the unruly mass to pin it up. She sighed looking in the mirror. "Why does it have to curl in every direction," she thought. There goes the elegant hairstyle she hoped to have when she met Esmeralda.

"Janine! We have to leave now," Joan demanded as she opened the door on the patio.

Janine sighed again and turned away from the mirror to jam her hat on and slide her sunglasses into place. She had wanted to be the perfect American visitor when meeting the neighbor, but it just wasn't meant to be.

Joan, intent on reaching the house before they were late, set out at a pace much like the one Alberto had used earlier. Recalling the near heat stroke from this morning, Janine stopped her. "I can't walk that fast."

"Of course you can, you walk all the time."

"Not in this place. The altitude, or whatever, slows me down. If you go this fast I'll be a mess by the time we get there."

Joan smiled. "Oh, you mean to meet the neighbor."

"Have you met her before?" Janine asked, trying to hide the anxiety she felt about meeting the woman so openly accepted by Constancia.

"Yes, I have, but she's never around unless Alberto is present," Joan explained. Then she added with an impish grin, "It isn't often that Berto comes around if he knows in advance that Esme is here."

Janine smiled. She felt like a weight had been lifted off her shoulders. "I'll bet Constancia isn't too thrilled about that."

Joan laughed. "Alberto doesn't pay any attention to what Constancia wants. He flatters and dotes on her like a good son and then does exactly what he wants. Constancia does think she's the only one who knows what is best for each member of the family, but she's doing it with love."

"What do you mean about Berto?"

Joan shrugged. "Alberto has his own plans, and he's a pretty determined young man."

"Are you talking about his plans or yours?" Janine asked slyly.

Joan gave her a blank look.

"Today I found out he swims at exactly the same time you told me to go swimming. He also told me that you have passed each other on many mornings since you arrived here."

Joan frowned and said dryly, "Well, he certainly didn't need to share that information with you."

Janine laughed. "You are so obvious, mother, and have been all along. I can't believe you think I don't know what you're up to."

Joan didn't bother to make up an excuse. "It's not that," she said over her shoulder as she pressed on toward the house leaving Janine lagging behind. "I want you to be with Alberto. Somebody has to wake you up."

Janine hurried after her. "What did you say?"

"Nothing," Joan said. She walked inside holding the door open for Janine.

The two women stood in the cool interior of the house for several moments.

"Whew, I do believe this is the hottest it has been since I arrived," Joan admitted, breathing deeply. "I don't think I could handle much of this kind of humidity, but then that's why the people here rest during the hottest part of the day."

Janine removed her sunglasses. "It isn't even the hottest time of day." She looked around the hallway. This was a part of the house she hadn't seen yet. Wide stone hallways branched out from the entryway in several directions. Joan set her hat and glasses on a bench by the door. "The meal will be served in the dining room at the front of the house."

"They have more than one dining room?" Janine asked.

"Of course," Joan explained, exasperated that Janine didn't understand, "meals are eaten away from the sun. They eat in the coolest dining room depending on the time of day. Come on, we'll meet the rest of the family on the front verandah."

At Janine's inquiring look, Joan explained, "Well, that's how they explained the arrangements to me when I first came. It's logical isn't it?"

They walked past bedrooms with beautiful antique furnishings. "This is where the family sleeps if it becomes too hot upstairs," Joan told her when Janine paused to look inside one of the rooms. They were sparsely furnished. Each room had a bed with a crucifix on the wall above it but that was it.

"The cottage has central air, but the main house is too large."

"How do you know all of this?" Janine asked.

"Frederico. He gave me a tour when I first arrived. He never stopped talking."

Janine wondered why she hadn't been offered a tour by Frederico. He seemed so friendly.

"Alberto is in charge of your tour," Joan grinned, reading her daughter's mind.

"He is?" she said in surprise.

"I guess he started with the pool this morning, not the house.

It's a great old house, Jani. You'll love it when you get to see all of its secrets."

"Really, it has secrets?"

Joan nodded. "And secret passageways."

"Really, are any of them in this area?"

"I don't think so, this part of the house isn't used that much. I come through here because it's quicker, but it's out of the way of the main rooms."

"Is the family sleeping down here now?" Janine said. "The heat can't get much worse than today."

Joan shrugged. "I think it takes many days of intense heat to warm the house. The builders are masters at constructing buildings to keep the cool in and the heat out. Centuries of learning have gone into their technique."

"I read a little about it at the library," Janine said. "Do you think you've adjusted to the heat? I find this miserable."

"I've learned to avoid it," Joan replied. "The day starts earlier as you've already seen, and during siesta I do what I'm supposed to and rest. Life on the ranch has a definite routine. It's slower than what we're used to up north but I don't really miss it too much. Well, at least not yet," she added.

Janine stopped. The stairs were in front of them and on the wall was a painting of the hacienda. It was the only decoration in the long corridor, and the only painting she'd seen in the house. How odd when Alberto seemed to enjoy art so much.

This painting wasn't professionally done, but the colors were bright and it caught the lines and details in the architecture that Janine had found so attractive. Once more, she had the urge to pick up a brush and paint the same view of the house but with her own perspective and in watercolors.

At the top of the narrow stairway, they walked into a patio room. Dark green ferns lined the windows providing much needed shade. Constancia and Carlos were relaxing on cushioned rattan chairs, holding cold drinks. The frosty liquid looked refreshing to Janine. She was hot and thirsty.

The Casilda family looked cozy and content, and Janine felt like an intruder bursting in on them. Even the younger members were quietly playing a game with pegs and a ball on the floor at their parent's feet. Alberto was not present and neither was their other guest.

"Señora, señorita," Frederico called joyfully when he caught sight of them. "Come join us. An iced coffee will relieve any thirst."

Janine smiled a greeting at Frederico and then turned to Constancia to greet her in Spanish. When she looked at Juan Carlos, there was kindness in his smile.

"Buenos días."

"Good day to you, señorita."

Constancia abruptly stood and glanced at her watch. "We will go to the table now," she said briskly. "Alberto is late." She swept gracefully out of the room without waiting for Carlos.

"Rico, please bring their drinks into the dining room for them," Carlos said. The family patriarch leaned over to scoop up the little girl playing at his feet. "Come, Mia." He looked at Janine. "You must be hungry. It's late for lunch."

Janine nodded in agreement as she watched the child in his arms. The girl's hair was in two braids that hung down her back. Her dark eyes shone like buttons as she snuggled under her father's chin to smile shyly at Janine.

Frederico was already in the dining room with his mother. He moved to hold Janine's chair and then did the same for Joan. He sat down next to Janine. "How do you like our hacienda, Janine?" he asked, shaking out his napkin before placing it in his lap. He looked exactly like his older brother when Alberto had asked her the same question.

Janine needed no pretense. "What I've seen is absolutely beautiful. Alberto and I met at the pool this morning and after we swam he showed me your grandfather's grotto. It is so amazing that he built it for your grandmother and uncle." She stopped when she realized everyone was listening to her. Her gaze dropped to her lap. "We don't do things like that for our dead...deceased relatives."

"Not many do it here either," Frederico replied. He glanced at his mother.

Constancia sat rigidly in her chair as she stared at the centerpiece and then at her husband until they were interrupted. A young woman carrying a tureen of soup came into the room, and

Constancia smiled at her.

"Set it here," she directed. Then Constancia took over and began to ladle the soup into bowls and passed them down the table. It was a cold soup called gazpacho, and Frederico immediately began to spoon it into his mouth. Janine gingerly tasted the oil and vinegar based soup and found it good. Not too spicy considering there were red peppers floating around in it.

Juan, the youngest son, who was about seven, sat across from his big brother and mimicked everything Frederico did. He wasn't shy like his sister Maria, and he blurted out answers to questions and asked a good many questions of his own. After awhile, all of the conversation stopped while everyone concentrated on the main course of tender roast beef. Throughout the meal, Alberto and Esmeralda's chairs remained empty.

Janine watched Constancia interact with Maria. The sometimes fierce woman was gentle and spoke with a soothing tone whenever she addressed the child. It was the mother side of Constancia that Janine hadn't seen before, and it came as a bit of a surprise considering how Alberto's mother had been so abrupt earlier.

When the dishes were cleared, dessert was brought in, and Frederico let out an exclamation of delight. "Watermelon ice!" He turned to Janine. "You are in for a treat, or have you had this before? It's Berto's favorite. He will be sorry he missed it."

Just as Frederico said his name, his brother strode into the room. He stopped next to his mother's chair and took her hand. "I apologize for being tardy," he said with a grin.

Constancia snatched her hand away. "Oh you…I should be used to it," she admonished him. "I know you always have a good excuse so spare me from having to listen to it. Go sit down."

Alberto nodded a greeting to his father and then walked around the table.

"Berto, where is Esme?" Constancia asked. "I thought she was with you at the stable."

Alberto shook his head. "I wasn't at the stable." He stopped behind Janine's chair.

"Will you please excuse us?" he asked Joan. "I have arranged my schedule so I am free to give Janine a tour of the house this afternoon." He pulled out Janine's chair, she hastily set her napkin on the table and stood. She awkwardly thanked her hosts before following Alberto out of the room.

"How are you?" he asked.

Janine smiled. "Fine, thank you. Are you sure you wouldn't rather eat first? Lunch was delicious." She hesitated. "I didn't insult your family running out on dessert like that, did I?"

He shook his head. "No, and I've already eaten in town." He took her hand as he led her down the hall. "I'll tell you a secret. I've arranged for dessert to be served in the solarium. The ceiling fans keep it cool in there and after that we shall go on your tour."

Janine smiled, feeling incredibly happy. Suddenly all of her worries seemed unimportant.

27

Once Alberto and Janine had left the dining room, Constancia saw that all the adults at the table were staring at one another in a stunned silence. "Esme's not coming," Constancia thought.

Frederico was the first to speak. "Who at the de Martés house did you make the lunch arrangements with, mama?"

Constancia frowned. "With Esmeralda, of course, on the telephone this morning. Of all the inconsiderate…" she began, then stopped herself. "I must have misunderstood her. There's no harm done. Alberto obviously had other plans anyway."

"You know Esmeralda. With us she feels no obligations," Carlos said.

"She takes care of Esmeralda first and last," Frederico said under his breath.

Carlos gave Frederico a disapproving look and then said in a soothing voice to Constancia, "She feels we are family and has probably just forgotten the time or the date, my dear."

Constancia frowned. "Always when Esmeralda is involved everything turns into chaos. That girl will probably arrive here at sundown expecting supper." With a sigh, Constancia stood and began to pick up the dirty dishes that remained on the table. Maria and Juan fidgeted impatiently in their seats.

"Go and play, you two, but stay inside the house," Constancia said. She watched the children scramble to their feet, dodge around the table, and dash out the door.

Joan was quietly picking up the dirty napkins from the table.

"Joan, please, you don't need to do that," Constancia said. "The girls will be out in a moment."

Joan, holding the linens in her hands, said, "But I enjoy helping, if you don't mind. I'll just bring these into the kitchen. Carlos said I could choose a book from the library. I'll go there after that."

"That will be fine, and thank you," Carlos broke in when it looked like Constancia might argue the point. After Joan's hurried departure to the passageway that led to the kitchen, Frederico asked suspiciously, "You don't really think Esme will show up for supper tonight?"

"I cannot say, Rico, but knowing her, that would fit, wouldn't it?" Carlos said coldly.

"Esmeralda, you foolish girl," Constancia thought. "If you only knew how much you have hurt me. Would that you would grow up and appreciate what I have done for you."

After the death of Esmeralda's mother, Constancia began to nurture a relationship with the girl, but it hadn't been easy. Esmeralda, even then, had an obstinate nature, but Constancia persisted. She was busy raising her own children but knew it was important to Esme to make the effort.

The Casilda's were the de Martés family's closest neighbor. The de Martés' had never been overly welcoming to the Casilda family, but Constancia felt the right thing to do was to include the motherless girl in family gatherings. As the months after Esme's mother's death went by, it became increasingly obvious that Constancia's efforts to keep some normalcy in the child's life were futile. Constancia realized she couldn't continue the struggle to help with the troublesome girl when the girl's own father was causing so much damage. He indulged his daughter with every material possession she demanded until, to Constancia, his indulgence became almost indecent. Yet, he never bothered to fulfill his other duties as a father. When the strong hand of discipline was needed to curb Esmeralda's increasingly improper and, at times, truly offensive behavior, Luis de Martés preferred to stay locked up in his home or away on business while his daughter ran wild. It was inevitable that, as Esmeralda's bad behavior became widely known, the neighbors, to protect their own children, began to shun her. The only family in the area who continued to socialize with the de Martés' was the Casildas.

"Responsible isn't in Esme's understanding," Frederico said with a short laugh. "Why do you think she is different now?"

Constancia shrugged. "I don't really. I just continue to hope that maybe, if she had a strong husband to replace her indifferent father, and someone who would not stand for her behavior, she will have a chance for happiness."

"I don't think any man's strength could be enough to influence Esmeralda to change," Carlos said.

"When a woman is in love with a man, anything is possible,"

Constancia disagreed.

"And Esmeralda has told me of her love for Alberto. It began when she first met him as a girl and has continued all of these years. She would change for Alberto."

Frederico shook his head as he listened to his parents. He definitely didn't agree with his mother. Nothing would change Esmeralda, and if she spoke of love it would be because she would then have control over Alberto. Frederico knew any match between Alberto and Esmeralda would never happen. Alberto refused to be in a room alone with her. He hid his feelings well, but Frederico knew Alberto despised their neighbor.

Frederico remembered when Constancia first began inviting Esmeralda to the hacienda to be a playmate for Juanita. All Esmeralda did was find ways to torment her until, in tears, Juanita would run away and hide. Alberto, who was much older than the other children, wasn't around much, but one time he caught Esmeralda in the middle of one of her malicious tricks. Frederico had never found out exactly what she was doing, but after Alberto finished talking to Esmeralda, she stayed away from Juanita. Esmeralda's visits to the hacienda became less frequent after that incident until she passed her teenage years and her aging father began to look for a husband for her.

Alberto was in Madrid most of the time but when he returned home for a visit, Luis de Martés and his daughter would arrive at the hacienda using any pretext. Constancia always invited them to stay for the next meal, and they always accepted. Frederico would watch Esmeralda attempt to engage Alberto in any possible way. He blatantly ignored her. Her frustration was obvious to Frederico, but she didn't stop going after Alberto.

Frederico sympathized with his brother. Luis wasn't the only local parent who began to parade their eligible daughters in and out of the Casilda's home. But Esmeralda was one of the most persistent suitors. None of their efforts accomplished anything. Alberto remained aloof.

Alberto was not a man to publicly display his feelings, even with his family, but since he returned from the United States he had changed. When Janine showed up at the hacienda it became quite clear to Frederico. For the first time, Alberto was in love, the love that jealousy protects and possessiveness shields from harm.

Alberto, as the eldest Casilda, was the heir to the hacienda. Frederico, far from being jealous of his brother's status, pitied him. He preferred the less tiresome role of the second son. In the family, the title heir meant only that Alberto shouldered the burden of the family business.

Alberto had chosen to give up his life in Madrid working for their Uncle Armand. Armand Casilda was a distinguished art critic and owned one of the most prestigious art galleries in Spain. Frederico knew art was one of Alberto's true passions, but two years ago, when Juan Carlos asked Alberto to return home and take over the family business, Alberto walked away from the art world.

28

The fans faintly moved the heavy air in the large room. It felt larger due to the cathedral ceiling. Janine perched nervously on the edge of the brightly flowered settee with her eyes lowered. The night before she had had cocktails with the family in this very room, but it looked much larger now in the daylight without shadows obscuring the corners. The furniture coverings were bright. Huge crimson and orange flowers decorated every cushion in the room.

"What are you thinking?" Alberto asked, watching her still figure.

Footsteps in the hallway warned them that someone was coming. The same girl who had brought lunch to the family carried in two delicately fluted glasses filled with the watermelon ice dessert from the dining room. She set them on the table.

Alberto smiled and nodded to the girl. "Gracias, Carmen."

Janine had learned she was Marisol's daughter last night. She was quiet but polite. She smiled at Janine before she left.

"What is wrong?" he asked abruptly.

Janine watched the girl leave. She jumped at the sound of his voice. "I was just wondering if it's alright, for us to be here alone, without the rest of the family?" She felt guilty about being alone with him.

Alberto gave her a studied look. "Who has told you about such things?"

Janine, with nervous fingers, smoothed the fabric on the armrest of the couch. "At lunch, your mother was talking generally of how the Spanish people view proper decorum. I don't want to cause any problems," she said, her voice low.

"The guidelines for my sisters are very different than for…"

"Yes?" Janine looked up.

Alberto paused. "In a household where the adult children remain to live in the family home with their parents, there are common courtesies that..." he raked his fingers through his hair, trying to think of a way to explain this tradition to her. "There has to be some kind of an understanding between the young and the old when many generations live together in one house. A certain amount of privacy must be given to the young, all within reason of course. I am well aware of what is proper and not. I do not know what my mother was talking about. I do know it is not something for you to worry over."

"I guess I understand," she said.

"There are seven generations of Casildas who have lived and died in this house, Janine. Surely you are not such an innocent not to know how this is possible?"

She hesitated. "I didn't mean I don't understand that part!" she cried. "I just wondered…oh nothing, forget it," she declared. Feeling frustrated, she flew from the couch and walked over to the window to stare out at the gardens. She couldn't say what was really on her mind.

After a moment he stood next to her. "If you want to know, I have never required that kind of privacy in my family home before today. I have never asked any woman to stay here until now."

Janine closed her eyes tightly. The relief she felt at his answer overwhelmed her.

"Never?" she said without realizing she'd spoken the word out loud.

"Never," he said firmly. He ran his hands lightly up her back to hold her shoulders. He turned her around touching both of her cheeks with his lips. "Now we must enjoy our dessert before it melts and then we shall begin our tour."

She moved with him, his arm slid down to rest around the curve of her waist. They stopped at the table where Alberto released her. He handed one of the glasses to her.

Janine held the cold crystal. "This room is lovely. Your mother has a talent for decorating."

He glanced around. "No, this is the decorating of my grandmother, maybe my great grandmother. Who remembers such things?" he shrugged.

"But the cushions look like new. They must have just been covered," she said, walking over to the couch to run her hand over the cushion. "This material can't possibly be that old. Are you teasing me?"

Alberto savored the melting ice in his mouth before he answered her. "I am sure it has been recently recovered but it would have been done with material that my grandmother had bought." He emptied his glass and set it down. "With all of your questions you haven't even tasted the dessert."

Janine lifted a spoonful of the dripping ice into her mouth and then another. She felt terribly self-conscious with Alberto watching her and hurried another bite. Abruptly she set the glass down.

"Have you had enough?" he asked.

Janine nodded as she swallowed the mouthful of ice.

"It is good, isn't it?"

Janine nodded again unable to speak.

"I'm glad you like it. It is my favorite, but you should eat it more slowly, it's very cold."

Janine felt the intense cold in her mouth and cringed. His warning came just a fraction of a second too late. She could already feel the pain beginning in her head. She swallowed the last bite more slowly and the feeling passed.

"There is a special place I'd like to show you where my ancestors kept their stores of goods. Would you like to see it?" he asked.

Janine nodded. "I'd like that."

He took her hand and led her down winding stairs. At the bottom were the French doors leading onto the patio and then the pool, but Alberto walked past it to a short wooden door. He reached up to pull back the dead bolt at the upper corner before he opened it. Inside was a dark narrow hall that smelled dusty. He reached inside to flip on the light switch and a dim glow emitted from the low wattage bulb. With the light, she could see only a short distance inside. The walls were constructed of rough looking cement-like material. The ceiling was so low Alberto had to stoop so he wouldn't hit his head. The narrowness forced them to walk single file, and as they rounded the first corner, she felt the musty dampness increase.

"This is a part of the original structure of the house," Alberto told her over his shoulder, "so it is three hundred years old."

"People must've been a lot shorter then," she said. Her back was already getting sore from hunching over, and she wasn't nearly the height of Alberto.

He chuckled. "Probably, but what is more likely is they didn't want to dig out more of the rock than they had to. This was all that remained after the fire. The solid rock is why it survived."

There were no windows in the passageway. The shaded lamps were spaced along the walls, and there were small cloth bags hanging off each one.

"What are these?" Janine asked.

Alberto stopped and lifted one up. A huge-bodied, long-legged spider hiding behind it darted away and disappeared along the wall into a corner. Janine gasped at the sight.

Alberto wasn't surprised. "There are a lot of spiders, but most cannot hurt you."

"What a relief," Janine quipped. "So they won't bite?'

"Well, yes, of course they bite, but they aren't poisonous."

"Oh," she shivered.

"The bags are hanging here to absorb the dampness from the air," he explained, releasing it. "A trick learned from the past. They have hung here ever since I can remember."

"A medieval dehumidifier," Janine said with a laugh.

"So it is," he agreed, smiling at her. "There are herbs inside to absorb odor and volcanic ash that absorbs moisture. This passage isn't used often, so it becomes quite fetid in here."

"Are the walls made of adobe?" she asked, touching the graceful swirls that decorated the stone. It felt sharp against her fingertips though it looked smooth. She had read about adobe but had never seen it.

"Yes, this was a part of one of the original farm buildings built on the property. There was a very large room used for cooking and living and then a small sleeping room and this was the tunnel to their storage room for everything, even food."

"It's hard to believe that something made by man can last for so long. This is exactly what I would imagine one of the secret passageways in some old castle to look like."

"That could well be, except this would probably be more what a passageway to a dungeon would look like."

"Like something out of the legend of Zorro," Janine exclaimed.

"You speak as a romantic," Alberto said.

A note in his voice caught her attention. "Why do you say it like that? Did something happen in this tunnel?" She paused and whispered, "Your grandmother, did she…"

Alberto took her hand. "Watch your step," he warned. "From now on the floor begins to slant upwards. If you're not careful you can trip."

Janine stopped, pulling him to a halt with her abrupt movement. "Tell me what happened in here. I won't go any further, Berto, until you tell me." Chills ran up her arms and it had nothing to do with the tunnel. She was convinced that his grandmother had died in there. Without their voices, silence settled around them leaving nothing to hear but their breathing. She waited anxiously for him to answer.

Suddenly, Alberto laughed.

Janine jumped at the sound.

"What happened was nothing, chica, and had nothing to do with my grandmother."

Janine shook her head. "I want to know."

"Alright, I will tell you. Some years ago, I was left in here," he said with a shrug of his shoulders.

"Left…what does that mean?"

He sighed. "You are full of questions today. I was locked in here."

"How awful," she breathed. "How did it happen? Was it a prank?"

Alberto began to walk again. "It is not much further to the storeroom. I do not think it was a prank. Rico promises that he had nothing to do with it. My father was so angry at the time it happened, Rico would have denied it no matter what. But to this day he does not change his story. He was very young, I think six or seven at the time. I don't believe he could have done it. It is an unsolved mystery," he said with grimness in his voice. "If we had a family ghost, then I could blame it on that, but alas, we have no ghost, that I know of."

"If Frederico was seven, how old would you have been?" Janine asked softly.

He stopped so suddenly it startled her into stillness. The tunnel had shrunk in height and width as they had continued through the many twists and turns. Ahead of them it completely disappeared. Alberto stepped aside to show her a staircase where the tunnel ended. It was really only a make-shift wooden ladder that had been made stationary against the wall with metal bolts. The stairs led upwards into the ceiling of the passageway.

"This is unbelievable," she gasped and then choked on the dust.

"The family history says this tunnel was carved by hand out of the rock," Alberto told her.

"That's exactly what it looks like."

Alberto went up the ladder first. "Be careful, this part is a little more difficult."

Janine grimaced. "More difficult? I'll never make it."

Alberto chuckled as he lowered his head in order to avoid the overhang of stone the staircase led to. As they moved slowly upward, the air in the confined space changed. It became denser and dry with dust, so it was hard to breathe.

Janine had already lost her romantic images of the place and now all enthusiasm about the mystery ahead withered. She'd never before been afflicted with claustrophobia in her entire life but right now, she felt like the walls were pushing the very breath out of her lungs. She fought the panic that gripped her.

"Don't worry, in a moment we'll be out of this," Alberto said over his shoulder.

Janine took a deep breath and numbly continued to climb.

He stopped after a few more steps to push his shoulders against a trap door. The metal hinges creaked a protest as he gave one hard shove against it. It slammed on the other side with a resounding bang. Dust trickled down from above, landing on them. Alberto scrambled up the rest of the steps, and Janine followed as fast as she could. Coughing, she reached the last rung of the ladder. Alberto reached down to take her hand, and she stepped off and into a room that rose above her. Clean air cleared the dust from her throat and cooled her hot skin.

29

They were standing inside a cave, a cave lofty enough for Alberto to stand.

"The story is that this was a natural cave and my family enlarged it to be a storage area. In here, everything was safe from animals or thieves, and the temperature remained cool."

Janine stepped away from him. "I never would have guessed this huge space would be on the other side of that horrible tunnel."

"'That horrible tunnel,' as you describe it, has stopped many people from coming in here. The only woman I know of that made it all the way through the passage is my sister Juanita, and she did it only as a dare. Never did she do it a second time."

Janine didn't know why he was telling her this, but a feeling of satisfaction crept over her as she realized she had done something on the hacienda Esmeralda hadn't.

"You have been asking so many questions about the history of the house and my ancestors, I thought this place would interest you."

"Is it okay to look around?" she asked. Piled up along the slanted walls were steamer trunks, the kind pirates always found filled with gold coins and magnificent jewelry.

"This is unbelievable," she murmured. Her desire to open the containers and look at everything inside made her smile. "It's like Christmas when you didn't know what was inside all of those wrapped packages."

Alberto nodded. "I always felt that way about this place too, but unfortunately, looks are deceiving." He walked over to another corner of the cave where wooden cupboards with huge drawers had been built. He stopped at one and pulled open a drawer. Janine followed him and smelled the aroma of strong herbs filling the air. He pulled a large roll of material out of the drawer and carried it back into the light of the exposed overhead bulb. It was the very material the couch was covered with.

"See, it is the same," he said, holding it up for her. "My great grandmother kept bolts and bolts of this material. Why, we have no idea, but each time my mother recovers the cushions, this is what is used." He grinned at her before returning the roll to the drawer. "So, you see, my ancestors did pick the fabric. And the only things hidden in all of the chests and drawers that you see are household materials that have been used over the years for making repairs. In the old days, shipments of goods to the country were scarce. The people found it necessary to keep large stores of what they needed to survive, in case they missed a few shipments. The dictatorship caused the same problem during the fifties. Embargos against Spain stopped most imports into the country. The family began to use the supplies in here. When the foreign governments who were against the dictator renegotiated trade relations and the embargos were lifted, we could buy most of what we needed. My mother didn't want to change the hacienda so she has been content to use what was left in here."

"Why haven't I noticed this from outside of the house?" Janine asked. "I've never seen any sign of it before."

"You've been exploring," Alberto raised an eyebrow.

Janine lowered her gaze, embarrassed. "Well, I've sort of been thinking of sketching the hacienda and wanted to look at it more closely."

Alberto smiled. "I would be honored if you would sketch my home. But, to answer your question directly, it is not as visible as you would expect because it has been carved mostly into the ground. The cave itself is a mound covered with small trees just past the orchards. There is only one way in and out of here, and it is through 'that horrible tunnel.'"

"How old were you when you were locked in here?"

"I was fourteen. The worst part was there was no electricity in this part of the house at the time so I carried a candle. It went out when the door slammed shut."

"How did you get out?" her voice sounded hollow.

"I was in the tunnel not in here. I doubt I could have made it up the stairs in the darkness without breaking my neck."

It was not easy for her to picture him as a boy in this tomblike place. To be in here now, even with Alberto present, gave her the creeps.

"The tunnel was not the same. As children, Rico and I would play in here with our cousins, but it was dangerous, and Papa discouraged it." He pointed to the light switch near the door. "Father had electricity installed as soon as he could."

"Turn off the light," she said suddenly. Her voice hushed. Why she said it, she didn't know.

Alberto looked at her and laughed. "Why?"

"I want to see what it was like for you being in total dark all that time."

"No, I do not think it is necessary. You have already shown your bravery by coming here with me. I think we have both had enough of disturbing old ghosts from the past." He took her hand as they moved back to the steep staircase. When they reached the bottom, he returned up the ladder to shut the door and then jumped down beside her. "I doubt it will be disturbed again until Mama wants to fix something."

The return trip through the tunnel went fast and wasn't as tiring as Janine expected. Soon they were able to walk upright. Janine stretched and rubbed the ache in her neck.

Alberto happened to glance back and saw her. He slowed his steps. "I thought this would be enjoyable for you, but instead it has turned out to be a miserable time. You look hot and are covered with dust."

Self-consciously, Janine brushed at her clothes. "That's not fair. I can't help it if I look a mess, and it has been fun. Hard work, but fun." She was surprised when she blurted the words out and found them to be true. A feeling of elation at accomplishing something explained the lifting of her spirits. "It's been awhile since I've done so many scary but exciting things. I convinced myself that I couldn't try anything new anymore. But I was wrong, and now I know for sure because I've done them."

"Why would you think you are incapable of doing new things in the first place? You're intelligent and in good health. What stopped you?"

Janine chewed on her lower lip before answering. "I was afraid. If I didn't try something new then I wouldn't fail." She laughed. "And all this time I was failing myself."

"And now how do you feel?"

"Like I'm free, I don't have to be stuck doing the same things. And if I do feel like trying something different, I'm not sure what, then I will."

"Like being in the dark in a tunnel with spiders."

"You shouldn't tease, it was a horrible thing to happen," she protested. "I certainly wouldn't ever be able to brush it off like you have." Ahead of them she saw the outline of the door. "When you got to the door was it easy to open?"

Alberto shook his head. "No, the wood swells in the humidity. I tried to open it for quite some time before I figured out it had been locked."

"Locked. Then you know for sure it wasn't an accident."

"Exactly my thought," Alberto said.

"Who let you out?"

He sighed. "The restoration on this part of the house had not been done yet. Without the patio and swimming pool, this area was unused. I really had no idea how long it would be before my family realized I was missing, probably not until the next meal. The passage was filled with cast-offs from the house that had been thrown in here, like old furniture, broken baskets, but nothing I could use to help myself escape. There were also a lot of spider webs that I disturbed when rummaging around in the dark. When the neighbor girl heard my cries and opened the door, she found me standing in the dark passageway covered with dirt and spider webs, and there were spiders crawling all over me." He shook his head and laughed. "The sight sent Esmeralda flying off in a fit of hysteria. Rico swears he could hear her screaming all the way to her house."

"How awful," Janine gasped.

At her stricken expression, Alberto slipped his arm around her shoulders. "You can brush aside all the tender feelings you have in your mind for the poor boy. I have since survived many mishaps, most of them more dangerous than being locked in the dark."

Janine held up a hand. "Spare me the details," she cried, "I don't think I can handle hearing about anymore."

They stopped when they reached the door. He turned the handle and pushed against it. It didn't move. Alberto frowned and with more force tried again. His weight caused only a dim thud, barely heard, against the heavy plank door.

"Is it jammed?" Janine asked, a feeling of panic rising in her throat.

"It cannot be," he said. He grasped the handle and twisted it hard before again throwing his weight against it. It flew open and after a second the two were out and in the hallway.

Janine laughed breathlessly. "Thank you," she said.

"For what?" Alberto asked with a puzzled look.

"Thank you for leaving the lights on in the cave. It's obvious now I would have panicked if you turned them off. You saved me from embarrassing myself."

Alberto shut the door and reached up for the heavy bolt. "I very well could have been saving myself from embarrassment," he said as they walked away.

Janine laughed. She was sure he had said it as a joke, but there seemed to be an undercurrent of truth in his words.

All she felt right now was relief. She had her fill of the Casilda's history and had no desire to see or learn anymore about their past.

30

Alberto stopped her at the French doors of the guest cottage. "I almost forgot. I wanted to talk to you last night and then this morning about something. Early in the evening is a perfect time to go horseback riding, and I was wondering if you would join me tomorrow before supper? Do you ride?"

Janine's eyes widened with dread. "No. Never!"

Alberto frowned briefly and then smiled. "That will be easy to change."

"I don't think so," Janine stepped back. "Horseback riding isn't something I've ever really wanted to do. I'm sure it was necessary for you, living on the ranch, but in Duluth it's very expensive. I was always interested in art." She avoided looking at him directly, fiddling with the curved metal handle of the door. "How old were you when you learned to ride one of those beasts?" she asked, suddenly curious.

"Three or four."

"Years?" she exclaimed. It horrified her to think of a small child being forced to sit on one of those animals.

"All Casilda children learn to ride almost as soon as they learn to walk," he smiled. "I would like to teach you how to ride, Janine, just as I taught my sisters."

"Your sisters? Do you mean little Maria is already riding horses?"

"Yes, she is." He stepped closer to her. "Will you allow me to do this for you?"

Janine's eyes flew to his face. Her nightmarish fear of horses didn't stop her from giving in to him. "Yes," she whispered but not without a lingering feeling of fear.

After he left, she quickly regained her senses. "How can I get out of this?" she cried out loud. She needed a fool-proof excuse to save herself from the total humiliation of getting near a horse. It wasn't going to be easy after she'd confessed her newly achieved freedom to try new things. "What have I gotten myself into?" she muttered to herself.

The sun was sinking in the sky the next day when Janine walked with Alberto down the dusty path toward a long white-washed building with brick-red roof tiles. Sweat trickled between her shoulders from nervousness. Two horses stood outside the double doors of the barn tied at a wooden rail with saddles on their backs. With their heads down they lazily switched their long tails back and forth. The taller of the two horses was flame red with deep grooved muscles in his body. The other was small and a muted color of gray and brown with a dark black mane and tail.

"This will be your mount for the first lesson," Alberto said as he led her to the smaller horse. "Her name is Sophia."

"What color is that?"

"Buckskin, isn't she a beauty? And, she is very gentle."

Janine was briefly relieved. Sophia looked old, which Janine took to mean this horse couldn't hurt her.

A moment later she was uneasily sitting on top of the horse where Alberto had bodily placed her in the leather saddle. It cut into her flesh in places she didn't want to think about. On the horse's back, she stared straight ahead, afraid to look around. She must be a long way off the ground, and she really didn't want to find out.

Alberto remained standing on the ground next to her. He held the long leather reins and said, "The back of the saddle is called a cantle. Hold onto that with your right hand and put your left hand on your knee." When Alberto led the horse forward, Janine could feel every step and tried to grab the saddle horn several times.

"Janine, if you do that you will only throw yourself off balance and that makes it easier to fall off," Alberto explained.

She immediately dropped her hand and grasped the back again.

"You see, Sophia has a steady gait. Once you relax you will find it easier to sit. Now if you would take hold of the reins."

Janine shook her head clinging to the back of the saddle. "I can't hold both," she told him.

"Of course you can. Here take them." He draped the reins across Sophia's neck and stepped back. Sophia moved forward to follow him.

With clumsy hands, Janine grabbed for the reins and pulled back. Sophia stopped.

"Now loosen the reins," he prompted her.

Janine, with her insides shaking, did as he said. "I think I've done enough. I'm ready to get down now."

"Just a bit longer, I think you have a very good start."

Janine could barely control her growing apprehension.

"Good. Now shorten the reins just a length…that's right," he said, watching her hands. "I knew you would have a gentle grip, and the mare feels it too. Relax your shoulders, this isn't a military drill, and then she will even her gait."

"How will I stay on if I let myself move?" Her words shook with each of the horse's steps.

He reached over and grabbed the bridle to stop the mare. "You have it backwards, chica. The stiffer the rider's seat the easier it is to lose the beat of the horse and end up in the dirt."

Janine stared down at him in disbelief. She looked up at the horse's ears that were waving back and forth. "You're serious? Okay, I'll try, but I'm not sure if I can or not."

When Alberto began to walk the mare again, Janine forced herself to slouch her shoulders. She relaxed into the curve of the saddle. Janine was amazed at how much more comfortable she was. After a turn around the fence line, she didn't need to make herself relax. She was enjoying it. With the reins in one hand, and the other still on the cantle like Alberto showed her, she began to look around. The green field across from the barn seemed to lead directly to the ridge of mountains.

"Alberto, how long does it take to drive to the mountains?" she asked.

There was no answer. Alberto was not at the horse's head where he'd been before. Instantly, her body tensed and the reins tightened on the mare's mouth. Sophia immediately shook her head in protest. Her long ears flicked back and forth uneasily.

"Alberto," Janine hissed, afraid to scream like she wanted. The scream might scare the horse, and then Janine would fall to her death. "Alberto, where are you?"

Behind her she heard hoof beats. Paralyzed with fear, she couldn't move her head to see what was happening.

Alberto rode up next to her. The mare suddenly broke into a disjointed trot, tossing Janine in the saddle until Alberto reached for the reins to stop Sophia.

"I am right here," he said. "Now relax like you were doing

before. You were enjoying yourself. Admit it to me."

Janine, from sheer relief, laughed. "Si señor, you're right. I was enjoying myself." Her eyes shone with joy when she turned to look at him.

Her eyes widened in admiration at the sight of Alberto mounted on his flame red steed. She felt weak at how handsome he was.

"Ahh, I love it when you speak my language. I do so enjoy hearing the lilt of your northern accent."

Suddenly Janine looked around. "We aren't in the paddock!" she exclaimed in alarm.

"No, I wanted to take you a short distance to the village where my relatives live. They are curious about the American señorita, the one who haunts the garden walks and speaks to the servants in remarkably good Spanish for an American. But we will not go too far. You shouldn't ride too long the first time or you will suffer sore muscles tomorrow."

The sun smoldered above the ridge of the horizon. It was a fiery ball above the land that created colors Janine couldn't name but would never forget. Children played alongside the road she and Alberto rode down. Alberto called out to them, and they ran over, speaking rapidly to him and swarming around the horse's legs. Janine watched, fearful that his horse might step on one of them. Alberto paused to introduce her to the entire group. The children looked up at her and nodded. Some even gave a good imitation of a bow before they ran off. As soon as they were gone, Alberto swung his horse around to return. The mare followed him at a trot that almost jarred Janine's teeth loose.

"Tighten your knees and keep your heels down," Alberto said.

Janine did as he said and didn't flop around as much.

"The children, are they related to you?" she asked.

"Distantly," he said. "I would have brought you to visit the homes of my cousins, but it is almost suppertime, and the families are busy."

Janine was disappointed. She was curious about what a Spanish home looked like. Without a doubt, the Casilda hacienda could not be considered a conventional home.

The conversation between them died as they rode across the darkening land. The lack of light played tricks with her eyes. Janine stared down at the ground and realized it was jumping at her because she was falling forward. She clawed at the saddle horn with both hands, dropping the reins, which bounced across the horse's neck and fell out of reach to the ground. Sophia began to trot. Alberto was nowhere in sight and without a sound Janine fell like a stone to the ground.

She landed in the dust, her breath knocked out of her. She sat unmoving, her eyes clenched shut, waiting to be trampled under the mare's hooves. Nothing happened. Slowly, she opened her eyes and sat forward, stunned that she was not hurt.

"Janine, are you alright?" Alberto called, riding up a second later. "Sophia ran back to the barn without you." He swung off his horse and knelt beside her. "Are you injured?"

Janine reached to grab his shirt-front. Anger washed over her.

"You knew I didn't know what I was doing. How could you leave me?" she cried, tears streamed down her cheeks.

"You were doing so well. If you give riding a chance, you will be a natural horsewoman."

She shook her head. "Never, never will I get on one of those things again."

"Everyone feels that way the first time they fall off, but it will pass. I am sorry," he said cheerfully, "but you must."

She looked at his face, hidden in the shadows of evening. "No," she said. "I don't care how far away the barn is, I will walk back if it takes me all night."

"We still have a mile to go before we reach the barn," he said with a shrug and helped her to her feet. Janine clung to his arm but quickly realized she could stand.

"You can ride. I don't mind," Janine said.

Alberto held her arm as they started to walk, leading the stallion behind them. "There are many things on meseta hiding in the grass," he said.

"Oh right, like what?"

Alberto remained silent momentarily. "The horse would warn us if there were any snakes, but mostly the ground is a danger. Until the moon rises, we cannot see any holes. It will be easy to fall into one."

Janine stopped and crossed her arms defiantly.

"Fine," she said. "I'll ride, but I am not having anything to do with steering this thing." She gave him a look as she tried to mount the steed. "Don't you dare lift me into the saddle like you did before. I'll climb in by myself," she muttered, "if it kills me."

Alberto chuckled. "I would not think of doing anything more to upset you."

Alberto tossed the reins over the horse's neck. He stepped aside to allow Janine past. She grasped the leather straps and put her foot in the stirrup before hauling herself into the saddle. Out of breath, she sat upright and looked around. If she'd thought Sofia was tall, this horse was mammoth.

"It seems you can do much when you are angry, señorita. Now, you need to move behind the saddle," Alberto said from the ground.

"I would have to trust the horse to do that," Janine said, "and I don't."

"Then you will have to steer."

"Oh, all right then. If I must," she said, gingerly inching herself backwards out of the saddle and onto the horse's back. Alberto swung up into the saddle and clucked gently. The horse began to move. Janine grabbed his waist and closed her eyes, hanging on for her life. "This is completely crazy," she gritted out.

31

Pinpoints of light sparkled like tiny stars in the distance. Janine could not guess how far from the lights they were. The stallion's easy stride, as she and Alberto rode on his back together, had lulled her into a feeling of security even when she was perched so high above the ground. She sat so close to him, the heat from his body radiated through the cotton of his shirt, every movement of his body turned her thoughts to the times he held her in his arms. The sensation was so overwhelming she released her grip on his shirt and dropped her hands onto the cantle.

"What are you doing back there?"

"Nothing."

"It will not be long before we reach the barn. You have no reason to fear anymore," Alberto said. His voice sounded loud in the hush that surrounded them.

Janine almost laughed. Not only was she still afraid of the horses, but she was also afraid of the way she felt about Alberto. Now that she wasn't touching him, the sound of the horse's quiet, steady hoof falls, the bright stars blanketing the sky above, and the fact that she was completely alone with Alberto filled her with pure satisfaction. She gave a sigh of contentment.

"What was that for? Are you tired?"

Janine smiled. "No," she exclaimed, "quite the opposite. I think you're right. I could learn to enjoy horseback riding."

He turned to look at her over his shoulder. "You do? What brought this change of heart?"

Janine shook her head and laughed. "I don't think I can tell you exactly, except that as long as I don't have to worry about where the horse is going or how fast, it's great. Look over there, Berto. The full moon is just rising, and it's the most beautiful golden color."

Janine stared at the sky and wished she didn't ever have to go home. It would be so nice just to stay here horseback riding and swimming. She realized as long as it was just her and Alberto, she could be happy.

Alberto interrupted her thoughts. "It looks like our arrival is expected."

Janine peered around his shoulder and saw the lights outside of the stable had been turned on, completely illuminating the darkness of the yard.

Approaching the front of the barn, Alberto murmured softly to the horse, “Whoa, Diablo.” He stood in the stirrups and swung himself to the ground.

Janine remained unmoving. The muscles in her legs already ached from the unaccustomed activity, she didn’t know if they would support her once she was on the ground.

“Here, Janine, I will help you,” he said as he dropped the reins and held up his hands.

Janine winced as she slowly moved herself away from the saddle and leaned forward. Her legs wouldn’t move, and she could hardly get her leg over the horse’s rump to slide into his arms. “Ouch,” she cried. Her feet were numb when she hit the ground and pinpricks shot through them.

Alberto held her by the waist. “The riding lesson turned out to be satisfactory, though there were some unexpected twists.”

Janine tilted her head back to look at him and smiled. “I’d say very satisfactory, señor.”

“I must say, I was surprised that the pupil rebelled on several occasions,” he added keeping her close in the curve of his arms. Then, in the next moment, he pulled her against him and kissed her.

Janine ceased to breath, ceased to function. She felt herself drown in the swirling physical emotion this man was causing inside of her. The pleasant kisses they had exchanged before were nothing compared to the hungry passion in his lips when he claimed hers now. She clung to him, slipping her hands behind his back. She responded completely to his lips.

Alberto abruptly withdrew. His breathing heavy when he lifted his head, the sound of voices reached them.

Janine could only stare up at his face silhouetted in the light. Her fingers moved to touch her bruised mouth. She felt her breath warm and fast against her hand. She was stunned at how she could not control herself when he touched her.

The people walking to the barn from the hacienda could not see as Alberto gently brushed loose strands of hair from her face.

His hands remained touching the sides of her face as he met her gaze and smiled.

No words were necessary, and Janine smiled back feeling ridiculously happy.

He gathered the reins and clucked to the horse leading the way into the barn, "Pietro, vamanos."

A lanky youth dressed in baggy blue jeans and a dark tee-shirt hurried outside. His dark hair curled around his forehead, and his smile was so like the other members of the Casilda family she knew he was related and not distantly.

"Si, Berto," Pietro replied.

Alberto barely had time to hand over the reins of the horse before they heard Constancia's voice from the other side of the fence.

"Alberto, what is going on?" her voice held a sharp edge. "Galeno sent word to the house that your…guest's horse returned to the stable riderless and quite wild. What happened? Is she alright?"

Alberto laughed. "I hardly think Sophia has acted wild in many a year." His warm hand held Janine's as he walked toward the fence.

"Sophia's behavior is not important, what matters is…is the señorita unhurt?" Constancia demanded. As Janine came fully into view, Constancia said, "Oh, there you are. You look like you are limping. What happened?"

Janine opened her mouth to answer when an extraordinary voice interrupted. A heavy Spanish drawl slurred the English as if the language was unfamiliar. Janine's heart plummeted. She knew all of the Casilda's were fluent in English, so the speaker could only be Esmeralda.

"Alberto, how do you do it? Your mama asks me to come and meet the American señorita and each time some terrible mishap prevents it. Now the girl has fallen off of Sophia." Mocking laughter was heard from Esmeralda de Martés. She moved forward out of the shadows to stand next to Constancia, her hands rested on her narrow hips.

Janine couldn't stop staring no matter how unwilling she was to see the woman Constancia had designed to make Alberto's bride.

The shadows hid the fine details of Esmeralda's face but nothing could hide her height. Next to Constancia, she looked as tall as an Amazon, with long legs that were completely bare to her mid-thigh. The voluptuous curves of her slender figure were outlined in the glare of the light, but the outfit she wore hardly looked decent for a family supper invitation. Shocked by her first glimpse of Esme, Janine openly gaped at her. The woman was everything Janine wasn't, and she wanted to shrivel up and hide.

"I do not feel this is the appropriate time for introductions," Alberto said, his voice cold. "Papa, please will you escort the ladies back to the house. Señorita Janine needs a chance to prepare to meet the guest. And you, Rico, don't just stand there, go with your father and be entertaining."

Carlos agreed and spoke to Constancia as he took her arm and quite deliberately turned her back in the direction of the house. "We will wait in the solarium, Berto, until you are ready to join us."

Constancia opened her mouth to argue but remained strangely speechless as she walked beside her husband.

Esmeralda remained where she was and cooed in a smug tone, "Berto, are you certain the American señorita is able to make it on her own? She does not look well."

Alberto turned to Janine. His broad shoulders completely blocked her from Esmeralda's sight. He leaned close. "Tell me señorita," he asked with mischief dancing on his face, "are you certain after your ordeal that you have the strength to walk to the cottage or shall I perhaps carry you in my arms?" He lifted one dark brow in question.

Janine quickly shook her head. "Gracias for the offer, señor, but I am quite well."

"No? How disappointing, but I am not surprised, since you would not allow me to help you mount a horse, even one as tall as Diablo. Let me assure you it would not be a hardship for me."

Janine laughed and shook her head no again.

"Well then, I shall have to be content with simply holding onto your arm. Rico, we will see you at the house."

32

Esmeralda silently watched as the couple walked away. Hot anger gripped her. Her throat closed, stopping the fury of words she wanted to scream after them: "Alberto is mine. No woman will take him away from me." She saw how the woman clung to Alberto's arm. "You are trespassing on my territory. For that you will be sorry," she snarled under her breath.

Suddenly, Frederico stood right beside her. "What did you say?" he asked.

Esmeralda tightened her lips and refused to answer.

"Come, we might as well return to the house and wait," he said. "There is no reason to remain. My mother will be expecting you, and there is the matter of why you did not grace us with your presence at lunch the other day. I am quite certain you have a perfect excuse. You always do."

With a toss of her head, she ignored Frederico and said with a sneer, "It is cold out here. I will now return to the hacienda." She kicked off the absurdly high stiletto heels she was wearing and glanced speculatively at Frederico. He was no Alberto, but maybe she could use him to get Alberto's attention away from the American. She masked her irritation and her expression changed to a pout. She moved closer to him.

"Rico, you are such a tease. I do have an excuse about yesterday. I hope Constancia will not be too angry after she hears it. You all know my father's health is not what it should be, so there are many times I am forced to stay by his bedside in case something," she lowered her voice to a whisper, "terrible should happen. I would never forgive myself if I was not by his side."

"I knew you would understand," Esmeralda cooed as she moved closer. "There has always been this little understanding between the two of us. I have a feeling that the time might be ripe to see if this feeling might turn into something more."

Frederico narrowed his eyes and remained silent as he lit a cigarette.

"Alberto did ask you to walk me to the hacienda, Rico." She slid her hand slowly over the curve of Frederico's arm until she had wrapped her fingers securely around it.

"I will be more than happy to, Esme," Frederico said. He slowly blew the cigarette smoke between his lips before he reached down to pry her fingers from his bicep. "But first I will make this perfectly clear. There has never been anything between us, and there never will be. Neither I nor Berto will fall for your vicious little games, so you might as well give up."

"You damn Casildas," Esmeralda said hotly.

"Why do you say that, dear Esme?" Frederico asked innocently.

"Why do you care?" she spat out.

"You're upset. Obviously it is out of concern for the well-being of Señorita Janine. I must tell you she is under the best of care, as you well know."

Esmeralda seethed at his taunting remarks. "I do not care if she lives or dies. And why do you think I am after you or your brother? It is ridiculous. We are like brothers and sister."

Frederico laughed loudly and began walking toward the hacienda.

Esmeralda winced at the sound and joined him.

"There is no way we have ever felt that way. You might as well put your claws away, Esmeralda, and behave yourself around my family. If you know what is good for you, you'll just forget about Alberto and the American."

Esmeralda clenched her fist so tight the length of her nails cut into the flesh of her inner hand. She feigned a careless laugh. "Rico, you have to be joking with me, but if it will make you happy, then I have forgotten about Alberto and the girl. There. It is done."

Frederico flicked the cigarette into the dirt. "For your sake, I certainly hope so."

"Why are you so concerned with her?" Esmeralda asked him slyly. "Perhaps it is you she really wants to be with and not Alberto."

Frederico's voice softened. "I would be honored to find a woman like her. She is gentle and innocent and has the most agreeable temperament. Everyone in the family agrees with Alberto's choice."

At Frederico's words, a flash of violent rage clouded Esmeralda's thoughts and she closed her eyes, stumbling to a halt. Slowly, she opened her eyes as she gained control over the feeling.

"Where is the liberated woman I hear all the Americans are? This one, she is an infant. An innocent as you say, but perhaps it isn't because she is virtuous," Esmeralda spat the word out. "Alberto may be mistaken. She is probably just dumb or a mute."

"She works in a library."

"Then I am right," Esmeralda exclaimed triumphantly. "If the American government employs her, she must be handicapped in some way."

Frederico laughed again just as loudly. "Your ability to manipulate the little knowledge you acquire is truly frightening to me."

Esmeralda turned to him with a movement so filled with violence Frederico stepped back.

"You are such a fool, Rico," she spit out through tightly clenched teeth and stalked off, disappearing into the shadows that surrounded the front porch.

33

Standing in the bathroom, looking at a starry-eyed stranger in the mirror, Janine touched her lips remembering Alberto's passionate kiss. She didn't look any different. Somehow she thought being in love was supposed to change a person's appearance, but it only caused a deep ache in the pit of her stomach.

"How can I be such a fool to fall in love with him?" she cried and turned from the mirror. Continuing to talk to herself, she said to the walls, "There is no hope for us and I know it. He can never leave his home, and I can never live with a resentful mother-in-law." She dragged a comb through her wet hair while she looked over the clothes laid out on the bed. She slipped the filmy skirt over her head, and it settled around her waist. The silk made her feel very feminine, and the brilliant colors of the matching top shone like precious stones; sapphire, ruby, and emerald. The material looked expensive even though it wasn't. This was going to be a difficult evening for her to get through with the neighbor waiting to attack. Janine had heard the hatred in her voice and knew she was no match for the beautiful Spanish señorita.

Outside, clouds scudded across the sky. The humidity in the air rose as the rumble of thunder could be heard over the mountains. There was the promise of a storm in the near future, especially when the wind shifted, moving briskly through the thick leafy trees overhead. The rustle of the leaves hid the soft tread of high-heeled shoes along the stone path leading to the guesthouse. The rhythm of the high-heeled step stopped for several moments as the walker peered through the swaying tree boughs to study the shadow of Janine in the second story window.

A flash of lightning outlined the face of Esmeralda de Martés. Her features were so distorted that few would recognize her. Some, like the Casilda men, suspected a trace of insanity existed in Esmeralda, but even they had never seen this evil surface. With her scarlet painted fingernails clenched into the flesh of her hand, Esmeralda stopped still, hidden in the shadows. She didn't have a plan, but she knew there was no way this American was going to stop her from marrying Alberto Casilda. She had pursued him far too long. Not only was he rich and destined to become richer once he took over the estate, his most important quality was that he was going to help her have her long-delayed revenge, and the only way to be successful was for her to become Señora Casilda.

Alberto was the first cousin to the King of Spain, Juan Carlos I. With his direct lineage to the royal family, becoming Alberto's wife would give her tremendous power. The mere thought of it sent a thrill through her.

As Señora Casilda, the blue-blooded women and men who had shunned Esmeralda all her life would be forced to accept her. No longer could they refuse to welcome her into the social gatherings that she craved. No home in Spain, in Portugal, or in South America could turn her away. With Alberto's money and prestige, she would be free to do as she liked.

This fantasy of Esmeralda's had been building in her mind since she noticed how differently people treated her. No matter what explanation people gave, she knew it was because she wasn't from the right family. Tonight's duty was to dispose of the pesky American.

She had thought Frederico would be a problem. He always seemed to get in the way of her schemes, but he had gone on by himself. She waited outside the hacienda until the Casildas and the mother of the American were settled in the solarium. It was then she made her way to the guest cottage. She knew that woman, Janine, was alone.

Esmeralda removed her shoes and crept around the porch railing and up the guest house steps. A movement out of the corner of her eye caught her attention, and she stopped. Instantly, she relaxed her tightly wound body to hide her emotions.

A tall man with a thick build stepped from underneath the flowering arbor that hung over the porch near the patio door. Esmeralda found it hard to control her shock at his appearance. She would have screamed if she hadn't become such an accomplished actress.

"Señor," she exclaimed with a husky laugh. "The wind must have hidden the sound of your arrival. You surprised me." She spoke in a pleasant tone, but that was all. With him she knew not to waste her time with flattery or seduction.

"Si señorita," he replied, his squashed features unreadable. He stood silently with his arms crossed over his massive chest, blocking the patio door Esmeralda had been planning to enter.

"Constancia has sent me to walk with the American," she glibly lied. "She was worried that the storm might upset her. She must be a flighty woman to let a little storm bother her." Esmeralda shrugged her thin shoulders as if such weakness was beyond her understanding.

Galeno's expression didn't change. "The señorita already has an escort."

Esmeralda bit her lip to hold back the scathing comment she longed to say. Instead she forced a smile. "Then I shall see what is taking her so long." She stepped forward.

Galeno moved closer at the same moment, looking as impassable as a brick wall. He shook his grizzled gray head. "The señorita is not to be disturbed." His voice was a deep rumble from his chest.

"This is nonsense, Galeno," Esmeralda argued. She tried to keep her voice from becoming shrill. "If I return to the house alone and inform Constancia that you refused to allow me to help the señorita in any way, she will be displeased, very displeased."

Galeno didn't bother to reply this time. He merely kept his dark eyes on Esmeralda.

Esmeralda clenched her teeth. She did not want to lose this opportunity to stop the American. There was no question about it, she would never get past Galeno nor would she try. She was afraid of the man. In Madrid, he had proven his unfailing loyalty to Alberto. She had pushed him too far only that one time, and she never wanted to be the object of Galeno's loyal wrath again.

Finally, with a heavy sigh, she tossed her head and turned to leave the patio entrance. "I have no choice but to go back alone. The family will not be happy about this," she warned as she walked along the circular porch of the house to go around him.

Galeno fell into step directly behind her.

With an angry snort, she spun around to glare at him. His face, with its thick features and misshapen nose looked sinister in the shadows. Esmeralda stamped her foot. "What are you doing?" she demanded, not bothering to hide her aggravation.

"The señorita is not to be disturbed while she remains on the hacienda."

Esmeralda's eyes narrowed. She read in his words the warning and knew she was wasting her time. "Fine. I shall return to the hacienda!" Esmeralda attempted to push past the man's massive body. He blocked her path.

"Get out of my way, you idiot," she cried.

Slowly, he stepped aside, and Esmeralda darted past him up the path.

A slight smirk crept onto Galeno's grizzled face as he stared after Esmeralda. He was about to follow when Janine appeared in the kitchen window of the cottage. He watched as she slipped a bracelet around her wrist and then picked up her handbag.

34

Janine turned off the lights and opened the sliding door. "Galeno," she exclaimed.

She was startled to see him for the first time since she had arrived in Spain but smiled, genuinely pleased to see his familiar face. "How nice to see you," she said as she stepped outside.

Galeno moved quickly to step behind her and slide the door closed.

"I thought I heard voices out here," Janine said with a glance past him hoping to see Alberto.

"Buenas noches, señorita," Galeno said. "Perhaps it is the wind you are hearing?"

She looked skeptical. "I don't think so. You aren't out here waiting for me, are you? Oh no, I've taken too long to get ready. Have I kept the family waiting? It doesn't matter, I've kept you waiting, I'm sorry."

Galeno shook his head as he held his arm out to her. "I am here to escort you to the hacienda at your convenience. Time does not matter."

She looked up at him. "Do you remember the first time you waited for me?" She laughed as she remembered their first meeting on the bus.

The wind blew in heavy gusts that carried moisture in them. They added an unexpected chill to the air and she shivered.

"Galeno prefers not to be reminded of that, chica," Alberto said, joining them. He stepped from between the hedges beside the path that led from the shrine. "I am afraid his ego still suffers from the fact that you so easily lost him."

"As a stranger in a strange land, I think Galeno did a marvelous job tracking me down." Her eyes were on Alberto until he turned to look at her. Her breath caught as she wondered if he remembered as clearly as she their kiss.

"Janine, will you excuse us for a moment?" he asked.

Janine dropped her eyes, suddenly too shy to do anything but nod.

The two men walked several steps up the path toward the house.

She waited, looking up at the threatening sky. She glanced back at the men anxiously as lightning flashed, giving the clouds an eerie yellow glow. Galeno spoke quickly while Alberto listened. Galeno suddenly turned and bowed to Janine before he stepped away into the darkness.

Janine hurried up the path. A peal of thunder rolled above them. Janine flinched.

"It comes from the mountains," Alberto explained. "We still have hours before the rains will cross over and reach us."

Janine shaded her eyes from the glare of the spotlights on the house. "I don't remember ever seeing those lights before."

"The torches will not remain lit in this wind," he explained. "They are to light the path."

Alberto entwined their fingers as he faced her. "Buenas noches, beautiful señorita. You look exceptionally pretty in your finery." He reached to cup her chin in his hand. His thumb smoothed the skin along her bone moving up her cheek. Her face heated from his touch. He chuckled softly and said, "You still blush when I speak the truth about you."

"A compliment should never be taken for granted, but I think you're far too generous."

"I speak as I see." He lightly brushed her lips with his.

The contact was nothing like this afternoon, but Janine still felt her flesh tingle.

"Come, we must get to the house."

They began to walk. Within minutes, large drops of water began to fall around them. Alberto grabbed her hand, and they began to run as the clouds burst open to dump a steady sheet of rain. Out of breath and dripping, Alberto flung open the patio door, and they fell inside.

Janine stood dripping while water puddled under her nose and chin. Her hair hung in lank tendrils clinging to her wet skin. She pushed it aside to give Alberto a look. "How long before the rain?"

He shrugged. "The rain must be traveling faster than I thought."

Janine laughed and then shivered. "That's an understatement. I'm just glad this didn't happen when we were riding. I could never have handled Sophia in a storm."

Alberto laughed. "You seemed quite able to do what you

wanted once you lost your fear."

Janine watched the rain slide down the glass door and saw her reflection in the glass. She dreaded going upstairs. She knew how the two women would watch her with malicious eyes. Now that she was completely drenched, they would get quite an eyeful, and she could do nothing about it.

"It will not matter," Alberto said, seeing her concern. "You are beautiful."

"Señor Alberto," a voice called breathlessly from the hallway.

"It is Carmen. The meal must be ready," he told Janine. "Carmen, please come here and help Señorita Janine. We were caught in the storm."

Carmen's quick staccato footsteps could be heard long before she came into view.

"Oh, señorita," Carmen gasped. She moved closer, pushing Alberto out of her way. "How could you do this to her?" she admonished him angrily. "Go upstairs and explain to your mama what has happened."

Then she ignored him as she gestured for Janine to follow her. "Hurry, my dear, before you catch a deathly cold." Shaking her head in disapproval toward the nonplussed Alberto, she opened the closest door in the hallway.

Janine glanced at Alberto, who, without a word, turned away. There was nothing for Janine to do but follow Carmen.

In seconds, Carmen had pulled a large bath towel out of a dresser drawer and handed it to her. "If you blot the material it will dry faster," she explained as she wrapped another towel around Janine's trembling shoulders. "Such a lovely outfit. How inconsiderate of Señor Alberto to allow you to be caught in the rain."

With Carmen's assistance, Janine's clothes were only slightly damp when they silently walked up the stairs.

Janine already had a picture in her mind of what awaited her. The family would be seated at the table. Everyone would stop to stare at her when Carmen brought her in like a drowned rat.

Carmen left her at the door as she hurried down the hallway to the kitchen. Janine took a deep breath and walked inside. The long trestle table had been covered with a white linen cloth and tall white candles decorated the length of it. The candles added a cozy, festive atmosphere to the dining area. The rain lashed against the windows. Janine quickly glanced around the table and saw that Joan was sitting at the end of the table next to Señor Casilda and across from Frederico. The chair next to her was empty. With a smile, Janine eagerly moved to take the seat. The two men stood for her.

Alberto moved out of the shadows to hold her chair. "That was not so bad, was it?" he whispered to her.

Janine glanced at him and their eyes met. "Not when you're here."

Alberto grinned, and spoke up. "Rico, trade places with me."

Down the length of the table there was another empty chair positioned next to Constancia and across from Esmeralda. Frederico was still standing and, without a word, picked up his soup bowl and wine glass to do as Alberto asked. Before he sat down in his new seat, Frederico held his glass out to Janine and inclined his head to her. Then he drank.

At his silent salute, Janine gave him a smile that showed the depth of her gratitude. Deliberately, Janine stopped herself from looking in the direction of Constancia and Esmeralda.

As the meal progressed, Alberto and Carlos discussed ranch matters. Both Joan and Janine were captivated by the conversation, asking questions about the business end of running a vast enterprise.

At the other end of the table, the fury inside of Esmeralda was hidden behind a mask of boredom. Esmeralda needed a chance to think about this situation. As she watched Alberto, she knew he wasn't going to leave the señorita alone tonight. Galeno had told Alberto the whole story about the confrontation at the guest house, so now they would all be watching her. Her thoughts stirred up her rage again, and she hissed through her teeth loud enough for Constancia to hear.

"Is something wrong, Esme?"

Esmeralda brushed at her arm. "I must have been bitten by a gnat," she explained, though in her mind, she thought, "The sooner I escape the better." Esmeralda lifted her glass and looked toward the other end of the table. She caught Frederico looking at her with that smirk on his face. She knew he was laughing at her. If Frederico was able to read her thoughts, then she needed to go. Esmeralda jumped out of her seat before the dessert was brought in.

Everyone at the table stopped talking and looked at her, which is exactly what Esmeralda wanted. "I have just looked at the clock. I didn't realize it was already so late. Of course we did have to wait," she gave Janine a look that showed her displeasure, "but I must leave. I have left my dear father alone far too long, and I need to check on him before he falls asleep."

Carlos set down his fork and napkin. "Someone in town told me that you had said your father was in poor health." Carlos gave Esmeralda a direct look. "I went to see him today and found him in perfect health. He still does not leave the house often, but he assured me he felt fine."

Esmeralda did not even blink. "He is embarrassed. He doesn't want anyone to know. I am sorry that you did not ask me, Señor Carlos. I would have told you everything because we are like family to each other."

She stepped away from the table and moved to the door. "Perdon, Señora Constancia. Perdon, Señor Carlos, but I must go."

The silence from Esmeralda's unexpected exit lasted only seconds.

"Do not be alarmed, Janine and Joan," Frederico called cheerfully from his seat. "Esmeralda is always blowing in and out of here. She is unpredictable. I think that is something all of us can agree on," he added, looking at Constancia.

Constancia shrugged and took a sip of her wine.

35

"Mama, how could you accept without speaking to us first?" Frederico protested. He stood to pace. "Alberto, why don't you speak up," he implored.

Alberto leaned against the door frame. His head was back and his eyes were closed.

"Your brother has a tongue in his head, Frederico," Carlos said quietly. "If he objects, he will speak for himself."

Alberto shifted his shoulders but didn't open his eyes.

"What exactly is your objection, Rico?" Constancia asked. "The last summons the family received infuriated Alberto, but you were more than ready for the excitement of the festivities in Madrid."

Frederico stopped at the bar to pour sherry into a delicate crystal glass and walked over to hand it to his mother.

Constancia touched his hand. "You realize we must go, Rico. This is a summons from the royal family. It cannot be ignored. If you are worried about Alberto's guests, I am sure they will find the Spanish court very exciting. Americans always do. The señorita will find much to see at the royal palace."

Silence fell over the room. Everyone seemed to be considering the implications.

"It will work, Rico," Alberto said, moving suddenly into center of the room. "It is only a day earlier than we had planned to leave for Madrid anyway. I am sure the Nielsen's won't object to an early departure, especially with this foul weather."

Frederico, after drinking his brandy, asked, "What could possibly have caused Juan Carlos to bring everyone to Madrid at this time of year?"

"Probably a wedding in the family," Carlos said with a glance at Alberto. "Or maybe the king is going to become a grandfather."

Alberto smiled. "A new baby. That is a reason to celebrate. Another heir. I hope you are right, Papa."

"If it is a new heir to the throne, I lose all hope of inheriting Hacienda Casilda," Frederico said, pouring another splash of the amber liquid into his glass.

Everyone in the room turned to him.

Frederico glanced up and sighed before he laughed. "What? There has always been the chance that Alberto might be called to Madrid to take his rightful place."

Alberto stood in front of his brother with arms crossed. "I find this sudden desire to be more involved in the ranch a refreshing change, Rico. Papa and I have been discussing a business venture, and now, with your newfound enthusiasm for the business, I will be able to investigate it further. We'll discuss it in more detail when this royal summons distraction has been taken care of." Alberto turned and looked at his father.

Carlos nodded at his son in approval.

Frederico's dismay was evident.

"Now, do not be too worried, little brother," Alberto grinned, "a little responsibility will not kill you."

"Alberto, Frederico, and you," Constancia interrupted with a look at her husband. "I will need your uniforms tonight. It takes two days to have them ready for the presentation. There are so many details I must see about."

Carlos stood up. "Don't worry dear, we all know what has to be done, and it won't help anything if you worry about it all night," he assured her before leaving the room.

Constancia stood with a sigh and followed him.

36

Long before sunrise, the Casilda household teemed with life. Everyone was busy with preparations to leave the hacienda and make the journey to the royal courts in Madrid.

Alberto welcomed the sun. He had slept little and spent most of the early hours working in the barn office to clear his ledgers before the family and their guests left. As he walked briskly from the barn up the gravel road he kept one eye on the sky's threatening clouds. From the farm to the horizon in the far distance there were huge masses of dark clouds roiling, but directly behind was a barely visible line of golden light—the promise of blue sky and sunshine. He laughed at himself. "After last night's drenching, Janine will never believe any weather report from me again."

Alberto's mind turned to the task he had to face now. He needed to talk to Janine about the change in plans. Could his mother be right? Would she take it in stride? In the last ten days, had the routine of the ranch become mundane for her? If Janine became easily bored with life at the hacienda, he had a problem. If this was true, she would never be happy living here.

It was not the first time he had doubts about following his heart in pursuit of Janine, but now he needed to face reality. Janine must accept not only him, but his family and the hacienda. It was a package deal.

In Madrid, everything would be completely different. There was always a lot of visiting family and old friends stopping in at the house. There were the shopping excursions and long meals spent dining in restaurants. And now, to complicate things further, the formal visit to court. All of the activity in Madrid would be a sharp contrast to the leisurely morning swims and peaceful walks in the garden or any of the other activities they had been enjoying.

In court, the rules of behavior expected between single men and single women were stricter, and Alberto intended to closely follow these rules of propriety. His behavior with his future wife must be exemplary. Alberto smiled at the thought of Janine Nielsen as Mrs. Alberto Casilda. He ducked under the low hanging branch of flowering crimson azaleas that clung to the porch roof of the guest cottage.

Janine stood at the kitchen counter of the guest cottage and drank a glass of orange juice. She was still half asleep. She hadn't yet bothered to dress. The cotton pajama shirt that hugged her curves revealed her mid-thigh and the faint beginnings of a golden tan. She stretched and turned to look through the full glass door at the early morning. Alberto was striding up the walkway.

Janine almost dropped the glass. Frantic to remain unseen, she crouched down behind the counter and peered around the corner to watch him. He knocked and glanced at his watch. Janine, barely breathing, hoped he might go away. He knocked again. After several minutes of frozen indecision, she decided he was not going to leave, but she didn't know what would bring him to the guest cottage at that hour. When Alberto looked away, Janine jumped up and, cheeks hot and bright pink with embarrassment, she rushed to unlatch the lock. She felt practically naked although he'd seen her in much less at the pool.

"Buenos días, señor," she murmured shyly as she slid the glass door open.

"Perdon, señorita, for disturbing you so early," he said, absently brushing past her. He wore his work clothes and brought into the small room the smell of leather and horse.

Janine looked at him, alarmed at his abruptness. "What is it? Has something happened?"

He shrugged. "No, nothing is wrong. I apologize for arriving unannounced and smelling like the stable, but there is something I have to discuss with you." He paused, frowning. "I wonder... should we call Joan? It concerns her also." He glanced at the doorway leading into the main part of the guesthouse.

Janine shook her head. "Mother isn't here. She's gone for a walk in the garden."

Alberto turned back to Janine. His dark eyes slowly traveled up the length of her.

Janine remembered what she had on and casually stepped behind the counter as if seeking protection. "If you give me a minute, I can get dressed and by then mother will be back."

He shook his head, an appreciative gleam in his eyes and a half smile on his lips. "I am sorry, Janine," he said, "but there is no time. I hope the change will not upset you or your mother too much, but we must leave for Madrid earlier than planned."

Janine laughed. "Is that all? Goodness, Berto, I couldn't imagine what you were going to say. Of course we can go whenever you want. I'm sure my mother will be fine with the change."

He moved closer. "Are you feeling restless here at the hacienda?

Janine looked up and realized how tall he was when she didn't have any shoes on. "No, of course not."

"I hope you feel the same after Madrid," he murmured.

Janine frowned. "Is there something wrong with Madrid?"

"It is not like here, but Madrid has its compensations. There is plenty of excitement, crowds, and more diverse entertainment. That is important to many people."

"It must be pretty amazing," Janine said, "but none of that sounds more exciting than what we've been doing here. I've learned to ride a horse, I've swam everyday in a private pool, and I've walked through gardens that seem to go on forever. I've had a great time."

Alberto fell silent.

The coffee pot growled loudly in the sudden quietness.

"Would you like a cup of coffee?"

He inhaled deeply. "Yes, gracias, only half." In a quick movement, he sat down, settling his long legs around the stool.

Janine busied herself with the cups and saucers. It was distracting to have him watching her when she had to move carefully to keep her pajamas in place. "Is the entire family coming with us?"

"Everyone. The house will be closed."

"All because we have to leave for Madrid early?" she asked in disbelief.

Alberto choked on the coffee he had swallowed. "No, of course not. The month of August is a time for families to prepare for the harvest. Every year they take the month off and return to their homes. The family would usually take over the work around here. But this year, since we were going to Madrid, anyway, mama has decided to stay. Only a few of the caballeros will remain to care for the livestock, but even as we speak, the entire house staff is leaving to return to their own homes."

"When exactly are we leaving? I'll have to tell mom."

"After siesta today, Janine."

The cup in her hand rattled. She sipped the hot coffee too fast and burned her tongue. "Three o'clock? My, that is soon," she mumbled, then hastily added, "but of course it doesn't matter. I've barely unpacked my suitcase, and mother's so efficient I'm sure she's already repacked her own." She watched him expectantly and had the feeling he had not finished.

"There is something else, and now is a better time to bring it up. When we travel with the family, there will not be a lot of time for conversation."

Janine pictured a cross-country car trip with a boisterous family, the rambunctious children. She completely understood what he meant.

"I know we have never spoken about money. I believe you do not give it much thought."

Janine couldn't help laughing. "That's easy when you're a hard-up librarian. I think it's better to say I have a healthy respect for my limitations where cash is concerned. Why?"

"Madrid is not like here," he began slowly, choosing his words with care. "We plan to stay in our home and will eat most our meals in, but there are a few formal occasions that the family must attend."

Janine's mouth fell open. "Formal? How curious, I certainly never expected there to be any formal occasions. Did my mother know? She never told me."

"No, this was completely unexpected."

"Really? An unexpected formal occasion, now I understand what you meant when you said Madrid is exciting. But you mustn't be concerned about us, Berto. We certainly don't expect to be included, especially when the occasion requires formal dress."

Alberto shook his head. "You and your mother will be honored guests at every gathering my family attends. The Spanish are noted for their hospitality, especially to representatives from another county. The only reason I brought this up is, you and your mother did not come prepared for such an engagement, and I wanted you to know arrangements for suitable garments have already been made. There will be nothing for either of you to worry about."

Janine remained silent, every fiber inside of her protested against the thought of him providing them with clothes, but she found herself agreeing.

"What else can we do?" she quipped, sounding unusually logical.

Alberto stood. "That is settled then. This morning will be rather hectic so I will not be at the pool."

"Goodness no," Janine exclaimed. "I'm sure I won't be able to make it either."

"Until later, adiós, la bonito."

When he left, Janine groaned and laid her head on the counter. Now that he was gone she remembered why she did not like to travel. Packing, arranging good-byes, she disliked the whole thing. "Three o'clock, we are leaving here at three o'clock," she muttered out loud. "I'll never be ready."

And at the same time she wondered if she would ever be ready to leave the Hacienda Casilda.

37

Joan seemed unaffected by the abrupt change of plans. "Madrid has so much to see. I've been reading all about it."

Janine listened but did not comment. She was putting her purse back together. She had taken everything out to be certain she hadn't misplaced anything of importance: passport, plane ticket, or traveler's checks. Their suitcases were packed and waiting outside on the verandah to be picked up and stowed in the car.

Joan sighed. "I know it's ridiculous, but I've become quite fond of this cottage. I'm going to miss being here."

"Not ridiculous, I was just thinking the same thing," Janine said. She was filled with regrets. There were so many things she had wanted to do but had not found the time. Soon the two of them would walk up the stone path to the main house for the last time. "Did you read about Madrid in the travel books?" Janine questioned. It was hard for her to have any interest in Madrid.

"No, I found some books in the family library."

Joan looked in the mirror as she carefully placed her hat over her faded blond curls. "I don't know why I bothered to curl my hair. It will fall flat as a pancake as soon as we leave the air conditioning. Did you see the library, Janine?"

"No," Janine sighed. Another lost opportunity now that they were leaving the hacienda.

Joan frowned. "I was wondering why you never mentioned it. You wouldn't believe the books they have on art and art galleries. I never asked, but I think somehow the Casilda's have more than just a passing interest in the art world."

"That's just one more thing I never got to do," Janine gave a frustrated cry. "I wanted to sketch the house so I can paint it once we're home, and I never did. Alberto promised to take me to the shrine again, but we didn't make it.

"The first morning Alberto and I sat together on a stone bench in front of the shrine, he told me that a shrine is a chapel under the sky." Janine sighed heavily. "He explained that it was but one of the shrines on the hacienda. They're scattered all around. It is a tradition that the eldest Casilda son, after his wedding, builds and dedicates a shrine to Our Lady. 'One day I will take you to visit them all and together we will read the plaques dedicated to the women loved by the Casilda men.'"

Joan looked at her daughter with mild disbelief on her face.

Janine remembered feeling the peace of the place, and she could not wait to return, but now she was leaving. If only someday she could come back.

Joan interrupted her thoughts. "You were busy learning to ride a horse instead of visiting shrines or reading. I've been here three weeks longer than you, and I never rode a horse."

While she knew Joan would never say it out loud, Janine could practically hear her mother's reminder: "You, too, were invited to come and visit for a month."

They closed the door for the last time, and Joan led the way up the path to the house.

"Why are we going the long way, mother? It's shorter to go through the pool area."

"Frederico stopped by when you were in the shower. He said that the pool area has already been locked up."

As they got to the front of the hacienda, there was no car waiting. There was no Galeno, no Frederico, nobody. "Where is everyone?" Joan asked. "Siesta ended half an hour ago."

The wide stone porch shaded by tall palm fronds was empty. No cars waited in the driveway.

"I prefer to wait for them rather than making them wait for us," Janine said. She walked up the stone step and sat down in one of the white wicker chairs. It was hot, but the front porch was out of the sun and it felt cooler. She looked around and said softly, "It's hard to believe that in just a few months this will all feel like part of a lovely dream."

Joan didn't hear her. "I don't know what is keeping them, but it's too hot to wait out here. I'm going inside to see what's going on."

"I'll wait here," Janine told her. She leaned back in the chair. It was nice to have a few moments of peace to just look at all the beauty surrounding her. She reveled in the solitude. The heat encouraged only the insects to move about, to interrupt and buzz around the abundant flowers.

"Señorita," Janine heard from the doorway. "Oh, American señorita, are you out here?"

Janine sat forward in alarm. It was Esmeralda. She scrambled to her feet. Once she was up, she grabbed her purse and turned to run. The front door stood open, and a shiver of apprehension ran through her when she faced Esmeralda de Martés.

The whip slender woman stood just inside the door of the house. She smiled, the gesture almost a grimace, thin lips, covered with bright red lipstick, stretched across her teeth. Esmeralda looked like a gypsy. She wore her hair bound in a crimson and black scarf that revealed her slender neck and high cheek bones. Her wide-spaced eyes, slanted at the corners, added to her exotic appearance. The crimson blouse and black skirt she wore were like the outfit from last night and left nothing of her figure to the imagination.

In her own sleeveless white cotton sundress with her golden brown hair cascading in long curls down her back, Janine suddenly felt overheated and insignificant, with little sex appeal.

Esmeralda took a step closer to Janine and gave a short laugh as she towered over her. "Have you not dressed for the trip yet? The family does not like to be kept waiting."

Janine didn't answer, but suddenly felt her resentment rising at the woman's behavior. No person with any modicum of decency spoke to other people this way. And whom did she think she was directing Janine on good manners. She was the rudest person Janine had ever met. "Are you waiting to say good-bye?" Janine asked coldly.

"Oh no, I am to travel to Madrid with the family. Constancia would not allow me to say no to the invitation."

A lump formed in Janine's throat. She was sure the special formal invitation Alberto had spoken about included Esmeralda. "I see. Well then, if you will excuse me, I have to find my mother." She would have said anything to be out of the woman's presence.

"Wait, señorita, I have a message for you. Rico asked me to find you. The family wants you to choose a memory of the hacienda since you will never be coming back here," she sneered. "I am to show you where he is," she said and turned to leave.

Janine clutched her purse tightly, hesitating to go anywhere with Esmeralda. “Where who is?”

“What are you doing?” she heard Esmeralda’s voice from inside.

Janine stood her ground. “Who wants to see me?”

“Alberto.”

Still Janine was uncertain. There was this jealous anger Esmeralda felt toward her. Janine did not know why. Esmeralda was fantastic looking and had Constancia eating out of her hand. All of the things Janine wished for, Esmeralda possessed.

“Come, come,” Esmeralda snapped. “Everyone is anxious to leave and the longer you keep them waiting the more angry they will be.”

Finally, Janine gave in. Her curiosity won over her distrust. Besides, what could Esmeralda possibly do? She had to stop letting her imagination run away with her. Janine hurried down the hall.

38

The house was big, and Janine was certain she had never been in this section before. The passage was narrower and the doors on either side of the hall were closed. There weren't any windows. Once she thought she heard muted voices, but she couldn't place where the sound was coming from.

"Where are we?" she asked after following Esmeralda's lead for several minutes.

Esmeralda barely glanced back at her. "In the staff quarters. This is where all the staff sleep, except the stable hands, they stay in the bunkhouse. You did not get to see much of the house while you were here. I suppose you were never upstairs," she said, her tone smug. "You missed seeing the most beautiful part of the house. Alberto's room is…." She gave a low laugh. "Well, you wouldn't be interested in knowing about that."

Janine glared at the woman's back as they wove their way through the many, many rooms of the hacienda. She was sick and tired of Esmeralda's little innuendos and wished she had the guts to tell the imperious neighbor off.

"Alberto said you liked all the old stories about his ancestors that everyone else is sick and tired of hearing."

Janine's resentment grew at Esmeralda's mocking tone. She felt betrayed thinking that Alberto would share their personal and private conversations with Esmeralda.

"I am sure he will give you some awful trinket from that old storeroom. Has he told you about it?"

"Yes," Janine nodded.

"Then you know there is nothing in there but old junk," Esmeralda said sharply. "Alberto should not dishonor you by doing this, but he does not listen to anyone, even his mama. You will have to pretend that you like his gift or you will hurt his feelings."

Janine smiled, thinking of what Esmeralda would say about the watch that Alberto had wanted to give her. A nasty desire to flaunt the beautiful gold watch under Esmeralda's nose made her feel slightly better. As they came around the corner, Janine finally recognized where they were.

The door of the tunnel stood open and the lights were already on. Esmeralda stepped aside. A tight smile flickered across her face when Janine looked at her.

"I will go no further," Esmeralda said with a distasteful look on her face. "I do not like this small space. It is dirty and filled with spiders."

Janine was actually relieved she didn't have to suffer Esmeralda's presence through the tunnel, although she was surprised Esmeralda didn't want to chaperone. "Thank you for bringing me," she said.

"I did not do it for you but for Constancia," Esmeralda said.

She paused for a moment to look down the passageway. There was no sound coming from inside, but that did not surprise her. The cave was far away from the main house.

A deep, impatient sigh from behind hurried Janine into the passage and once inside, she moved fast to get away from Esmeralda's dark, suspicious eyes.

Janine's ears quickly became attuned to the silence. She was awaiting a sound that would indicate Alberto was nearby. She hurried as much as the low ceiling allowed. The thought that Esmeralda might decide to follow her made her nervous, but all she had to do was get to Alberto. Finally in the distance, she saw the door to the storeroom. She was getting hot, and she stopped to catch her breath. As she recovered and took a step forward, ready to call out to Alberto, the tunnel went black.

Janine's heart jumped into her throat. She closed her eyes, squeezed them tight and opened them. It was dark. The only sound was her panicked breathing. She tried to quiet the ragged noise, but that caused her gasping to sound even louder. Her heart slammed against her ribcage, and, recalling that he refused to turn the lights out when they were together here earlier, she called out hopefully, "Alberto, turn on the lights, I'm in here."

"Please turn on the lights," she pleaded, her voice falling to a whisper. More panic clouded her thinking, and the dark disoriented her. Dizzy, she leaned against the wall. She didn't care if it was crawling with spiders.

"There are switches along the passage," she remembered excitedly. "Where? I don't remember where!?" The sound of her voice didn't echo. It was hollow and then gone. Silence fell again. Obviously, Alberto was not in here, and Esmeralda had done this. "I am such an idiot," she exclaimed, smacking the wall.

All she needed to do was turn around and follow the wall back to the outside door. Once she was there somebody would let her out.

Gingerly, she pushed herself away from the wall. It was rough, almost cool against her hands. With a quick prayer to Alberto's Lady in the garden, Janine began to move back along the way she had come. Her progress was steady but the stifling darkness confused her thoughts. How long have I been in here? Why isn't Alberto looking for me? Why hasn't anyone come looking for me?

As a child Alberto had been found in this place by Esmeralda. It was Esmeralda who had gone to get Frederico. It was Esmeralda who had locked him in this horrible place so many years ago. A sick feeling filled Janine. What had she accomplished then? What did Esmeralda think she might accomplish by locking her in here now?

"Okay, so I'm stuck in the dark, but I will get out." She continued to talk to herself. It was slightly calming to break the heavy silence filling the tunnel. "It's just a matter of following this wall to the door."

A sharp pain stabbed her finger, and she jerked it away. "What was that?" she whispered. "I hope I wasn't stung by something. What did Berto say about poisonous spiders? I can't remember what he said," she cried, shaking her hand, curbing the urge to put the stinging finger in her mouth.

She kept moving, afraid if she stopped, she would just give in to her fear. "I know I'm going in the right direction or I'd have fallen into the ladder by now," she confirmed.

When she could walk upright, she moved faster. Without warning she fell to her knees. She cried out in pain. The air down at her feet felt cooler. She must be close to the door now. Scrambling to her feet she hurried forward.

Gradually the darkness became less of a black blanket. Even before she felt the solid wood of the door in front of her, she sensed it. "Finally," she said, as, carefully with her hands, she felt along the door frame until she found the electrical wires that led to the switch. She raised the switch and the dim light blinded her.

Grateful the nightmare was almost ended, she fell against the door and began pounding the rough wood. After a minute, she stopped. Blood was smeared all over her arms. She held out her hands and found dozens of small cuts and scrapes. She looked down at the front of her dress smudged with brown dust and red blood. The door was too heavy. The feeble sound she was making wouldn't bring any help.

The heat and fear and the sight and smell of her own blood took their toll, and Janine collapsed on the dirt floor, leaning against the door. "Nobody is around," she thought hopelessly.

"The pool and patio area is already locked up," her mother's words echoed back in her mind.

"As we speak the house staff is already packing up to return home," Alberto had told her earlier.

"I'm in the servant's quarters," she said aloud to the cold stone walls.

"So this is what Esmeralda planned," she thought in a daze. The tomb-like atmosphere of the tunnel and the horror of starving to death cloaked her in a suffocating blanket of desolation. She covered her face with her hands and buried her head in the curve of her shoulder, desperately wanting to hide herself from the panic swelling like a summer storm inside.

39

A bang outside of the tunnel disturbed the silence. Janine slowly lifted her head. She had no idea how much time had passed or when she had stopped listening and become lost in her troubled thoughts. Now that someone was nearby again she filled with hope. She sat forward with her ear pressed against the wood of the door straining to hear another sound. The wood shuddered, and Janine attempted to stand, but off balance, she stumbled forward as the door abruptly flew open. A pair of strong hands reached out. She was caught in them and held steady.

"Alberto," she breathed. It had to be him holding her.

"Janine," Alberto cried. He lifted her to her feet.

Janine was unable to look at him. She buried her face in his crisp, clean shirt. She could feel his heart beating. His arms were around her shoulders and he held her. There was no sound until Janine pulled away and began to laugh. It was a high-pitched, unnatural sound. "I hope I don't look as bad as you did when they found you here," she managed to say.

"Janine what happened? Are you alright?" Joan's voice, full of concern, asked from behind Alberto's back.

Janine looked around and saw Joan and Constancia hurrying toward them. With a quick brush down the front of her dress, she instructed Alberto in a whisper, "If I have spiders crawling on me please get them off."

"None that I can see," Alberto said as he brushed the webs from her hair and shoulders.

"What a relief," she said, moving away to meet her mother.

Joan cried, "Darling, you look awful. What happened?"

"I was locked in the passage to the storeroom. I'll need to change before we leave." Glassy-eyed, she remembered, "And all my clothes are packed."

Joan glanced at Constancia and then Alberto. He frowned and stepped closer to Janine. "After you have cleaned up and your cuts are taken care of, we will then decide what should be done. Bring Janine to the bedroom down the hall. I will go tell Papa what has happened."

In a matter of minutes Alberto returned carrying a professional-looking black medical case. "Papa has decided, since all is ready, to take the children and leave for Madrid as planned. Rico will ride with him. The four of us can leave whenever we are ready."

"Carlos will love that," Constancia smiled. "Traveling that distance with the children and Frederico, I do not know who will be more trying for him."

Joan bathed Janine's hands with a warm cloth that smelled of antiseptic. Janine fought to conceal the pain of the cleansing. Joan struggled to gently remove the grime and dried blood encrusted in the sores.

Constancia leaned over Joan's shoulder watching the progress. "I think Alberto should look at this one," Constancia said to Joan when Janine's hands were clean.

Joan gingerly held the finger Janine had thought was bitten by a spider. The cut was ragged and quite a bit of the fleshy pad of her finger was gone.

"Berto, this cut looks rather deep," Constancia said, turning to him.

The two women stepped aside. Alberto moved over to the desk where Janine sat with her palms resting awkwardly on a clean towel, feeling like a sinful child. He gently took Janine's hand in his. "It will have to be bound tightly, and that will hurt," he informed her.

Janine shrugged.

With a competency that only comes from experience, Alberto quickly pulled the separated skin together with adhesive and then covered it with another bandage. "The adhesive should remain undisturbed for a few days so the skin has a chance to mend. I am afraid when it is done healing you may have a small scar," he said. "I would have come for you sooner, querida," he said, leaning over to kiss her cheek, "but I was certain you had become lost in the gardens. It was not until I saw the hill in the orchard that the storeroom came to mind."

"Alberto, it was Esmeralda who locked you in the tunnel when you were a boy," Janine gasped, remembering everything. "I know because she is the one who did it to me now, today."

"I know, Janine. Galeno caught her leaving the house. When we could not find you, he knew in some way she was responsible.

I have always known it was Esmeralda, but I should have told you. Then you could not have been fooled by her. If Galeno had not been busy preparing for the trip, she would never have been allowed near the house. I am sorry, but I assure you this is the last malicious act she will ever have the opportunity to do on the hacienda." He turned to look at his mother for confirmation.

Constancia's lips were pressed firmly together and she nodded her head in agreement. "I tried giving Esmeralda allowances for losing her mother but this is inexcusable," she said tersely.

"Do I get my suitcase so I can change?" Janine asked hopefully. She was filthy and could feel things creeping across her flesh. Only by getting out of her clothes and showering would she be absolutely certain there were no ugly black spiders still hiding in her clothes. "Wouldn't it be best, so we can leave as soon as possible?"

The three of them gave her a look. She felt like a child who did not know what was good for her.

"We can always leave in the morning if you do not feel well enough to make the journey," Alberto told her.

Only a few hours before, Janine couldn't bear the thought of leaving the hacienda, but everything was different now.

"No, please I am ready. I am ready to leave today, now."

40

Steam rose from the pavement into the air in wispy clouds. The street was empty of people but crowded with compact automobiles parked haphazardly along the endless stonewall. The lovely dome of a basilica rose in sharp silhouette against a sky that was so blue it looked like a painting, not something that really existed. A few stray clouds left over from the early afternoon rain sailed out of view. The narrow sleeping streets of the city of Madrid were lined with shuttered shop windows and closed restaurants. Only the churches remained open to the public at siesta time.

Janine enjoyed walking through the quiet streets at this time of the day. Gone were the local residents and the endless throng of tourists. It was entertaining to watch the yawning waiters in crisp white coats as they wiped off the outdoor furniture and prepared their restaurants to re-open for the evening crowd. She walked slowly. The heat didn't seem to be quite so bad after the rain. By the time she reached the Casilda's home, about ten blocks away, the streets would be dry.

She followed a now familiar track through the business district into an area with walls that surrounded well-tended gardens and homes. Tall trees shaded the cobblestone sidewalk. Olive bushes, with their branches protruding through the iron fences, hung in her path. She brushed them aside.

The clock tower had already started the first of its three long and foreboding peals. She was late. She had taken too much time walking through the marketplace. She hurried as she followed the sidewalk into a much different area. A six-foot yellow stone wall covered with green moss hid the only residence on this block. The entrance of the estate was enclosed with an iron gate that was manned by staff at all times.

When they had first arrived from the hacienda, Janine had been intimidated by the gate, the guards, and the grandeur of the house. She had thought it to be more like a fortress than a home but not any longer. On the other side of the wall was a beautiful garden that surrounded a small castle in the heart of the city of Madrid.

Her preconceived idea of a gray-walled stone structure, cold, damp, and dismal with a legendary dungeon in the basement, certainly didn't accurately describe the Casilda's formal family residence. It was simply a charming old stone house. Even more charming than the hacienda and filled with all the beautiful statues, artwork, and family mementos that they didn't have at the hacienda.

Most of the rooms on the first floor were small and intimate. The house was set up for the old style of social gatherings. There were rooms set aside for the men—a smoking room, the library, and a game room. Then there were rooms for the women—pretty parlors for greeting guests, a tea room filled with flowering plants and palms, and the room most used by the women, the sitting room. It had huge windows and doors that led out onto a patio and the garden beyond. All of the rooms had fireplaces and central heating that kept the damp out.

Janine was having a wonderful time meeting the family members and the large number of friends that stopped by at any time for endless cups of tea. The small, intimate family meals at the hacienda simply did not happen here. There were always at the least thirty people at supper. The conversations were spoken mostly in Spanish, but the family and guests did make efforts to remember to use English.

After a meal ended, they would go into the sitting room where a piano was uncovered and at least one member of the group would volunteer to play while dessert was served. The evenings moved slowly, dressing for supper, eating the delicious courses, which took over an hour, and then the quiet entertainment before going to bed. The people at these meals did not have that constant drive to search out the most exciting diversion to keep them entertained. They were all ages, early twenties to late eighties, like Alberto's Dowager Aunt, who was usually asleep before dessert had ended. These people were content with refined conversation and music or a cool evening stroll through the gardens.

It was all an experience she never expected. The life of the rich was supposed to be dictatorially, restrictive, and full of pomp and circumstance. Instead she found this world filled with charming people who had good manners and good taste.

Janine walked up to the gate and waved at the guard. He never smiled. He had a gruff military demeanor that Janine found reassuring. "Buenas tardes, señor," she called a cheerful greeting to him, and he lifted the brim of his hat and nodded.

She rushed down a narrow sidewalk that led to the left wing of the house and began to remove her hat in the shade of the garden walk. This brief walk at the end of the siesta was the only opportunity Janine found to be out in the city streets alone. Since coming to Madrid, whenever she left the house, Janine was always accompanied by several people. She needed this time to peacefully enjoy wandering around the streets to do exactly what she wanted to do and not worry about anyone else.

When Janine mentioned her desire to get out alone, Joan hesitated. "Constancia told me that it isn't wise for young, unmarried women to be out alone. It has something to do with the culture and, of course, your safety."

"I don't believe it," Janine scoffed. "There are American women all over the place, and I know they don't follow the rules of this culture."

"Honey, you're in a strange country, what's so important that you want to go walking through the streets of Madrid by yourself? These streets are worse than the maze at the garden at the hacienda. How can you be sure you won't get horribly turned around and lost?"

"I have a map," Janine protested, "and I'm not going anywhere but to the plaza Alberto brought us to. The one by the basilica with all those charming stores."

"The Prado Museum is right around there. Haven't you spent enough time in that museum looking at all the artwork?"

"No I haven't. I hate being rushed through when there are so many things to see, and I don't want to bore anyone while I'm looking."

"Why don't you ask Alberto to take you?"

Janine shrugged. "He's never around. I've barely spoken to him since we got here."

"Oh, so that's it," Joan nodded with an understanding look at her daughter.

"That's what?" Janine snapped.

"I'm sure Frederico isn't busy. He would take you."

"Haven't you noticed since we've been here the men are only around at meal times. I never even see Carlos."

"Nonsense, Alberto took you to his uncle's art gallery just yesterday, and you had tea at that café. You should have brought it up then."

"How? With his uncle and aunt and some other men I couldn't understand even when they spoke English? There wasn't a chance to talk to him alone."

The whole truth was that Janine did not even want Alberto with her when she went through the art exhibit. Alberto's knowledge of art far surpassed her amateurish interests, and she was nervous about making some ridiculous remark and embarrassing herself.

Today was the second time she slipped away to visit the museum. The brief hour where she could become lost to the exquisite beauty of famous paintings from as early as the fifteenth century was worth it. The colors and scenes became an inspiration to Janine. The desire to create her own scenes, the ones she found in the streets of Madrid, filled her with delight. Maybe the talent she left behind so long ago was not completely lost.

Janine swiftly ran up the back staircase that led into the suite of rooms she and her mother shared in the old house. She quietly shut the door of her lavish bedroom and removed the colorful scarf from her hair. She began brushing her hair with swift strokes, to better hide that she had, once again, been out alone.

The ceramic basin near the door with a pitcher of water and towels next to it served for a quick clean up, at least to get rid of the dust and sweat. Her mother would join her soon and then tea would be served in the small sitting room that adjoined their bedrooms. Janine hurried into the flowery sitting room. She would find a book to read until her mother appeared from siesta.

"Did you have a pleasant walk?"

Janine jumped in surprise. "Berto!" she exclaimed, giving a shaky laugh. She saw him sitting on the window ledge watching her. "Why, yes I did, gracias."

She felt tense with the disapproval she read on his face.

"I'm sorry. I've made you angry, haven't I?" she said quickly.

"You are a guest in my house, not a prisoner." He reached into the breast pocket of his shirt and removed a cigar. "Why have you kept these afternoon walks a secret?"

Janine's mouth was dry. She looked toward the small bar in the corner of the room. "Before you grill me, could I get myself a bottle of water?"

Alberto stood and moved toward her. "I am not going to grill you. You are mistaking my concern for something else. The heat in the city is intense, and you are not accustomed to it." He walked to the small refrigerator behind the bar. With quick movements, he opened a bottle and poured the contents into a tall crystal glass then walked to where she was still standing in the middle of the room.

"Janine I just want you to understand, siesta is a tradition that is practiced for a reason. I don't recommend you ignore it."

Janine sipped her water and smiled at him. "Especially since I come from the far north end of North America. We do have hot summer days there, too, you know."

"I see," Alberto grinned. "I must be treating you like one of my siblings again. How I continue to make that mistake amazes me," he admitted, his eyes on her as he sat down on the couch and pulled her down to sit next to him. They both relaxed back into the couch cushions.

Janine sighed. "Not really amazing," she said then took another sip of the cold, bubbly water before she set the glass on the heavy wood coffee table near their feet. "I admit I'm a novice to your Spanish traditions," she said in a teasing voice, "so there are times I suppose I deserve to be treated like a child."

"Ah ha, this is a first. Now if I could only trust that you would heed my advice," he said. He kissed her hair. His fingers lightly stroked the skin of her arm.

Janine didn't resist his attentions. She had come to enjoy the contact between them. Since coming to Madrid, the times they spent alone were brief. This was the first time he had been in her sitting room. Lately they were together with many people surrounding them, never alone. The casual caresses that had become a part of their relationship were pleasant. None of the passion Janine was only beginning to recognize surfaced to frighten her. She could relax and enjoy being held in the strength of his arms with her head resting against his shoulder. She didn't know what the future would bring, but she was here with him now.

Alberto looked at the palm of her hand then pressed his lips against it. "You have fully recovered?" he asked softly. "I see mostly pink skin. That is a good sign. Are there any inner scars left from what happened in the tunnel?"

"No, I'm not harboring any claustrophobic tendencies or fear of the dark. It was nice of Esmeralda to send me a formal apology. I never thought she would do something as civilized as that."

Alberto didn't answer as he rolled the cigar through his lean fingers before returning it to his shirt pocket.

"Are you ready for the festivities tonight?" he asked finally. "You found the gown you chose will be suitable for you? You are pleased?"

Janine smiled. "More than pleased. It is absolutely gorgeous. I can't believe your aunt allowed us to borrow dresses from her shop. That is so generous. What if I spill something on it?"

Alberto threw back his head and laughed. "I do not think she will be upset."

"She might not be, but I certainly will," Janine protested.

"Then you will pay to have it replaced," he said.

"Oh, right, I can do that."

"Of course you can. Where is your mother? Is she equally pleased with her attire?"

"I haven't spoken to her since siesta began. I think she might be in her room. She's thrilled, of course. She hasn't had a new dress in more than ten years."

Alberto stood to leave. "I think you should rest awhile since you didn't rest during siesta. Tonight there will be a long dinner and some speeches, then dancing. We will be up very late." He glanced at his watch and suddenly became brisk and distant.

"A light meal will be brought up for you both. We will not dine until nine or ten o'clock. It is the custom."

Janine walked him to the door and he left.

She wandered away from the door through the room straightening the pillows askew on the couch and returned her glass to the bar. There was only one full day left in Madrid, and then they would be getting on the plane for home.

41

The library was large but, situated as it was in the mansion, inconspicuous, located at the back of the Casilda house, out of the main flow of people traffic. The business matters of the estate and the hacienda all took place amid the austere decorations of long highly polished bookcases filled with thousands of books stacked on shelves to the ceiling. Delicate porcelain statues of matadors and bulls confronting each other sat at various intervals along the shelves. Every inch of wall space was covered with dark wood paneling. The room smelled pleasantly of lemon polish. A couch and several deep-seated chairs covered in leather surrounded the fireplace. The smell of cigar smoke foretold that someone else was already waiting when Alberto, followed by Frederico, entered the room. Frederico immediately moved to the wooden sideboard that held numerous liquor bottles and a crystal decanter filled with sherry. He poured the sherry into three glasses.

"Your guests are ready for this evening, Berto?" Carlos asked. He stood by the window and was partially hidden from view by thick damask curtains.

"Si, papa."

A movement outside the door warned them that the man they waited for had arrived.

"What did you hear, amigo?" Alberto asked the moment Galeno appeared in the doorway.

Frederico walked over and handed Galeno one of the crystal glasses.

"Señor de Martés has taken his family to South America for an extended visit. The main house has been closed, and the livestock have been brought to the auction yard. At the next sale, they will be put on the block."

"Did you hear if Esmeralda has gone with him?" Frederico asked. "She has never obeyed Luis before. I find it hard to believe she will do so now."

"It doesn't matter if Esme is playing her usual games, Rico," Alberto broke in. "I spoke to Juan Carlos today at the rehearsal. He will be sending an official letter to Luis from his office stating that it would be wise for them to stay in South America. The estate and the land adjoining it will be put up for sale as soon as can be arranged. If Luis does not agree, criminal charges will be brought against Esmeralda." Alberto looked at Frederico. "I am not sure what price will be set, but I believe purchasing the property adjoining the hacienda would be a legitimate investment. What do you think?"

"My thoughts exactly," Frederico grinned. "I decided it was time for me to look for a place of my own."

With the attention of the other men centered on Frederico, Alberto walked away to look out over the shadowed garden. He lit a cigar and stared silently out the window.

42

Janine pressed her forehead against the cold glass of the arched-pane window and gave a deep sigh.

"Tonight is the last social engagement we have in Spain. I can't believe it's time to go home," she whispered. She turned around when she heard Joan's footsteps and hoped she had not been heard.

"You're ready. I'm so glad. Come and do this clasp for me," Joan said.

Janine quickly crossed the room and took the gold bracelet that was heavy with large stones from her mother's hand. For such a cumbersome piece of jewelry, the clasp was thin and awkward to maneuver. It took Janine several tries to secure it.

"Finally, thank you. Now let me take a look at you."

Janine smoothed the delicate transparent overlay of crepe that shimmered silver against the peacock blue silk of the dress. "It's a bit flashy," she said.

"I know!" Joan exclaimed. "What a great choice! You look absolutely stunning. What do you think of me? I'd fit into a scene of Romeo and Juliet, wouldn't I?"

Janine smiled. Her mother did look elegant in a full-length gown of navy, trimmed with gold at the waist and sleeves.

"Isn't this fun! We never get to deck ourselves out like this at home!"

Janine did not answer right away. "Mother, are you getting at all homesick?"

Joan stopped and tilted her head, seriously considering the question. "I am ready for the change of seasons. In Duluth, the trees will just be turning, apples ripening, and the big lake will be giving off a breeze during the night that gets rid of the hot August heat. The harbor will be busy. The shipping lines will be hurrying to finish their deliveries before the ice comes. It seems like a long way off, but I think I'm ready. For awhile, I just didn't care about home. But being here has helped to put my life back into perspective."

They were interrupted by a knock. Joan walked over and opened the door. Alberto stood in the hallway, looking splendid in a military uniform. He wore a white jacket with a crimson sash and two gold braids on his shoulders. His hands were shoved into the pockets of the pleated white pants. "Buenas tardes."

"Buenas tardes, señor," Joan said in a brisk tone. "I'm ready, Jani, so I'll start down to meet the others." She smiled at Alberto as she stepped past him. "Adiós."

Janine paused to give Alberto an inquiring look. "I'll meet you downstairs," she said to Joan.

Once Joan was gone, Alberto started quickly. "Janine, I am sorry to interrupt, but I must tell you this now."

"You're not interrupting anything. Do you want to sit down?"

"I can tell you as we walk," Alberto said, taking her arm. "It is about tonight. I have duties at the royal palace that will keep me occupied. I will be unable to escort you to the assembly."

"At the royal palace?"

"Yes, that is where we are dining tonight. We are the guests of King Juan Carlos and his wife Queen Sophia. Juan Carlos is my cousin."

Janine's mind went blank for an instant, and then the realization of what he meant flooded in.

"This is worse than I ever imagined," she muttered softly. She raised her voice. "We're going to your cousin's house for an assembly, and he's the King of Spain?"

As they made their way through the mansion, Alberto spoke quietly but firmly. "I know it sounds overwhelming, but you have to trust me when I say you will do fine. I am the first-born male of my father's family and will be expected to stand with the royal family. Once the reception line ends, then my duties are done. It usually does not take more than an hour."

"Why haven't you told me all of this before?"

"I should have explained, but it has been very busy," Alberto said.

As they approached the top of the wide staircase leading to the foyer, the general confusion and conversation of the family gathering at the bottom of the stairs hid her silent bewilderment.

Constancia was busy straightening the lacy white scarf on Maria's dark head while Carlos held the charming girl.

"Hola," Carlos cheerfully welcomed Alberto and Janine as they descended the stair into the pleasant chaos. "Berto, I know you must leave. The rest of us will follow in two vehicles. With everyone in formal dress we take up more room than we normally do," he laughed.

Alberto moved away from the group. "Gracias, papa. It is time then. I will see all of you at the palace."

Frederico extracted himself from the back of the group to move next to Janine. "Señorita, I find I shall have the honor of driving you to the assembly tonight."

Janine gave him a blank look and then nodded.

Galeno appeared in the doorway. His presence signaled to everyone that it was time to leave. Constancia paused to look at her family to be certain each one was presentable before she led the group outside. Two black, distinguished cars waited in the drive. The group separated. The family climbed into one vehicle and Frederico escorted the two Nielsen women in the other.

43

The royal palace was a long, white building that had the same look as all the other government buildings in Madrid. Once inside, the massive columned hallway glowed in a soft, reflected golden light. Huge crystal chandeliers in close succession lined the ceiling, making the white walls with gold trim seem miles long. When they exited the hallway, they stood on a narrow balcony above an immense ballroom spread out below them. Slowly they moved down a wide expanse of stairs toward the reception line.

Banners of red, gold, green, and white adorned the balustrades of the staircase and archways of the massive room. This along with the sparkle of the finery worn by the couples on the dance floor took Janine's breath away.

The reception line moved quickly. The Casildas and their guests were rushed through as quickly as everyone else. Janine's only impression was that the king and queen looked extremely normal. Their adult children stood next to them followed by the lengthy string of relatives, including Alberto.

After the reception line, they lined up to watch presentations of traditional dance from the different Spanish cultures. The outfits were spectacular and the dexterity of the dancers, some of whom were small children, was astounding to watch. The food, set out in a separate room, was served in buffet style that was replenished throughout the night.

Well after midnight, Janine, who had danced most of the night with strangers, found herself in Alberto's arms. The music started, a slow, hypnotic beat that was easy for them to follow as their bodies swayed together to the dreamy music. Janine's head fell naturally against his shoulder as he gathered her closer.

It took her a moment to hear through the music that Alberto was speaking to her. "There is only one thing I want that I do not have," he said, "and that is you. I want you to become a part of my life, Janine."

He moved her slowly across the floor before saying, "A permanent part of my life, as my wife."

"Your wife!" Janine stopped moving and exclaimed.

Alberto chuckled. "This is why we could never be alone in public here in Madrid. I planned to ask for your hand in marriage. I needed to follow the rules so this could be honored."

"But... But... I'm an American," Janine shook her head sadly, "and...and...your mother is so concerned about who you marry because of the royal line."

"It is not my mother who is asking you."

"No, that's true, but it's important to her. What about the royal lineage?"

"I do not care about it."

Her words caught in her throat as she fought back the tears. "Oh, Alberto. I just don't know. I thought it wouldn't matter. I thought I could throw caution to the wind and allow this to happen but, I am so sorry."

"You do not need to be afraid."

"To leave Duluth forever and move here? Spain is absolutely paradise, but Duluth..." her voice trailed off.

The room seemed to spin. The music played. There were people all around them.

"I don't think it would be right to marry you knowing there would be a good chance that we both would become miserable. It wouldn't be fair. I just don't think I can do it," she continued as Alberto danced on in silence.

Alberto broke his silence. "I see. I thought...it doesn't matter what I thought. You seem ready to make up your mind right now at this moment, so I must honor you by accepting it."

The music faded, and Alberto released her. "Gracias for the dance, señorita. You will understand when I ask you to excuse me." He strode off, disappearing into the crowd.

The night did not continue like the dream it should have been. This dream had turned into a nightmare that would not end. By the time Joan found her and they made their way to where Galeno was waiting, Janine's head throbbed. They followed him to the limousine. Frederico joined them as they climbed into the car. Alberto was already sitting inside.

As Galeno drove them through the city streets, Frederico asked him, "How late did mama stay, Galeno?"

"The family returned home several hours ago. The children were ready for bed."

"They were so good during all of those presentations," Joan said with a yawn. "I can definitely say I've had enough excitement to last me for ages."

Frederico turned to Janine, who sat across from him. "And you, Janine. Did you enjoy tonight as well?"

Janine was very aware of Alberto's silence, and her heart ached because she was the reason for it. In a strained voice she said, "I don't really know how to answer. It was unbelievable. I haven't any words to describe how I feel right now. I'm sorry, Rico, I'm tired and not very good at hiding it."

"There is nothing to apologize for," Frederico clucked sympathetically. "I, too, am tired. It affects me all of a sudden once the excitement has died down, and I always feel rather empty."

"That is exactly how I feel, Rico," Joan agreed from the dim light in a sleepy voice. "Has Alberto fallen asleep already?"

"No, I am here and wide awake," Alberto said. His deep voice resonated from the shadow of the corner. "I am only thinking how nice it is to hear a conversation between a few people instead of many."

The car slowed to turn into the narrow drive leading to the house. When the car stopped, Frederico stepped out to help the women. Alberto was last. He gave them a formal bow but said nothing.

Janine glanced back at him regretting the hasty words she had unthinkingly said to him. He gave her no chance to say anything before he turned his back and walked around the car to the other side. Slowly, Janine turned and followed her mother into the house.

44

A folded newspaper slapped the wooden desk in front of Janine. "That professional hockey player's house on Lake Superior sold," Connie said, her voice thick with excitement. "Two and a half million dollars. Have you ever heard of anything so outrageous? I don't care if the house was built for one of Chester Congdon's daughters. No house is worth that much."

Janine's eyes slowly moved down the small, even print of the society column article. "Why is real estate in Maddie Flowers' gossip column?"

"Because the buyer is a friend of the Jacoubi's, and you know that whole family is absolutely Maddie's favorite subject. In her eyes, they are the golden family of Duluth. Look, she says that the house was bought by an undisclosed family to use for their seasonal home."

Janine glanced up to catch the look on Connie's face. She knew some kind of response was expected.

"Wow, for that much money, huh? Didn't Chester Congdon build that house for his daughter...for a wedding present?"

"Yes," Connie said. "I can't believe someone would drop that kind of money for a part-time house, and in Duluth? Who knows, maybe Duluth will become the Martha's Vineyard of the North. Just think how exciting that would be."

"Martha's Vineyard is an island," Janine said.

"Whatever. Who cares? Our little city could become a stomping ground for the rich and famous. After all, wasn't your Spaniard one of the rich and famous?"

Janine's throat painfully constricted as she nodded.

"It figures, he did act pretty high-handed."

"What do you mean?"

"Oh, come on, Janine. He waltzes in here with his stretch limo and basically takes over your life. Didn't he convince your mother to leave and recuperate in Spain? Does that sound like something your sensible mother would do?"

Janine frowned. "I found out my mother isn't all that sensible. But, you know what? I'm glad. I'm glad she's decided to start living again. I didn't realize how boring our lives were until we left Duluth."

"I say he was way too presumptuous. He was so, so overbearing. It makes my liberated soul furious just remembering how he treated you."

Janine kept her face impassive as she carefully thought of a reply. It was unfair for Connie to keep that impression of Alberto.

"It may have looked that way, Connie, but it wasn't. For the first time in my life, I didn't have to worry about merely surviving. He took away all my boring, everyday worries. I didn't just drift through the days any more. I was free. I remembered dreams that I'd completely forgotten. It was amazing," she laughed with a wistful note in her voice. "I even felt brave enough to try some new things like horseback riding and ballroom dancing. I would never have had the guts to try anything like that before. I knew without a doubt Alberto was a man I could depend on. Don't know why. I'm not exactly experienced where men are concerned."

"That's the first time you've talked about how you felt, Jani. I didn't really know. I'm so sorry."

"What help does talking about it do? Nothing. Whining about how lost I feel and how my heart is broken into tiny bits only makes me completely miserable. I'm not a big fan of misery loves company. Misery's just plain boring."

"I don't know," Connie said. "I read in some magazine that the first step to curing a broken heart is admitting it."

"That's ridiculous," Janine gave a bitter laugh. "Admit it to who? The guy who dumped you? It must've been an advertisement in some woman's magazine drumming up business for some psychotropic drug. I don't bother to read women's magazines."

Connie stopped talking. She had never heard such resentment in Janine's voice before. With nervous movements, she folded and refolded the newspaper edges, creasing it tight. Studying Janine's solemn face, Connie's thoughts raced. Connie knew about broken hearts, but she also knew there was nothing she could say to make Janine feel better. The pain would pass after a short time. It always had for her.

But, Janine was different. She had never been involved with a guy. The Spaniard literally swept her off her feet, and she fell hard.

Connie didn't know any of the details. Janine had been predictably close-mouthed about what happened in Spain. But it was clear the relationship had ended.

When she first came back to work, Janine's appearance absolutely astounded Connie. She looked golden. A golden tan, sun-streaks of gold in her hair. Even her preference in clothes had changed. Her first day back to work she showed up in a bright colored outfit that actually flattered her.

Janine's spirit did not match the change in her appearance. Gone was the sparkle of excitement she had before the trip. She looked downright defeated.

Connie changed the subject. "What's that on your fingers?" Connie asked in her brightest voice.

Janine held up her hand to look at her fingertips. Stains of sienna brown and orange paint decorated her fingers. "Paint," she mumbled.

"Are you painting the house or something? You never said your mother was remodeling."

"No, this isn't wall paint."

"Then what is it?" Connie asked impatiently.

"Oil base. I couldn't get the colors I was looking for with water colors, so I'm working with oils now."

"Clarify for me what that means?" Connie asked, frowning. "You are painting…like on a canvas? You're an artist?"

Janine nodded carelessly. "I used to paint in high school. I've decided to give it another try."

Connie gave a short laugh as she stood up. "I must say I'm shocked. I had no idea. Good for you."

"I do like the subject I'm working on, but I can't seem to get the colors I'm looking for."

"What do you paint? Landscapes, people?"

"Right now I'm working on buildings. Houses, like the ones I saw in Spain. They were so beautiful. Made from the most beautiful stone you've ever seen."

Connie heard the note of enthusiasm in Janine's voice. "Do I get to see it when you're done?" she asked.

Janine nodded. "I'm pretty much an amateur, but if you'd like to see it, of course."

"What a pleasant hobby to have," Connie said and glanced at her watch. "Darn it. Break's over. I'll talk to you more about it at lunch, okay?"

"Connie," Janine said quietly, "quit trying so hard. I'm all right. Really."

"I just want to help. I do know about guy problems."

"Thanks for the offer. The only problem is I've never met anyone like him before."

"Yeah, he's a pretty hard act to follow," Connie agreed, heading back to her desk.

With misery as her constant companion the past month, Janine thought these were the longest thirty days she ever remembered. She heard Connie's footsteps fade away then closed her aching eyes. There were no tears left to ease the dryness. Janine gave a deep sigh. The memory of him holding her, of how his lips felt against hers, and that he wanted to love her for life, left her physically and mentally aching. She needed to quit brooding. The pile of leather-bound reference books that had been repaired and deposited on her desk needed to be returned to the shelves. Right now, to be busy and lose her self in the silent, dimly lit book aisles where she could forget about Alberto would be a blessing.

After pushing the books onto the shelf, Janine reluctantly left the concealing shadows. The room was quiet except for the occasional murmur of pages being turned by the handful of silent readers. As she walked around the wooden divider that separated her desk from the main reading area, she saw a large object wrapped in plain, brown paper on her desk. "What can that be?" she thought.

A small hope crept into her thoughts, but she convinced herself the package was probably something for the new computer system. Not every mysterious package was going to be from Alberto.

Scrawled across the wrapping in black marker was her name, nothing else. The heavy paper was sealed with tape. With shaking hands, she pulled her letter opener out of the drawer. Janine slit the tape and undid the paper. She froze. In her hands she held the painting of the hacienda, the one she loved so much, from the hallway in Spain.

For a moment her heart soared with the hope that Alberto was near. She glanced around. Seeing nobody, hope quickly died. "He'll never come back," she thought. "Not after the way I treated him. I humiliated him. How could I have been so heartless?"

A familiar voice echoed gently from the shadows of the bookshelves. "I wanted to give you a memento from my home, so I chose the one I knew you liked and one showing that I, too, have lost some dreams. You see, Janine, I, too, wanted to be a painter. When I was young, I painted this picture, not very well, but it is mine. And now I give it to you."

The soft lilt of his accent caused her to shiver.

"I hope you approve of my choice."

Janine slowly turned. She peered into the darkness of the tall shelves. She shook her head, whispering, "It can't be you."

He moved toward her. The grace of his movements could belong to no other man.

Without thought, without a breath, Janine flew forward straight into his arms.

They held each other.

Janine, comforted by the physical contact between them, blurted out, "Berto, I'm so sorry. I was cruel that night at the palace. You didn't deserve to be treated so heartlessly. I should have had more sense. I should have waited to give you my answer, but I couldn't think."

"Actually, I believe I did deserve it, Janine. I was arrogant enough to think there was no chance you would refuse me, or else, I never would have asked you a question of that magnitude in the middle of a crowded dance floor. Your refusal caught me completely off guard." Alberto held her tight.

"Your mother called me," he continued. "She asked me to come to Duluth. It seems you never told her what happened at the royal assembly. She had no idea why we parted company without saying good-bye. Nor that you flatly turned down my marriage proposal."

Janine laughed. "How could I admit to my mother, of all people, that I'd made the biggest mistake of my life? If I'd told her, she would have killed me," Janine laughed again and blinked away the tears in her eyes. "And now look. She's the one who brought you here. What a meddler! But, it would have never happened except for her."

"Silly girl. Of course it would have. You are the only one I want for my wife. Haven't we already gone through this? I looked at your refusal simply as a roadblock. Not the end. I love you, Janine. Several months ago I arrived in this back country because I owed an old friend a visit and found myself captivated by a woman who stole my heart the first time I set eyes on her."

Janine rested her head against his chest. She could feel his heart beat, fast and strong.

"I have come to the library to speak with you in private because mama and papa are in Duluth with me. They are at your house visiting with Joan. They traveled this distance to welcome you, if you decide to accept my offer, into the Casilda family," he explained. "The strangest thing happened when we arrived at the hotel. My mother walked out onto the balcony. She took one look at the view and was captivated by the magnificence of the beautiful Lake Superior. After we arrived at your house and she saw the view from there, she convinced my father the cool climate of Duluth would be an ideal get-away for the family during the hot months in Spain. They immediately set about looking for a house. Papa has already made an offer on a house next to Lake Superior. Just before I left them, we found out his offer was accepted. I wanted to warn you before you see them so their announcement is not too much of a surprise."

Janine watched him in silence. Her anxious eyes moved over his face. "It's you?" she whispered. "Your father is buying that house and your mother approves?"

"I hope the impulsive action will not cause a problem?"

Janine's warm brown eyes were alight with happiness. She smiled at him. "What you're telling me is your mother doesn't object…in any way?"

"Janine, she never objected to you," Alberto chuckled. "She was blinded by the past."

"And now she isn't?"

"Mama understands that I will not run away to marry for love as my sister Juanita did. I will marry whom I love, whether Mama approves or not, and you, you do love me, Janine?"

Janine heard the note of indecision in Alberto's question and hurried to reply. "No one matters to me like you. I knew that on the dance floor the minute after I said no and watched you walk away. Yes, Berto, I love you more than I ever thought imaginable."

Alberto let out a deep sigh that sounded almost like a groan. "There. That is it then. Now there is only you and me. We can make plans about us."

"Where do we begin? It's astounding about your parents and Lake Superior. I remember on your first visit how the big lake fascinated you."

"My parents' house does not have to be our house. Once we are married, you may choose a house anywhere in Duluth you like."

"I don't know, Berto. I've always liked living on the lake, and your parents will only be in Duluth during the hot months in Spain. Besides, you can't possibly plan on leaving the hacienda? That wouldn't be right, Berto. Your family depends on you."

"I am glad that you do appreciate I cannot forsake the hacienda. Yet, I know how you feel about Duluth. It was never my intention to keep you from the place that is important to you. This way you and I will have part of the year to enjoy Duluth, and the other part we will spend in Spain. Papa and Rico and I discussed how the three of us will divide the responsibilities at the hacienda. We are also considering the purchase of a small cattle ranch in this area. I have a friend who found an extremely promising prospect close by."

"Your friend is one of the Jacoubi's?"

"Yes, Ajai Jacoubi. We played polo together in South America."

Janine's arms slipped around his waist. Instead of the depths of depression that she had felt moments before, now complete joy filled her.

Alberto kissed her hard and quick on the mouth. "Will you marry me, Janine?"

"Of course," she smiled. Her face flushed a rose petal pink, a beauty filled her that could only be found in a happily content woman. "I will marry you tomorrow if you like."

Alberto buried his face in the curve of her neck. His lips gently moved against her silken skin as he murmured, "That is all I need to hear."

Other Savage Press Books

OUTDOORS, SPORTS & RECREATION

Cool Fishing for Kids 8-85 by Frankie Paull and "Jackpine" Bob Cary
Curling Superiority! by John Gidley
Dan's Dirty Dozen by Mike Savage
The Duluth Tour Book by Jeff Cornelius
The Final Buzzer by Chris Russell

ESSAY

Battlenotes: Music of the Vietnam War by Lee Andresen
Hint of Frost, Essays on the Earth by Rusty King
Hometown Wisconsin by Marshall J. Cook
Potpourri From Kettle Land by Irene I. Luethge

FICTION

Burn Baby Burn by Mike Savage
Charleston Red by Sarah Galchus
Keeper of the Town by Don Cameron
Lake Effect by Mike Savage
Mindset by Enrico Bostone
Off Season by Marshall J.Cook
Something in the Water by Mike Savage
The Year of the Buffalo by Marshall J. Cook
Voices From the North Edge by St. Croix Writers
Walkers in the Mist by Hollis D. Normand

REGIONAL HISTORY, HUMOR, MEMOIR

Baloney on Wry by Frank Larson
eyond the Freeway by Peter J. Benzoni
Crocodile Tears and Lipstick Smears by Fran Gabino
Fair Game by Fran Gabino
Some Things You Never Forget by Clem Miller
Stop in the Name of the Law by Alex O'Kash
Superior Catholics by Cheney and Meronek
Widow of the Waves by Bev Jamison

BUSINESS

Dare to Kiss the Frog by vanHauen, Kastberg & Soden
SoundBites Second Edition by Kathy Kerchner

POETRY

Appalachian Mettle by Paul Bennett
Eraser's Edge by Phil Sneve
Gleanings from the Hillsides by E.M. Johnson
In the Heart of the Forest by Diana Randolph
I Was Night by Bekah Bevins
Moments Beautiful Moments Bright by Brett Bartholomaus
Nameless by Charlie Buckley
Pathways by Mary B. Wadzinski
Philosophical Poems by E.M. Johnson
Poems of Faith and Inspiration by E.M. Johnson
The Morning After the Night She Fell Into the Gorge by Heidi Howes
Thicker Than Water by Hazel Sangster
Treasured Thoughts by Sierra
Treasures from the Beginning of the World by Jeff Lewis

SOCIAL JUSTICE

Throwaway People: Danger in Paradise by Peter Opack

SPIRITUALITY

Life's Most Relevant Reality by Rod Kissinger, S.J.
Proverbs for the Family by Lynda Savage, M.S.
The Awakening of the Heart by Jill Downs
The Hillside Story by Pastor Thor Sorenson

OTHER BOOKS AVAILABLE FROM SP

Blueberry Summers by Lawrence Berube
Beyond the Law by Alex O'Kash
Dakota Brave by Howard Johnson
Jackpine Savages by Frank Larson
Spindrift Anthology by The Tarpon Springs Writer's Group
The Brule River, A Guide's Story by Lawrence Berube
Waterfront by Alex O'Kash

To order additional copies of

Summer Storm

or to
receive a copy of the complete
Savage Press Catalog,
contact us at:

Local calls:
(Superior, WI/Duluth, MN area)
715-394-9513

National Voice and FAX orders
1-800-732-3867
E-mail:
mail@savpress.com

Visit on-line at:

www.savpress.com

Visa/MasterCard Accepted

All Savage Press books are available at all chain and independent bookstores nationwide. Just ask them to special order if the title is not in stock.